FIRST SIGHT OF SUN

Desert Palm Press Trade Paperback Original

Desert Palm Press
4804 NW Bethany Blvd, Suite I-2, #148
Portland, OR 97229
www.desertpalmpress.com

ISBN: 978-1-63304-087-8
E-Book: 978-1-63304-088-5

FIRST EDITION: First Printing: 2026

Editing: Raven's Eye Editing
Formatting: Anne Battis
Cover: Lilia Dormichev

FIRST SIGHT OF SUN

By

Kayla Gornick

Desert Palm Press
www.desertpalmpress.com

Dedication

To all the girls who sat alone at lunch, you've got a seat saved at my table.

Chapter One

IN THE EARLY HOURS of the morning, before the sky was flecked with gold and pink, October was at its finest. The dark skeletons of branches were the only things that mimicked movement, though there were whispers of living things, or not quite living, creeping around in shadow at the witching hour.

She didn't need to feed that night, so the chances of her leaving the manor were equal to the chances of her receiving a visitor. That might sound like a lonely existence, but it didn't feel like one to her, if for no other reason than she could not remember any other sort of existence. She had many books in her library that featured descriptions of other realities, stories about family and friendship and romance. But why should she bother trying to relate to those things? Those were human things, and Beatrice Caswell was not human.

Perhaps this was a slight exaggeration. There was a point in time when she definitely was human. Bitten by someone, somewhere, for some reason—you start to lose track of the details after a few decades—her humanity was ripped from her body and replaced by something else, something cold. If it had bothered her at some point, it certainly didn't anymore. As far as she could figure, she hadn't had much to live for back then anyway.

Yes, it would appear Caswell led a lonely existence long before she became a vampire.

Another night alone was as good of an excuse as any to practice the piano, one of the few human pleasures she allowed herself to partake in. There was something soothing about music. If she had a soul, she would've poured it into the melodies. As she did not, she let them sweep her away from who or what she was, who she might've been once, and who she couldn't be again.

Her peace was interrupted by an enormous *BANG!* at her door. She sighed. Whatever dared to make that horrible noise was about to regret it.

She flew down the staircase, her cape swishing behind her like the wings of a bat, stopping halfway to give her spiel to the figure standing in the opened doorway, backlit by moonlight. "Foolish mortal," she said, voice rough from underuse. "Can you even fathom the misfortune you've wandered into? Your death is inevitable, but I can assure you it will not be swi—"

"HEY, DUDE, THAT'S COOL AND ALL," a rumbling voice interrupted her. The raised monotone was edged with a bit of panic. "BUT CAN I BORROW A BAND-AID?"

Dude?

Snapped out of her monologue, she was overwhelmed by the smell wafting up to her. The person who had interrupted her so rudely was soaked through with the stench of something Caswell couldn't put her finger on, but it was foul and hardly human.

Setting the odor of this unwanted visitor aside, her appearance was even more striking. She was doubled over, clutching her stomach, and her orange tracksuit was torn and stained with blood. Her face was smudged with blood and dirt, and behind large, clunky sunglasses, her eyes were wild from pain.

Caswell found herself at a loss for words. She ended up blurting out, "What the devil do you think a Band-Aid is going to accomplish?"

"PLEASE?"

Caswell watched ears folding back into the woman's skin and was pretty sure the question hadn't been heard. The woman's pupils slotted against freshly yellowed irises, and suddenly Caswell recognized the smell.

Werewolf.

She tensed up at the memory of her last encounter with the brutes. That was how she ended up in this dismal little town a few decades ago, fleeing from a conflict that never seemed any closer to an end. She had little interest in upheaving everything again. She'd just have to get rid of the beast before she caught the attention of the whole pack.

Caswell rushed down the rest of the stairs, trying to shoo away the uninvited were. "You've entered a vampire den by mistake. If you get out of here now, I will graciously let this offense slide."

The wolf-woman threw up on her before passing out at her feet.

Charming creatures, really.

The first streaks of daylight were pouring onto Caswell's newly bloodstained carpet. She shuffled around the body, getting behind the door to push it shut. She stopped briefly to consider her choices. She could throw the ghastly thing right out the door, but she didn't know why it came in the first place. Was it to declare war? Were more on their way? She sighed and shut the door. She would have to interrogate her before sending her on her way. Caswell cleaned herself up first, naturally, then turned her aim to the carpet. She covered the couch with an old sheet, then dragged the werewolf over to get her out of the way. Caswell paused to look at her. The thick, wild locks of dark hair and sharp jawline weren't unattractive. Her nose was sort of big, but it fit her face. If it wasn't for the pointed, hairy ears, she would still pass as a human. A pretty one, at that. Caswell felt a strange heaviness in her chest, but whatever happened to this stranger wasn't her fault and it wasn't her business, so she got back to cleaning.

"Huh, I didn't die."

Caswell jolted awake with the words several hours later. She glanced at her visitor, who sat checking over her hands and sounding slightly bemused but otherwise unaffected. "That's cool."

"Of course you didn't die," Caswell said. "That sort of injury could've only killed something as weak as a human."

She noticed Caswell and flashed a toothy grin. "Hey, you didn't kick me out! When I saw some angry old lady was living here, I thought you were going to kick me out for sure. Though I guess you're not that old. The white hair threw me. Sorry for bleeding all over the place. Did I throw up? I think I threw up. Sorry for that if it happened. My name's Vic, uh, Montana. I didn't pause because I forgot my last name. I wasn't sure if it'd be weird to give my full name."

Caswell was dumbstruck by the free flow of information from Montana's mouth and tried to stay focused. "Y...your name doesn't matter. Why did you come here last night?"

Montana stared blankly for a moment, then her eyes widened as she seemed to remember the events that brought her to this stranger's couch. "Oh man, I was out with my friend, Alison, and this huge dog attacked her! I wrestled it off before it could bite her or anything, but it was freakishly strong. Like, you can't even imagine this kind of power. I've never fought anything that vicious in my life, and I wrestled an angry pig once. It did a hell of a job on me. It finally ran off, but I don't think it was 'cause of me, since nothing I did seemed to hurt it even a little. So my friend already ran off, which is good because I told her to, but I definitely was going to die. I mean, you saw, I was real messed up. I...feel all right now, though..."

Montana began checking her body over for signs that last night's injuries were real, patting at her limbs and hair. "How long was I knocked out?" She unzipped what was left of her tracksuit, and lifted the once-was-white tank to find a singular mean-looking scar across the right side of her stomach. "Oh, there's that one! Yeah, he got me bad."

"The hyper regeneration doesn't apply to the bite, obviously. How do you not know that?" Caswell stopped Montana before she could open her mouth. "No, wait, I don't care. Just tell me why you came here of all places."

Montana shrugged nonchalantly. "Your house was the closest."

"It's not a house, it's a castle." Well, that wasn't true either, but it sounded better. "And you came here because it was the *closest*? Hasn't anyone warned you that a vampire lives here?"

There was a beat of silence. Montana looked unimpressed. "What, you?"

"Yes, me," Caswell sputtered, in total disbelief over this lack of respect. She straightened up to her full height, snarling so all her teeth were visible. "Did you not notice the *fangs*?"

"It's been a long day," Montana said, a halfhearted apology. "I'm sure you're very scary. It's—ah, do you mind if I take off my pants real quick?"

Caswell's annoyance vanished into confusion and mild horror. "What kind of question is that?"

Taking that as confirmation, Montana started slipping them off. "Real quick. Something's been bothering me"—She freed a fluffy tail, already wagging to reflect its owner's curiosity—"Huh. That's new."

Caswell scrambled to cover her eyes. "Just put your pants back on!" The command did not come out as sternly as she hoped it would.

"Well, I can't now. I've got a new body part to account for." Montana was significantly less distressed than a person ought to be when finding new limbs stuck to them. "It's cool. I've got undies on. Are you a virgin or something?"

"I am not a virgin." Still flustered, she reluctantly removed her hands from her face. "I simply don't care for strangers getting naked on my couch."

"We're not really strangers though. You know my name, I know you're a vampire…what is your name anyway?"

"Caswell." She responded without thinking. It wasn't like she wanted Montana to know, but the word slipped out easily. It had been a long time since she'd had a proper conversation.

Montana, still full of surprises, snorted at her. "Wait, really? What were your parents thinking?"

"It's my last name." She said, fuming.

"Oh, that makes more sense. What's your first?" Montana continued to smile pleasantly at her.

Caswell rolled her eyes, scoffing. "After that, you really think I'd tell you?"

"Aw, come on, don't be like that. It was just unexpected. With how you act and dress, I thought it'd be like, Alucarda or Morticia or something."

Caswell did not budge.

"If you don't tell me, I'll call you Ms. Vampire Caswell. Is that what you want? Is it?"

"I want you to stop making a mockery of a very serious situation. I hope you realize you're in enemy territory."

Montana stretched, raising her arms lazily above her head. "Uh, 'cause you eat people, right?"

"Humans, and I…I don't even eat them. I drink their blood." She didn't know why she was bothering to explain herself. There was something peculiar about Montana that sparked argument in her.

"So you want some of my delicious human blood or something?" Montana asked inattentively.

"You have a tail!"

Montana sat up a little. "Ooh, am I a vampire too now?"

"I don't have a tail! Vampires don't have tails! What do you think is happening right now?!"

"Not sure, but you don't have to yell." Montana held up her hands in defense. "If you know more, please, enlighten me."

If there was still blood in her veins, Caswell's face would have been redder than a cherry. "You're a werewolf! That big dog that attacked you was a wolf, and it bit you, and now you're a wolf! You're supposed to be angst-ridden, not lounging on my couch!"

"Ah, guess that makes sense." Montana nodded sagely, like she had heard a somewhat interesting piece of trivia and not the devastating news that her entire life had been irreversibly altered. Her talking pace and tail wagging quickened as she quick-fired, "So do I transform on full moons only or is that just a myth? Do I control when I transform? Do I know what I'm doing when I'm transformed? Did the guy who attacked me know what he was doing? If he did, why did he do that? Is my hair going to grow faster? What about my nails? Do I heal faster? Is that why I've got no cuts? If I met another werewolf, would I know they were one too? How would I know? If we were both in wolf form would I still—"

"I don't know!" Caswell spluttered. "You have too many questions, and I haven't got a single answer! I'll do some reading. I'll get back to you in a few days!"

Caswell caught her breath, and only found herself aware of her hasty promise after she spoke it into existence. What was she *thinking?*

Montana, either oblivious or apathetic to the fact Caswell had spoken without thinking, grinned again, sharp teeth glistening. "It's a date."

Montana hopped up from the couch, grabbing her discarded pants to shove her tail back in. "I'll do some searching of my own and find out some vampire stuff too. I better get home, so I'll leave you to your brooding or whatever in the meantime. See ya."

With that, she left through the same big, heavy doors that she had stumbled into the night before.

As Caswell watched her go, she only then fully processed what she had signed up for.

Chapter Two

CASWELL DIDN'T WANT MONTANA to come back.

There was no guarantee she would come back. Maybe Montana would come to her senses and realize how lucky she was that she made it out alive the first night and never return. Or maybe she'd forget. She seemed sort of scatterbrained, after all. She might go live in the woods for a while, dealing with the expected amount of angst. Maybe she'd be taken in by her pack or another, or perhaps she would simply drop dead. Werewolves were hardly invincible. Someone carrying a silver fork might trip and fall onto her, plunging it right into her heart. A hunter who was rich enough to splurge on silver bullets might mistake her for a deer in aviators. Anything was possible.

As Caswell mulled over every possible excuse for why Montana wouldn't show up, she still found herself listening intently for a knock at the door or that husky voice calling for her to open up. This waiting only made the silence more looming. Had it always been so quiet? Did one night with that woman really change the way her whole house felt?

Caswell didn't intend to read up on werewolf lore. But if, by some miraculous turn of fate, Montana still showed up at her doorstep, she'd be able to turn her away immediately. Caswell really didn't do much normally, but anything else she tried to do resulted in her mind wandering back to the Montana situation. She hadn't had a goal in so long, no tasks to accomplish. And she was sort of curious. The more she knew about werewolves, the easier it would be to ward them off, after all.

So she read the books, and she left the lock off her door, and she waited. But that didn't mean she wanted anything to come of it. It was just curiosity, mild interest. Nothing ever happened around Caswell's home, so it was natural for her to feel this way.

Nights came and went since their last encounter. Caswell didn't know how many. She wasn't one to keep track of time. It was all fleeting and insignificant to a vampire. But it must've been a long time, and she was still alone, so none of this wondering mattered. Montana wasn't going to show up.

But then she did.

"Anybody home?" Montana was already halfway through the door, shoving it open with her shoulder, hands full with a big flat box. She was wearing nearly the same outfit as last time, but this version was untorn. She was chewing on something and swallowed before continuing. "Did I come too early? You didn't really specify, but I assumed you'd be asleep during the day."

Caswell huffed and ushered her in, shutting the door behind her to avoid any incidents like the other night. She chided Montana, "Just because you can enter buildings without being invited in doesn't mean you should."

"Wait, can you not enter places without permission?" Montana smirked at her. "I thought that had to be fake for sure."

"That's beside the point." Once Caswell got past the oppressive wolf smell she'd let in, she noticed another horrendous smell, presumably coming from the box. Disgust was evident in her voice when she demanded, "What is that?"

"Oh, right!" Montana glanced down at the box, as if she had forgotten she was holding it. "Kind of a funny story. I thought I should bring you a thank you for offering to help me, but I didn't know what you like, so I thought hey, everyone likes doughnuts, right? And I bought you a whole dozen and as I was walking over here, I realized you probably don't actually like doughnuts that much since you don't eat. So now all I've got for you is the box."

Despite the fact she was rambling, Caswell managed to follow the story. "So you ate twelve of those on the way over?"

"Nah, I'm at eleven and a half. It's 'bout to be twelve." Montana balanced the box with one hand and a knee, as she took out the last bit of fried pastry and finished it off. She must have caught the way Caswell was staring at her, because she straightened up, laughing a little. "The box is temporary, I promise. I'll get you something nice once I know you a little better."

"Don't get me anything." Caswell waved her off. Things were moving too quickly. That seemed to always be the case when talking to this girl. Caswell needed to shut her down before she got caught up in another strange situation, but the words stuck in her throat. She cleared her throat and tried again. "I know I said I'd help you, but I can't."

Montana did not pick up the hint. "No worries, broski. I wasn't expecting you to have all the answers. It's just nice to have someone with me as I figure this all out."

"That's not what I mean." Caswell sighed. "I know you're new to this whole thing, but vampires and werewolves don't usually...get along."

"Why not?"

Caswell frowned. Montana couldn't make anything easy, could she? "I don't know. It's just how it is."

"Then what a pair we make!" Montana bounced on the balls of her feet as she walked deeper into the house, apparently trying to find a place to store the box.

Caswell followed after her. "That's not how this works. You can't ignore stuff like that. It's biology."

Montana snorted. "What do you know about biology? You dress like the atom hasn't been discovered." She set the box down on a table, nodding triumphantly to herself. "Yeah, this is a good spot. Out of your way, but still in sight." As if the topic of where to put her garbage was on par with the discussion Caswell was trying to have.

Her scowl deepened. "You're supposed to hate me!"

"Well, do you?"

"Do I what?"

"Hate me." Montana stopped bouncing off the walls, her full attention on Caswell. She bit at her lip absentmindedly, and Caswell found herself unable to return her gaze.

Caswell was caught off guard by this question. She knew Montana would leave if she told her she hated her, that much was obvious. She couldn't bring herself to say it. She settled on a soft, grumbly, "I should."

Montana smiled like she knew something that Caswell didn't. How infuriating. "So why don't we give this a chance?"

"What exactly do you define as this?" Caswell asked hesitantly, instantly regretting the words once they left her mouth.

"Us." Montana replied simply and followed it up with a wink. "And if you end up hating me, I won't take it personally."

Every reasonable part of Caswell knew this was a terrible idea, yet she found it a surprisingly tempting offer. Which meant some unreasonable part was in her that she wasn't normally aware of. That disturbed her but also thrilled her in a strange way. Montana was giving her the freedom to back out whenever she wanted, so perhaps there was no real harm in indulging this unknown impracticality in herself. She was admittedly curious to find what else she might discover.

"Fine. I'll give 'us' a try."

"Sick." Montana said, as if it were the easiest decision of her life. She held up her fist and laughed when Caswell gave her a halfhearted fist bump. "I'm actually surprised you knew what that was."

Caswell quirked an eyebrow. "What, did you think I only stay inside every night, brooding?"

Montana thought for a moment before nodding. "Uh, yeah, actually. That seemed to be your thing." She walked past her again, eyes scanning the corners where the walls met the ceilings. "Thought there'd be a lot more cobwebs too."

"When you can walk on the ceiling, cleaning it isn't so much of a hassle."

Montana couldn't hold back another full-sized smile. "Was that a joke?"

Caswell tried to hide her satisfaction. "You tell me."

"It was! You told a joke! You've got a sense of humor!"

Caswell took a step back as Montana started intruding upon her personal space. "Spare me. More importantly, did you cut a hole in your pants for your tail?"

"Huh? Oh yeah," Montana twisted around so she could get a better look. "I cut holes in all my pants. Pretty smart, right?"

Caswell did not follow her logic. "But what if you get turned back into a human? Then you're stuck with holes in all your pants."

"I didn't know that was possible." The near constant movement of her tail slowed a bit. "Is it?"

"I couldn't find anything definitive. But if you don't know, you shouldn't assume."

Montana stretched, yawning. Caswell had never gotten such a close look at a werewolf's mouth before. Those teeth of hers were certainly interesting. Montana said, "Man, you got my hopes up for nothing."

There it was. "So you do want to be human again!" It was not so much a question as it was a victorious accusation. Montana's anguish took far too long to appear, but at least it showed up.

"I guess?" Montana shrugged. "I mean, things seemed easier that way, but I suppose once I get used to this, it won't be that difficult."

"Don't you long for your life to return to the way it used to be? Your chance to live normally torn from you each night the moon is full? Everything you've grown accustomed to, lost, as you are tossed cruelly between two worlds, never fitting in with either? Are you not weighed down with the horrible guilt and shame of what you've become?" Caswell prompted her on, complete with dramatic cape swishing and hand motions.

"Nah, man, I'm chilling." Montana wandered off, exploring the manor. She spoke louder, as though unaware Caswell was following her so closely. "Are you like, projecting or something?"

Caswell grimaced and let the gap between them grow so Montana wouldn't yell in her ear. "Are you joking? I'd never want to be human again. So powerless and frail, as if asking to be attacked." For some reason, the thought popped into her mind that she couldn't remember what a heartbeat felt like. She refrained from mentioning it, continuing firmly, "No, it's not how I feel, it's how you're supposed to feel. All werewolves do."

"At least humans can enter 7-Eleven without a formal invitation." Montana fired back with a small grin. She placed her hands on the wall, then pressed the side of her face against it, ears twitching. "You got any secret passages in this place?"

"No. Why would I need one?" Caswell stopped herself from getting distracted. "Can you at least pretend to listen?"

"I am listening!" Montana pushed off the wall and continued to search for the oddities she obviously expected in such an old house. "I just don't have a lot to add. You know better than anyone that I don't know anything about being a werewolf. That's why I came in the first place, yeah?" She made her way up the stairs and started opening any doors that weren't locked. "Ooh, bathroom. You still take showers, right? I mean, I get you prob—"

"Yes, Montana." Caswell cut her off with an embarrassed hiss. "I bathe myself. Get out of my bathroom."

"First, get in here for a sec." Montana called back. Caswell sighed, begrudgingly joining her in the little room. Montana laughed. "Oh my god, you really don't have a reflection! Why haven't you removed this mirror?"

Caswell glanced into the mirror, seeing Montana's unadulterated delight and her own clothes with no body in them. It was a nice suit, but all her suits were nice. "Why should I? It might not benefit me, but it doesn't get in my way either. The wall would look rather bare without it."

"Do you not show up in pictures either? Oh man, imagine all the stuff we could pull." Montana's attention span did not let her dwell on this for long. She soon darted around Caswell to keep searching. "You got any paintings of like, your dead ex-husband or something?"

"I'm a lesbian." Caswell said dryly.

"My bad, any dead ex-wives?" Montana paused. "Is that insensitive to ask? What about alive ex-wives?"

"Marriage between women in this country has only been legal for what, a decade? But anyway, I've never...been intimate." For all the things she couldn't remember about being human, she was certain she'd remember something like that. But she couldn't really be sure. "Can't say I've got much of an interest now."

"Is it because without any blood you can't...you know...?" Montana made some rather unfortunate hand gestures as she spoke.

Caswell spoke through her teeth, "My sex life is, and will always be, none of your business."

"I was curious!" Montana increased the distance between them. Had she finally sensed danger? "Let's go back to talking about my werewolf stuff."

"Yes, let's."

"On a scale of An American Werewolf in London to Twilight, how does the actual transformation work?" Montana pointed to her ears. "Also, are these a permanent fixture? You could've warned me I had them before I left the other night. All the old people I saw on my way home were like 'aaah monster!' and all the young people were like 'aaah furry!'"

An excuse to flaunt her knowledge helped Caswell calm down. "I don't have the very best information on your kind due to all the tension between our species, but it's certainly better than what humans have available. The ears are permanent, yes. Transformations happen involuntarily on the full moon, and it happens the moment the moon rises, even if no moonlight touches you. There's really no way around it. A few older sources claim that, with training, you'll have more control over yourself in your other form and may even gain the ability to change back and forth at will. Obviously, I have no way of validating this."

"We'll figure that one out together." Montana's smile was so sunny it felt like it was burning Caswell. "Is there stuff I should be avoiding?"

Caswell started to pace as she spoke. "Silver, of course, will burn you. If it gets in your heart, lungs, or brain, you'll die. Luckily for you, no one in this era is packed to the teeth with silver bullets. Wolfsbane was already poisonous to you when you were human, but now you mustn't even touch it."

"When would I touch wolfsbane?" Montana scrunched up her nose.

"I don't know! I'm telling you what I read. Do you want to know everything, or shall I leave out random bits I deem unimportant?" Caswell huffed.

"Nope, my bad, keep going." Montana, seemingly satisfied with her impromptu tour of the manor, sat at the top of the staircase and motioned for Caswell to join her. "Am I gonna wanna howl at the moon? More than usual, I mean."

Caswell reluctantly sat beside her. "You already had the urge?"

"I mean, yeah!" Montana rolled her eyes, as if it were the most obvious thing in the world. "I mean, have you seen the moon? She's so beautiful that it makes me wanna yell a little. You should try it sometime."

"I have better things to do than scream at celestial bodies."

The sad thing was, she really didn't.

Montana nudged her playfully with an elbow. “It would get some of that stress off your shoulders. You and I should do it together sometime. We could be howling pals.”

“Sounds lovely.” Caswell’s voice dripped with sarcasm. “Now can you please focus? The night’s only so long, and we have a lot of ground to cover.”

Chapter Three

AFTER THAT NIGHT, MONTANA made frequent visits. Sometimes she'd have questions, but Caswell had a sneaking suspicion that she simply liked having someone else around. If there were other people awake so deep into the night, she'd probably be with them instead. But as it was, she was here.

Evidently, Montana had no trouble making herself at home wherever she was. It had been less than a month, and her clothes were already scattered on every surface Caswell owned. Every time Caswell would remove a tank top, a sock appeared in its place. The only arguable benefit she got from this laundry game was getting acclimated to Montana's reek.

"Can't you smell the vampire on me?" Caswell finally asked one night.

Montana looked up at her from her usual place lounging on the couch, some brightly colored magazine in her hands. "I don't need to smell anything, man. I already know." She cursed under her breath, "Ah, shit, you made me bite my tongue."

Caswell shook her head. "That's not what I mean. Your sense of smell should be heightened. Don't I smell different than a human?" According to the legends, werewolves had a much better sense of smell than their vampiric counterparts. It should've been Montana being overwhelmed every time Caswell entered the room, not the other way around.

Montana was poking experimentally at her tongue to see if she bit herself hard enough to draw blood. Satisfied with her findings, she said, "I mean, nobody smells the same to me anymore. There's not really a human smell. Maybe if I met another vampire I could tell you." She flipped the page of her magazine. "Or like, a really old corpse."

Caswell was too offended to press her any further on that one.

So her scent didn't seem to bother Montana. Nothing seemed to bother her, really. The only concern she had was Caswell's accent, voicing her opinion that a vampire ought to be Transylvanian, not

British. She wasn't satisfied with the explanation that Caswell had never been to Transylvania, and a few relatively sociable decades spent in England could give anyone an accent.

Montana's lack of fear and questionable level of respect were oddly refreshing, if not extremely irritating. No one else had the nerve to tell her to cut her "weird gross nails every once in a while."

Caswell was still asleep when she heard the two bangs that characterized Montana's arrival, one of her slamming open the door and the second of her closing it a minute later as she recalled the dangers of sunlight. The action would almost be appreciated if she hadn't shown up so early in the evening that the sunlight would be a problem in the first place.

"Hey, Cas, are you up yet?" She really did have a voice that carried well. Sometimes it'd be better if she didn't. Most times, in fact.

"No!" Caswell shouted back, muffled through the wood of the coffin she was resting in. When Montana first found it, she asked her if she was worried about getting splinters in her sleep.

"Come on, it's the full moon!" Montana paused. "Do you own a calendar? Do you even know what month it is?"

So that's why she showed up before the sun had totally gone down. It was a pretty good reason, if not the best one, but Caswell was tired. With a heaving sigh, she dragged herself up and started getting dressed. With each impatient shout coming from downstairs, she went spitefully slower. Finally, Montana gave up and came upstairs to find her.

"There you are!" Montana sounded a little out of breath, and Caswell wondered how many rooms she burst into before this one. "What's the hold up, dude?"

"I was trying to sleep." Caswell finished buttoning up her shirt.

Montana pouted. "I can't believe you forgot! You said you'd be with me for my first full moon."

"I didn't forget. I'll be right with you." Caswell felt like an exasperated parent. "You can wait downstairs. I'll only be another minute."

"Fine, but if you take more than a minute, I'm going to come back up here and never stop annoying you ever again." Montana spoke as she retreated.

"You're already doing that," Caswell shot back over her shoulder. She grabbed a cape. She hadn't forgotten promising to spend the first full moon with Montana, but she hadn't been keeping track of the moon cycle. If this became a regular occurrence, she'd have to start paying attention to the days. She couldn't remember the last time she did that. She wasn't even sure she could still name all the months.

Thinking about keeping track of time ironically caused her to lose track, and she realized the moon was probably already up. She made her way downstairs. Montana had gotten everything related to being a werewolf wrong so far, but at least this was the one thing she couldn't mess up. She'd turn into a horrible bloodthirsty monster whether she liked it or not. Perhaps once the reality of the situation set in, she'd take the whole thing more seriously.

When Caswell reached the bottom of the stairs, no bloodthirsty monster awaited her.

The smallest, fluffiest dog Caswell had ever seen was wagging her tail furiously. They stared at each other for a long stretch.

"Somehow, I should've guessed." Caswell sighed, wishing she was even surprised at this point. "You've been domesticated."

"Wuff!"

Caswell scowled at her. "You can't say wuff. It's either woof or ruff. You can't have both."

"Wuff!"

"The hate I feel for you right now is stronger than any hate I've ever known, and I hope that you know that." She got closer to Montana, crouching down. "You're not even a full-grown dog, are you? You're a puppy. You're an embarrassment to your entire kind." She pointed at her disapprovingly. Montana licked her finger. "Yes, yes, I'm sure this is positively hilarious to you."

Seeming to realize that Caswell was not going to give her the pats she desired, puppy-Montana ran off to find entertainment with more speed than a dog her size should have. Finding her own discarded clothes, she began chewing on one of her shoes.

"Oh, give me that!" Caswell went after her. "That's more disgusting than the stuff you usually do." Caswell gave the shoe a tug. Montana growled and tugged back, tail wagging furiously. "I'm not trying to play with you. Drop it."

Montana kept trying to pull the shoe free from her grasp. "You'll never win this. My strength is far superior." Caswell could only feel so high and mighty while trying to bargain with a puppy. She yanked the shoe away as carefully as she could. Montana was annoying, yes, but Caswell didn't want to hurt her. Especially when she wasn't even being annoying on purpose.

Montana got low to the ground like she was going to pounce. "What? I'm not going to throw it, if that's what you're hoping for." Caswell stood back up, and as she did, she was struck with an idea. "Perhaps you look odd but still function correctly. Let's go give it a try." She gave the shoe a little shake to keep puppy-Montana's attention and led her outside.

Montana looked thrilled to be out there, sniffing at everything and hopping around. "Wuff!" she barked, infuriatingly.

Caswell's attention was directed elsewhere.

A young couple was passing on the other side of the street, bundled up in coats and scarves against the stinging, autumn night air. They were making idle chatter and were completely unaware of their surroundings.

"There you go, a perfect set of targets." Caswell crouched down next to Montana. "Don't be nervous. You've got this. Sneak up behind them and make your attack. They'll never see you coming."

Montana tilted her head, tongue hanging out. Caswell sighed and grabbed the furry head, turning it toward the couple. Tail wagging began immediately. "That's the spirit. Go! Kill!" Naturally, Caswell wouldn't let her actually kill anyone. She'd step in if it got that intense. But Montana needed the encouragement. Caswell let her go and watched her run up to her poor victims. They spotted her before she had her chance and started cooing over her cuteness. Caswell still had faith that she could pull it off.

Montana, on the other hand, was not very interested in attacking them. She seemed more than satisfied with getting petted. She even rolled over onto her back so they could rub her tummy.

Caswell couldn't pretend this wasn't the most likely outcome, but it ticked her off that Montana still wasn't anything like a werewolf was supposed to be. She stormed over, her voice coming off a little more pissed than she meant it to. "All right, that's enough."

The couple screamed when they saw her, which wasn't that unusual. The one currently petting Montana, a redhead boy who couldn't have been much older than sixteen, scooped her up protectively. The girl, about the same age with dark hair, whipped out a tiny can and sprayed Caswell right in the face.

Mace would not kill a vampire, and the damage was not going to last very long, but it still hurt like the devil. She reeled back hissing, and the youths took this as an excuse to run off with their newfound dog.

Once Caswell wiped the pepper spray out of her eyes, she realized that all three of them had disappeared. She blinked a couple times. She certainly hadn't been expecting that. "W-Wait!" Caswell nearly tripped over herself as she chased after them. Being as easily flustered as she was, she was lucky that she didn't have to deal with the spontaneous nature of humans often. "You can't kidnap her!"

The pair didn't seem to care what she had to say and kept running at rather impressive speeds. She quickly calculated the fastest way to cut them off and transformed into a bat, flying a few feet in front of them before changing back. "There's been a misunderst—"

The girl, panicking but unafraid, kneed her in the stomach. Her strength was surprising. "Go to hell, zombie!"

"I'm pretty sure it's a vampire, but we can talk about that later. Let's move." The boy was all but dragging his girlfriend away.

"Ooh, I'm not done with this creep!" She cracked her knuckles. "This is what you get for picking on puppies."

"I wasn't!" Caswell held up her hands in defense. "I don't mean any of you harm. That's my friend." The words came out faster than she could think. Montana was most certainly not her friend, but if saying that would prevent her accidental kidnapping, then Caswell could swallow a bit of her pride. "Just give her back." She hoped Montana would realize the lengths she was going to for her. "Please."

The girl exchanged a look with her boyfriend, suddenly unsure and acting more her age. "Is that good enough for you?" she asked her boyfriend.

He shrugged nonchalantly. "Yeah. I mean, you showed me Twilight. Not all monsters are, like, monsters," He gently set Montana down on the ground. "Here you go, ma'am. Don't eat anybody or whatever."

"I don't eat people," Caswell muttered indignantly. But the couple was already walking past her, lost in their own little world again. Humans really were so strange.

She looked down at Montana, who continued to stick out her little pink tongue. "Don't give me that look. I didn't mean any of it. I only did it so you don't wake up in a pet shop tomorrow. And that means you owe me," she said unconvincingly, as if the whole situation wasn't her fault to begin with. "Let's go back. When the transformation wears off, I want you back in clothes as soon as you're physically capable of it."

Her snarky comments were a little less fun when she didn't get a playful response. Montana followed at her heels, curiously sniffing here and there but content to stay close. Caswell briefly wondered why Montana was coming with her, when those teens petted her and cuddled her. Maybe her subconscious preferred Caswell. That was a silly little thought to have. Whatever reason she might've had was most likely nonsensical, as were most things related to Montana.

Once they were back in the manor, Caswell let Montana run around like the tiny madman she was until she tired herself out. After a good couple hours of it, she finally passed out. Caswell promptly picked her up, moving her onto the couch. She bundled up Montana's clothes and placed them next to her. Deciding her job was done, she was about to get back to other matters.

A thought took hold in her mind and wouldn't let her leave the room. She reached out a tentative hand, double checking to make sure Montana wasn't awake before gently petting her head. She was unbelievably soft.

Caswell pulled her hand away like it had been burned, mentally chastising herself. She was acting as ridiculous as a human. No, worse than ridiculous, she was going soft. She wasn't supposed to plead with schoolchildren and pet puppies. She was supposed to be a monster.

Watching Montana fail so miserably at the same task, while having such a good time was...conflicting. She shook her head, trying to dispel the thought. She had made it this long without giving int o her feelings, and she couldn't start now. She knew exactly what would happen. If she pretended to be human, she'd eventually have to learn she was a monster all over again.

By the morning, Montana was still asleep. She slept right through her transformation back into her human form. Caswell whipped around quickly to avoid looking at her. Montana grunted as she sat up. "I feel gross. And naked."

"There's an easy solution to one of those." Caswell waited as Montana fumbled with her clothes. "Are you decent?"

"Huh? Oh yeah, I've been dressed for a couple minutes." In Montana's defense, she still sounded very out of it.

Caswell turned back around to face her. Montana smiled wearily. "So you didn't abandon me." For a heart-stopping second, Caswell thought Montana could recall everything that had happened. "I felt something happening and you were still getting dressed but now it's...What time is it?" Montana waved a hand at her dismissively and pulled her phone out of her pocket. "Never mind, you don't own any clocks. Shit, I should probably call in today."

"You have a job?" Caswell couldn't hide her surprise.

Montana made a face. "I'd ask 'you don't?' But you never leave the house during the day and I visit most nights. How do you buy stuff? I guess you don't need food or electricity but...You know what, I don't think I want to know. If you ever need actual money, I'll give you some, okay?"

"What kind of place would possibly hire someone like you?" Caswell was still in disbelief.

Montana sank into the couch. "Uh, hardware store. We sell stuff, like...for making stuff." She groaned stiffly, covering her eyes with her hands. "I feel like I've got a hangover. How was it?"

Caswell sat beside her on the couch and sighed. "You were a major disappointment."

Montana chuckled. "Coming from you, that tends to be a good thing. I was going to ask if you wanted to chain me up beforehand because I saw it in a movie, but I forgot."

"That would've been fun." Caswell nodded a little. "But no, you would've slipped right out anyway."

"You're going to have to elaborate on that one."

"Ah yes, well, you were only about this big." Caswell held her hands about a foot apart. "You weren't even a wolf. You were some kind of baby lap dog."

Montana stared at her for a moment before bursting into laughter, harder than Caswell had ever seen her laugh. Surprised, Caswell found herself feeling almost relieved. Nothing bad had happened. Montana didn't lose her laugh. Her first full moon had come and gone, and she was still just her. That wasn't the sort of thing Caswell thought she'd be relieved by.

"Are you serious? Oh my god, that's hilarious." Her attention drifted back to her phone and she started typing, presumably messaging someone about taking the day off. "Mind if I crash here this morning? I'm too wiped to go back home."

"You're turning into a permanent fixture on my couch." Caswell stood up, already heading out of the room. "Try to be quiet this time, at least."

"You got it, bro." Montana gave her a thumbs up as she shifted to lay down. She groaned again. "Is it going to be like this every time?"

"We'll figure it out together," Caswell assured her, hoping Montana was too sleep-deprived to notice her sincerity.

Yes, it seemed she'd have to invest in a calendar after all.

Chapter Four

ONCE THE EXCITEMENT OF a new year dies down, January rolls by as gray as the slush in the streets. Even around Dot, the walking disaster magnet, it was a slow and uneventful month. With little excitement to be found, children had to get creative and make their own.

Dot was a middle schooler, known for her cheerful disposition, her pixie cut that stuck out in every direction, and of course, her family curse. Surrounding her was an aura of bad luck, one that had been with her bloodline as far back as they could trace. Not everyone believed in luck and curses, but even those folks were cautious around her.

Most people preferred to keep their distance, but anyone brave enough to call Dot their friend was bound to be as loyal as they came. June, with red curls as wild and fiery as her personality and a permanently lost front tooth, and Cameron, with his dark, curious eyes and dazzling smile, were the only two who would call themselves her best friends, which spoke great volumes about their character.

"This is the place." June was a little out of breath, stopping her bike far enough ahead where she wouldn't have to worry about the others crashing into her, even if their brakes were to stop working or the like. "I saw it a few weeks ago when my dad took me up north for that astronomy talk. I asked around and turns out this is like, one of the most haunted places in Arlington."

"So you've said." Cameron released his kickstand, hopping off his bike. The house in question was old, dark, and definitely a good candidate for being haunted. It lacked windows, and two decrepit pillars stood like guards in front of a huge oak door. It took them longer than expected to get there, so the early dusk added to the eeriness. "I thought you didn't believe in occult stuff."

"Watching you two get freaked out will be fun." she shrugged. "And if there's any chance at discovering something that doesn't exist, it'll be with Dot. Where is Dot anyway?"

They looked behind them to see Dot walking alongside her bike. She waved at them. "Sorry, got a flat. I'll fix it before we go. See any ghosts yet?"

June grinned as Dot caught up to them. "Not yet, but we're still outside. You can fix flat tires now?"

"I'm prepared for anything." Dot puffed her chest out proudly.

"I believe it. You ready to go in?"

"You want the three of us to go inside there?" Cameron raised an eyebrow. He did not have to voice his concerns to make them known. They knew he was the reasonable one, which was a package deal with the one with complaints.

"No, not three." June shook her head, curls bouncing. "I was thinking we'd send one in and test the waters."

"No way." Cameron chuckled nervously. "We should not split up. Haven't you ever seen Scooby Doo?"

"Yeah, and they find the ghost every time they split up. It's foolproof." June turned to Dot. "I'll buy you an entire thing of Oreos if you can stay in there by yourself for more than five minutes."

Dot was excited enough to go in for nothing, but she was not about to turn down an offer for free Oreos. "You're on!"

Cameron tried to convince her it wasn't a good idea, but she wasn't deterred. Ghosts were nothing to be afraid of. Her dad always said, as long as you were prepared, you shouldn't be afraid of anything. And Dot was very prepared for ghosts. Flashlight, salt, night vision goggles, whatever you could imagine, she had it. She even picked up the Specter Deflector she found at the dollar store for extra security.

She carefully avoided the ice on the lawn, but her left shoe got stuck in the mud. She yanked her foot free, getting a spare shoe from her backpack and putting it on. She really was prepared for everything. "This doesn't count for the five minutes!" June warned her from the sidewalk. Dot gave her an affirmative thumbs up.

"Knock before you go in!" Cameron called out once she was at the door, a last-minute worry striking him. "In case it's not haunted and someone lives in there!"

"Good idea," Dot chirped back, lifting her fist to the door. Before she could knock, the lock broke and a strong gust of wind pushed the door open. "Ooh, spooky." She disappeared inside.

The interior of the house was as dauntingly Victorian as the outside, albeit a little better kept. If someone did live here, they cared more about internal cleaning than lawn maintenance. It was stuffy, though, which Dot attributed to boarded-up windows. She was always observant, especially when it came to possible escape routes. Light fixtures were on the walls, but none were on. A bulb exploded as Dot passed by, but she was pretty sure that was only her luck and not a poltergeist.

She pulled out her flashlight, deciding that it would be hard to spot a ghost in the darkness pervading the area. She shined it up and down the walls, looking at the chipping paint and expecting quite a few more cobwebs than she found. She continued her search, following the natural curvature of the hall into a foyer.

"Yo, kid," a voice too casual for a ghoul greeted her. She whipped around in the direction it came from, shining her flashlight directly into the eyes of a woman lounging on the couch, a bag of chips on her chest. She used her elbow to protect her eyes. "Could ya point that somewhere else?"

"Oh, sorry." Dot shut off her flashlight and lowered it.

"Thanks. Chip? Sour cream and onion." She held out the bag to Dot. Over the initial shock of seeing anyone in there at all, Dot took in the woman's appearance. She was wearing a hoodie and a tacky pair of aviators that covered a good half of her face. Her grin was sharper than it should've been, and though it was a little hard to tell in the low light, Dot thought she could see two animalistic ears poking out of her wild mess of hair.

When Dot did not take her chip offering, the woman went back to eating them. "So do you always break into houses, or only the creepy ones?"

Dot was about to respond when she noticed the woman's eyes flicker up. She was no longer looking at her but behind her, making a rather disapproving face. Dot glanced over her shoulder to see an imposing figure in Gothic clothes glaring down at her. The eyes were completely black, save for sharp, blue irises. Dot stepped backward, inadvertently moving closer to the woman on the couch.

"You dare to break into my home, acting rambunctiously and destroying my property, thinking arrogantly you'll get off scot-free? Well I—" The angry goth tripped over the carpet and fell flat on her face. The couch woman booed and threw a chip at her.

Sprawled on the floor, it became more obvious that the supposed monster was only another woman. Dot kept her distance but said, "That sounded painful. Are you all right? I've got Band-Aids or an ice pack if you need it."

"Do not offer me your pity, mortal," she said.

"Don't mind her. Her bark's worse than her bite." The couch woman snickered to herself before finally rising from the couch, stretching. "Kid's like, nine. She didn't mean anything by it."

Dot piped up. "Eleven, actually, miss...uh..."

"Montana." She smiled warmly at her. "Vic Montana, Vic is fine. This is Caswell, who may or may not even have a first name." Montana motioned to the woman on the ground, who had shifted to sitting up. "And you are?"

"Dot Liang! Nice to meet you." Dot extended her hand for a shake and Montana accepted.

"Likewise. Nice grip. Now how about you tell us why you came through here like a hurricane."

Dot rocked on the balls of her feet. "Well, my friends and I thought this place was haunted, and we were hoping to see some ghosts."

Montana hummed thoughtfully. "There're no ghosts here, unless I haven't found them yet. Cassie, are you housing any malicious spirits?"

"Just you." Caswell spat. She did accept Montana's hand to help her up, then brushed off her wrinkled suit. Her skin was the same stark white as her hair, but a close look suggested she was not much older than Montana, who Dot would wager was somewhere around thirty.

Montana nodded to herself. "So no ghosts, but a vampire lives here alongside the occasional werewolf. Still pretty good, right?"

Dot's eyes widened with excitement. The only vampire she had ever met was Mr. Drake, her mathematics teacher, and she wasn't even sure about that one. "You're a vampire?"

Montana snorted. "Nah, I'm the werewolf. She's the vampire. Thought it was pretty obvious with my ears and her fangs. Plus her bangs kinda look like a bat." She splayed her fingers out over her forehead to mimic it.

"But I thought vampires were supposed to have eternal youth." Dot's thought-to-speech filter had never been that strong. She clasped her hands over her mouth. "I am so sorry."

Montana let out a sharp, barky laugh. "Oh man, I love this kid!"

"Deeply sorry I can't be as childish as her." Caswell pointed a stiff thumb in Montana's direction, her voice soaked through with sarcasm. "But I'm hardly self-conscious about my appearance. That sort of thing is beneath me."

Montana shook her head, still laughing. "She's lying. She's self-conscious about everything. Just the other night she was all embarrassed because I found out—"

"That's more than enough, Montana." Caswell cut her off loudly. Changing the conversation topic, Caswell turned to Dot. "Shouldn't you be headed home anyway, young lady? It's late and you have school."

"No she doesn't. It's Friday. Why'd I get you a calendar if you're not even going to use it?" Montana made a face at her.

"Well, it is Friday, but I should also get going." Dot tried to soothe the both of them, used to being a mediator. "My friends are waiting for me. Ooh, next time I'll introduce you to them!"

"Next time?" Caswell crossed her arms over her chest with a quirked eyebrow, but Montana elbowed her.

"If you don't work on that attitude, I'm going to end up being your only friend."

"You're not my friend." They stuck out their tongues at each other like the overgrown children they were.

Dot smiled. A fan of romantic comedies, she simply adored couples who were so in love even their bickering was cute. "We'll visit next week! I think you guys will really get along!"

"Yeah, I'd mark it on the calendar, but I think it'd be pointless." Montana faked a sigh. "You need any help finding your way out of this cave? We should've turned on a light. Your eyes aren't adjusted to the dark. Not that I can see much through these." She pointed to her sunglasses with a half-smile.

Dot giggled. "No, I'm okay. I've got my flashlight anyway." She waved it back and forth, until it suddenly caught fire. The adults panicked, but Dot blew out the fire and returned the flashlight to her backpack. She pulled out a smaller, travel-size flashlight. "Don't worry, I've got a backup."

"I've never seen a flashlight combust. And how were you so calm?" Montana asked.

"Really? It's happened to me three times already this year." Dot tested the battery of her new flashlight.

"How come every time someone breaks into my home, they happen to be the most unfazeable people in the world?" Caswell shot an accusatory look Montana's way, as if her nature or Dot's arrival was her fault.

"Because if we got freaked out, we wouldn't be able to withstand your scariness." Montana smiled playfully at her. Despite her cheeks remaining the same ghoulish white color, it was obvious Caswell was flustered by the comment, even though it had clearly been meant as a joke.

Dot was distracted from their antics, daydreaming about her situation. "Real, live monsters! That's more exciting than last month's aquarium visit. Heck, maybe more exciting than the butter slide incident!"

"She said heck out loud." Montana smiled and turned back to Caswell. "Why don't you use fake swears like that? You're old-fashioned and straight-up old. That should be something you do."

Caswell glanced at Dot. "You should go before this turns into more of a farce than it already is."

"It was very nice to meet you both!" Dot waved, getting an enthusiastic wave back from Montana and a slight hand lift from Caswell.

Back outside, Cameron and June had played three games of chopsticks. They both won once, and they added so many rules to the third game that the victor was unclear. They'd argued about whether or not a worm would become two worms if split in half, gone searching for a worm to test their theories, then made the world's smallest snowman out of the wet mush that littered the sidewalk. Finally, they were just waiting, and Cameron's worry was starting to gnaw at him. "It's been double the amount of time you guys bet on. We should go in after her."

June brushed off his concern. "Cam, relax. This is Dot we're talking about. She probably thought she saw something and sent herself on a wild goose chase. If anything went wrong, we'd probably see it externally. This house can't be very stably built. At the very least, it's not Dot proof."

"Is that supposed to make me feel better? What if she fell through the floorboards or something?"

"Where would she go? There's only dirt underneath."

Dot came back out the way she entered, seemingly unscathed. "Hey!" She ran over to them. "You'll never guess what I saw. There's a couple living here."

Cameron winced. "Ooh, that gives me second-hand embarrassment. Sorry, we should've checked that out first."

Dot shook her head. "No, no! They weren't a normal couple. That doesn't sound right. They were perfectly nice. I mean they weren't human. I guess human shouldn't equal normal, that's hardly fair." She snapped out of her tangent. "Anyway, one was a werewolf and one was a vampire!"

"Those aren't real, Dot." June held up a hand before either could argue. "Mr. Drake does not count as a primary source for that argument."

"They really were though! They had sharp teeth and inhuman eyes and dressed weird. I said we'd visit again next week so you guys can meet. They can prove it to you then." Dot spoke eagerly as they walked back to their bikes. "And don't think I've forgotten those Oreos, June."

"How about double or nothing if next week they turn out to be a normal couple." June said to keep the wager going.

"What do you define as a couple anyway? Like, boyfriend and girlfriend, or married?" Cameron asked, less bothered than he would've thought by the idea of supernatural creatures living on the outskirts of his town. With Dot around, this was hardly the weirdest or most dangerous thing to happen.

Dot shrugged, thinking back. "I didn't see any rings, but they were dressed like it was the 1930s or something. Maybe they didn't use rings back then." She got to work patching her tire, so used to it she didn't even need to look while she worked. "And I hope you're a woman of your word, June, because I accept."

June grinned. "Always am. Pleasure doing business with you, Liang."

As they rode off, Cameron hoped whoever lived in that haunted house was prepared for the chaos that was their trio.

Chapter Five

"WELL, AREN'T YOU UP early," Montana murmured. She tended to hang out for around an hour after arriving, waiting for Caswell to wake up, but she was already shuffling around when Montana got there. "What's the occasion?"

Caswell straightened her collar. "It's Friday. That human girl said she'd be back with her human friends. Did you forget?"

The blank look on Montana's face said it all. "No, no I did not." she spoke slowly, an obvious lie. To save face, she changed the topic. "Kid has a name, you know. You wouldn't like it if she just called you vampire woman. That sounds like a really lame superhero." She thought for a moment before smiling a little. "Kinda cute of you to wake up early for 'em."

"It would've been impolite for me to not be up for them, that's all." Caswell deflected, embarrassed by the implication.

"I'm paying you a compliment." Montana laughed. "Though I guess your stubbornness is pretty endearing too."

This was unusual. While Montana was strange, she was predictable to some degree. She had patterns. She was always snarky and always unimpressed and always messy. But this? This didn't fit.

"Are you feeling sick?" Caswell furrowed her eyebrows.

"What? No." Montana's confusion was evident, as though the question were a non sequitur. Then the light dawned in her eyes. "Sheesh, can't a gal be friendly without causing a fuss?"

"I'd hardly call that friendly."

Montana stepped closer. Too close. That wasn't unusual in itself since she never cared about personal space. The feeling arising in Caswell was unusual. "Then what would you call it?" She could feel the warmth of Montana's breath.

Caswell stared at her for a moment, trying to make sense of her reaction. She didn't have a word for it. Bizarre. Disarming. "Hostile," she finally decided on, and stepped back to return her space.

Montana looked away, her face unreadable. Though with Caswell's lack of social skills and Montana's expression-hiding sunglasses, that didn't say much. "Whatever." Her ears twitched. "Oh, I hear someone outside. I bet that's them." She paused. "Caswell? You hear me? There's someone at the door. They're at the door. Caswell."

"I heard you the first time."

Montana started bouncing up and down. "Okay, but there's someone at the door. You should answer the door. There're people. Caswell, you gotta open the door. They're outside right now."

"I am so grateful I don't get visitors more often," Caswell said with a grumble. "Must you act like that even when you're in your person form?"

Montana didn't seem to focus on the question, although the answer was obvious. "I am going crazy, man. You gotta get the door."

"If it bothers you so much, why don't you get it?"

Montana's eyes widened, her tail wagging at light speed. "Oh my god, you're right. I've got hands. I'm gonna get the door." She nearly sprinted away.

Caswell sighed. There were only a few instances where Montana's wolf side made itself apparent. Those manifestations were beyond annoying. Not that her human half was much better.

Caswell followed after Montana, who swung the door open. There were the three children, Dot in the lead, with her small fist poised to knock. Montana smiled easily. "What's up? Make yourself at home."

"Thank you," Dot skipped in, calling out into the house, "Hi, Ms. Caswell!"

She was followed by another girl, who was sizing up Montana. "Hmm. Mhm, mhm. Hmm." She nodded to herself, rubbing her chin, deep in thought. She circled around Montana, then grabbed her tail and gave it an experimental yank.

The sound that came out of Montana's mouth was not unlike that of a squeaky toy. "Hey!"

The girl showed no remorse. "I'm not done with you." She pointed at Montana, maintaining eye contact as she slowly regrouped with Dot.

The boy who came in behind her apologized. "Dude, I'm sorry. She's always like this." He glanced around the room. "Nice place you've got here. Old school."

Montana peered out the door to see if there was anyone else there, then closed it behind them. She flipped on the light switch, which had been unused for a long time. Monster eyes saw fine in the dark. Better, typically.

"They've got electricity,." The boy observed, probably not as quietly as he hoped.

"Hello, Liang." Caswell came down to greet them. "I take it these are your friends?"

"Yeah! This is June Winters and Cameron Breaux." Dot made wide gestures as she spoke, nearly smacking the others in their faces. "June, Cameron, this is Ms. Caswell, and that's Ms. Vic."

"Ms. Vic," Montana echoed delightedly as she made her way over to Caswell, careful not to turn her back to June.

"Uh, hi." Cameron waved awkwardly.

June, evidently, did not ride her bike in the cold all this way to waste time. "So Dot claims that the two of you aren't human."

"That would be correct." For once, Caswell had not been thrown off guard. People usually noticed she wasn't human immediately, although she didn't tend to stick around for a conversation. "I'm a vampire, and my associate here is a werewolf."

"I see." June sounded less than convinced. "You realize, however, with the discoveries of modern science, vampires don't make any sense? You can't go in the sunlight, can you?"

"That's right." Caswell nodded.

"But the moonlight is okay?"

"I have to get out some time."

June grinned like the cat who got the mouse. "The moon doesn't create its own light. It's just a reflection of the sun's rays. So why is it different?"

"I..." Caswell blinked. After thinking for a moment, she bristled up indignantly. "I don't have to answer that."

"And why can't you see your reflection? According to Christian belief, it's because you don't have a soul, which is what I'm basing this whole thing on, due to the cross thing and the holy water and the origins of the myth." She counted off on her fingers. "Inanimate objects don't have souls either. It's argued between churches whether animals have souls, yet all those things show up in a mirror." She was on a roll now. “You hunger for blood, but you can’t bleed. How can your stomach function without a working respiratory system? How do you talk without needing to breathe?”

Everyone was looking at Caswell now. She finally stuttered out, “Your science can’t explain everything!”

“Like what?” June seemed certain she couldn’t lose this debate.

“Mystical things beyond your wildest imagination,” Caswell said, as if that answered anything.

“Name one.”

Caswell thought for a moment. “Shapeshifting,” she said, sounding rather proud of herself.

June snorted. “That’s not possible either.”

“I do it about once a month,” Montana offered up, and Caswell appreciated the support.

“Don’t worry. I’ve got plenty of concerns with werewolves too. We’ll get there,” June assured her. “But on this topic, do you remember this so-called shapeshifting? Do you have any recollection of it at all?”

Montana scratched her chin. “No, but I don’t think I’m supposed to.”

“So why do you assume you do the impossible?” June argued.

“Because I wake up naked with the worst headache, and it feels like all my energy’s been vacuum-sucked outta me. Also, I think I ate a squirrel once.” She shrugged. “I know what happens right before and right after, and sometimes she fills me in on the rest.”

“Montana’s vague accounts aren’t important right now, because I can shapeshift too.” Caswell waved her off, wanting to bring the discussion to an end.

“You can?” The chorus was more or less in unison, with various inflections.

Caswell was not expecting such surprise. A lot of the vampire stories got most things wrong, but the ability to change form at will was almost always included. “Of course. It’s as simple as walking.”

“Then do it.” June egged her on, still not inclined to believe.

“Please,” Dot whispered, barely able to contain her excitement.

Caswell obliged and turned into a bat. Cameron screamed, prepared for shapeshifting but not for a tiny, winged mammal. Caswell was so pleased by this, she failed to notice Montana sneaking up behind her, ready to strike. She grabbed Caswell right out of the air, clasping her tightly in her hands.

"Why didn't you tell me you could do this? You're adorable." Montana cooed.

"Unhand me!" Caswell squeaked at her, which only incurred more delight.

"Your little voice!" Dot sounded like she was about to scream, but for a very different reason than Cameron.

"You sound like a chipmunk." Montana couldn't stifle her laughter despite her best efforts.

"That's enough," Caswell grumbled, though it didn't sound much like a grumble with her pitched voice. When she transformed back, Montana's hands wound up on her lower back. They remained like that for just a moment too long, before Montana slid her arms back to her sides and took a generous step back, leaning back against the stair railing.

"That was amazing." Dot was practically shouting. "You're so cool, Ms. Caswell."

"Thank you, Liang." Caswell tried not to let the compliment get to her. Feeling validated through a human's fear was one thing, which she could only presume was perfectly normal, but wanting them to like you? To think you're cool? That was a dangerous slope. Still, she could give the kid a simple thank you. That was only being polite.

June, meanwhile, had been watching the whole thing slack-jawed. Cameron smiled at her and asked playfully, "Was that enough proof for you? Because I don't think I want to see what else she might have up her sleeves."

"That was impossible."

"Yeah, that was awesome," Dot agreed, as if impossible and awesome were interchangeable terms.

June shook her head, "I guess around Dot..." As if on cue, the railing Montana was leaning on broke and she fell.

"Are you okay?" Dot rushed over, peering over what was left of the railing.

"Yep," she grunted. "Just knocked the wind outta me." She stood back up, and this time all three children screamed. "What?"

Caswell reached over and pulled the offending chunk of wood out of Montana's shoulder, making her wince. It had been at a rather gruesome angle. Montana whined, "Warn me next time you're gonna do something like that. You're too rough. I'm soft and squishy and don't like you tearing things out of my body."

"Somehow, I think you'll manage." Caswell said dryly. "Would you kindly quit bleeding all over my home?"

"Build a better house and I won't have to bleed. What if it was one of them who fell?" Montana motioned to the three. "Then what would you have done? Eaten them?"

"Has anyone ever told you how horribly unfunny you are?" Caswell mocked.

"How are you alive?" Cameron finally gasped.

"Oh," Montana turned back to them with a smile, then readjusted so her injury was out of their line of sight. "My wounds heal really fast, unless it's caused by silver. Then I don't think it heals at all."

"How does that make any sense?" June wrinkled her nose.

"Hey, don't shoot the messenger. Or, you know, you could since I'd survive." She chuckled at her own bad joke.

"All right, I think that's been quite enough excitement for one night." Caswell still held the piece of railing at arm's length.

"How are you not going crazy in the sight of blood?" Cameron asked.

Caswell made a face, similar to that of a child who had been asked to finish her broccoli. "It's werewolf blood. It tastes like dirt."

"How do you know what dirt tastes like? Have you tasted it?" Montana snickered.

"Spoken like a true kindergartener." Caswell rolled her eyes. "And I'm not an animal. I don't go 'crazy' for anything."

"Can you control minds?" Dot blurted out. "Dracula could control minds."

"You've read Dracula?" Cameron glanced at Dot with a quirked brow.

Dot shrugged. "There's a lot of stuff you don't know about me."

"Dracula could do whatever he wanted to. He wasn't real." Caswell said unimpressively. The kids were not satisfied.

"How would you know? Are you in contact with every other vampire in the whole world?" June argued.

"Are you telepathically connected to every single vampire?" Dot ran her hand through her hair, as if the action could calm her frenetic energy.

"Have you been reading our minds the whole time?" Cameron questioned disapprovingly. "That's not cool, bro. You need to respect people's privacy."

"Anybody know how to get blood out of a hoodie?" Montana poked at her shoulder, which had almost totally healed by then. Her clothes were still ripped and bloody.

"I can't do anything," Caswell finally shouted, overwhelmed. "I can't read minds or communicate telepathically or do whatever the hell Montana is asking for."

There was a beat of silence. "Could you suck the jelly out of a jelly doughnut?" Montana pointed to her teeth.

"That's disgusting." Caswell sighed, exasperated.

"But you're not sure?" June required clarification, her grin growing.

"Doughnut, doughnut, doughnut," Dot and Cameron began chanting simultaneously.

Montana already had the door open. "We're going to the convenience store!"

The kids cheered and ran ahead. Caswell followed, tossing the piece of railing outside and shooting Montana a glare. "Being with you is worse than dying. And I would know."

Montana did not so much as blink at the accusation. Her smile was softer than usual. "When was the last time things around you were so lively? Isn't it nice to have people who could be doing anything in the world choose to spend their time with you?" She walked past, patting Caswell's shoulder. "If you weren't having so much fun, I wouldn't be teasin' ya, I promise."

Caswell did not have a response to that. She just stood there, watching Montana catch up to the others, then joining in their play as if it were the easiest thing in the world. Caswell's hand was over her chest before she even realized it. She clutched at the fabric. Her shirt was so thin, and she thought about how little there was standing in defense of her heart.

And if it got staked right through, it still wouldn't beat.

Chapter Six

IT WAS THE TWELFTH of February.

Montana had drawn a dog with angry eyebrows in the little white square of the calendar. Two squares over had a little heart scribbled on it. It was surprisingly easy to keep track of the dates when you couldn't stop thinking about them.

It all started with Montana telling Caswell the unprompted story of attending her friend's birthday party. Caswell was pretending she wasn't paying attention, as usual, but still pointing out the holes in the story when Montana got too excited and skipped little things. Really, she was a horrible storyteller. Caswell didn't know why she bothered.

"So I told Alison that he had said that they had said what she thought she heard was actually ice cream cake." Montana finished, as improperly as she began. She glanced up, and Caswell could almost see a thought crossing that scattered mind. A vast distance to cross, to be sure. "When is your birthday anyway?"

Silence spoke volumes.

"You don't know? That's crazy, even for you. We'll have to pick a new one."

Caswell frowned. "You can't pick a new birthday. That's not how it works."

"Eh, it's a celebration that marks the passing of another year, so I think it's totally fine," Montana said. "I definitely took you as a winter baby, but we don't have a lot of winter left right now. Basically only February...Ooh, how about the fourteenth? It's Valentine's Day, so you won't forget it again. Instead of spending the holiday thinking about how wifeless you are, you can eat cake—no, wait, you don't eat—you can have a party. I'd better check to make sure there isn't a full moon on the fourteenth."

Montana checked the moon phases app she had downloaded a short time ago. Caswell found she was unable to come up with a proper rebuttal against the whole thing. It was a ridiculous idea, yet she didn't entirely want to fight against it. Maybe it'd be nice to have something to celebrate.

And now here she was, two days away from her birthday. Caswell tried to swallow back a smile. What a silly notion. She didn't even know how old she was. If she did, could she even count the years when she wasn't alive? Should her age be split in two halves, before and after the turning? That would've been a fine excuse for picking a new birthday.

"The day I died," she muttered out loud to herself, ghosting through an otherwise empty room.

Waking before Montana showed up always felt strange. Some nights Montana was too exhausted and didn't show up at all. Not having one of those cellphone gadgets or even a telepathic connection, Caswell would wait up all night, having nothing better to do than fear the worst.

Montana would always pop in the next night with terrible anecdotes or silly questions or nothing but the offer of her company, and Caswell had yet to turn her down. Tonight she was sure to show since it was a full moon. The guarantee of her arrival was reassuring, and Caswell pretended it was for the sake of a set schedule.

She heard the door open in the other room, knowing better than to wait by the entrance when the sun was still up. What June had said about moonlight was still in the back of her head every time she thought about the sun, and it bothered Caswell that she didn't have an answer. "I'm in the foyer." If she didn't call out, Montana would search the entire house for her.

Dot came hopping through the door, rambling, "I was worried I came too early, but I wanted to visit, and this was the only day I could stay out late this week. June had homework, and Cameron caught a cold, so they couldn't come with."

"Don't you know what day it is?" Caswell got over her initial surprise of seeing her. Having Montana show up at her manor was strange, but now multiple people were popping in and out whenever they pleased. It was so different from the way it had always been.

"Uhh...Friday?" Dot shrugged. "The eleventh? No, that was yesterday, it's the twelfth."

"The full moon." Caswell sighed. "You came to visit a werewolf on the full moon."

"Oh!" Dot's eyes widened. "That's so exciting!"

"It is not exciting," Caswell scoffed.

"Is it dangerous?" Dot did not sound afraid. In fact, she sounded delighted. She was such an odd child.

"Not nearly as dangerous as it should be. Still, you need to think before you act. You might've gotten yourself into serious trouble. And even if you don't mind, imagine how guilty it would make Montana feel if she hurt you." Caswell lectured.

"You're right. Sorry." Dot rubbed at her arm, looking very apologetic, like a scolded child.

Well, she was a scolded child. Caswell realized she was acting like an overbearing mother, trying to keep Dot and Montana's feelings safe. How disgusting. If the idea was nauseating enough to make her vomit, at least it would answer one of June's questions, though doubtless it would also raise more.

The door opened again. Caswell didn't know how she could've mistaken Dot's entrance for the way Montana slammed her way in. "Foyer!" she yelled simply this time.

"Is she already a wolfman?" Dot's eyes positively sparkled.

"No, it's...I suppose it'll be easier to see it for yourself."

Montana entered the room, not visibly surprised when she spotted Dot. She waved a little. "Hey, Dot. You know it's a full moon, yeah?"

"Ms. Caswell just said the same thing," Dot said, as if it were some sort of crazy coincidence.

"Well, yeah, I imagine she would. It's kind of a big deal." Montana smiled. "You still wanna stay?"

Dot nodded her head vigorously. "I wouldn't miss seeing a werewolf transformation for anything in the whole world."

"Fine by me." Montana laughed. "I don't mind being looked at like a science project, as long as there are no dissections."

"I wouldn't, and June might say she would, but she wouldn't either, I promise."

"Good to know. Okay, you're going to wanna look away for this part, so Cassie, could you cover her eyes?" Montana turned away from them, cracking her neck in preparation for the body distortion that awaited her.

"That's not fair," Dot complained as Caswell lightly put her hands over her eyes. "Your hands are so cold!" There was some strange brittle snapping, and grunts that became less humanlike by the second. Caswell removed her hands and all that was left of Montana were her clothes. Dot gasped. "Where'd she go?"

Caswell went over and crouched down, sifting through the clothes and revealing the puppy hidden underneath. She gathered up the clothes and brought them over to the couch, leaving the puppy, who ran over to Dot.

"Is that Ms. Vic?" She was flabbergasted. Puppy-Montana rolled over onto her back, and Dot reached down to pet her tummy. "She's so cute."

"Yes, she's rather...unconventional." Caswell walked back over, looking at Montana with disdain.

"Does she still have the same brain, or does she think like a puppy now?"

"The latter. She won't remember any of this, either." This part was easy to explain.

"Oh, I see. You must worry about her."

"Why would I be worried?"

"Well, she's so small and helpless. And if she's friendly enough to run up to strangers, that makes this form especially dangerous," Dot said, stopping when she caught Caswell staring. "Uh...Ms. Caswell?"

"Hm?" Caswell snapped out of it. "Right, no, she's fine. She's a werewolf. They're practically invincible."

"Well," Dot spoke slowly, "it's good that you're here to keep her safe. With a vampire protecting her, I think that's the safest she could be." Dot had stopped giving belly rubs, so Montana righted herself. "Ooh, I have something I bet you'd like!" Dot began digging through her backpack. The tennis ball she pulled out set Montana's tail wagging. Dot gave it a toss, and Montana chased after it.

"Why'd you have one of those?" Caswell asked her curiously, joining her in her position on the floor.

"Just in case." Dot smiled. "You never know what's going to happen."

"Maybe I should get one too. She seems to be a fan." Caswell watched Montana fight with the ball, which was a little too big to easily grab in her mouth.

"You could have that one, if you'd like." Dot patted her backpack. "I've got more."

"That's...Thank you, Liang."

"No problem." Dot shifted so she could sit cross-legged. "You can call me Dot, you know."

Caswell chewed at the inside of her cheek. Instinctively, she didn't want to use the child's first name. That would imply they were close. But it was hard to bring herself to admit such. And if that was hard, it meant they were already closer than she wanted them to be. It was silly to pretend that calling her by her last name would dissipate that closeness. "All right, Dot." She glanced at the girl and quickly glanced away. "Is it...difficult, for you?"

"Is what difficult?"

Having finally conquered the ball, Montana returned. Dot stole it back with ease and tossed it again. Montana went scrambling after it.

"Having to carry around flashlights and, and tennis balls, and what have you. Always preparing for the worst."

"Oh no, I don't think so." Dot smiled, and it was hard for Caswell to understand how a person could smile so much. "I mean, it's normal for me. I'm prepared, but not scared. That's what my dad usually says. When things always go wrong, you see that even then, it's not so bad. So I don't know. I think I'm all right. I've got a lot of people who I know would help me even if things got really, really bad. So, like, as long as I've got them, it'll never be really, really bad."

"I see."

"Can I ask you a question now?"

"Depends on the question." Caswell responded uneasily. With how much June's questions had gotten to her, she wasn't sure she was ready for more.

"Well, I see werewolves versus vampires a lot and was wondering if that's totally made up."

"No, that's true. Werewolves and vampires don't get along. We're blood enemies." Caswell tried not to focus on Montana, who was currently trying to roll on the tennis ball.

"Is that hard for you guys?" Dot looked at her with an expression too wise for her years. It was evident Dot had experienced plenty of hardships of her own due to that unlucky curse of hers. She could claim otherwise, but it would be obvious to anyone who saw her that her life had not been the easy one a child deserves.

Caswell shrugged a little. "Vampires exist in isolation, so it's not like I have anyone around me to disapprove. Werewolves usually come in packs, but whoever bit her never came back around. So she's got no one to tell her how things should be except for me."

"Did you tell her?" Dot's voice was quieter than it had been all evening.

"I tried." Caswell tried to lighten it with a laugh. "She wasn't very inclined to listen."

"You guys deserve to be happy." Dot promised her. "And I think your love is a beautiful thing."

Caswell nodded a little before processing what Dot had said, and then she nearly choked. "Our what?"

"This wonderful spark you two have between each other." Dot held out her hands in front of her chest to replicate it physically. "In the face of such adversity, it's still so strong, and you should be proud of that. You were obviously meant to be."

"It's not like that," Caswell stuttered. "She and I—we're not—there's no way she'd—we're just friends. We're not even that, we're...acquaintances! I...I know her, that's all!"

"You don't have to hide it from me," Dot insisted. "I support it completely. I get that's probably not much coming from a human, since I don't know all the societal expectations on the both of you, but I mean it."

"There's nothing to...Isn't it getting a little late anyway? You should be heading home."

Thankfully, Dot was quite easily distracted. "Oh, you're right. I'll call my mom, and see if she'll let me stay over." Dot rushed into another room, already dialing.

"Dot, wait!" Caswell tried, but Dot had already made up her mind and was out of earshot. "I don't even own a bed." Caswell heaved a sigh. There was no helping it, she supposed. Montana dropped the ball in front of her, tail wagging with anticipation. Caswell picked up the ball, turning it over in her hand. "If you had something you wanted to say, you'd say it. Not now, obviously, but any other day. How frustratingly enviable."

"Wuff!"

"I knew you'd say that." Caswell gave the ball the softest throw she could, not wanting to break a hole through her wall, and Montana ran after it. "If only things were that simple."

Montana had expected to wake up naked. She did not expect the little piles of books surrounding her on all sides. "Am I in puppy prison?" Groggy, but delighted by the concept, she stood up with a groan. The stacks didn't even come up to her knees. "Was I really that short?" On the other side of the books were her clothes, so she got them on. She scratched at the back of her head and yawned as she went searching for Caswell.

She found her asleep, sitting up on the couch, with Dot leaning on her shoulder, also conked out. Montana walked over with a smile, gently shimmying Dot into her arms, trying not to jostle her too much. Caswell's eyes fluttered open, but she wasn't fully awake.

"Hey," Montana whispered. "Gonna get the little one home. Thanks for watchin' over the both of us, Caswell. You can tell me all about it later."

Caswell leaned back, and Montana assumed she was slipping back into sleep. She was halfway across the room, when she almost missed Caswell mutter, "Beatrice."

"What?" Montana turned around, keeping her voice as quiet as she could. Caswell did not move at all, and from this angle Montana couldn't see her face.

"You can call me Beatrice."

Chapter Seven

"IF ONLY I COULD use a mirror." Caswell idled as she tried to smooth out her waistcoat. It was the fourteenth, which meant it was her birthday, which could mean anything at all.

After finally accepting there was nothing else she'd be able to do about her appearance, she sat at the bottom of the stairwell to wait for Montana. She didn't show up yesterday, but that wasn't unusual. She was always exhausted after the full moon, and since she couldn't always take off work, she needed whatever extra sleep she could get.

If only she had shown up, then Caswell could've asked her what the birthday plans were to quell her anxiety. She was bound to be anxious no matter what, but knowing what was waiting for her would make her less anxious.

On the other hand, Montana might not have told her anything. She probably would've delighted in knowing Caswell was overthinking her weird little plans. Researching birthdays wouldn't have been much help either, since Montana lacked any sense for tradition. She could have anything in mind. It was a tad exhilarating.

So she waited.

And waited.

And waited.

Hours passed, and there was no sign of Montana. She usually came around sunset when she was going to show, and now it was midnight. Maybe she was busy. It was Valentine's Day, after all. Maybe she had a date. Perhaps some witty, charming, attractive man won her over and stole her away for the night. Caswell realized she didn't even know if Montana was seeing someone. Montana had an entire life of her own that didn't include Caswell at all.

She found herself imagining a pair of lips on Montana's mouth, a pair of hands on Montana's waist, a pair of eyes that only saw Montana. A pulse that could match hers as they sat in the sun. Someone she could eat junk food with, someone who was very good at all the things Caswell was very bad at.

She stood up, trying to shake her head clear of those thoughts. It wasn't any of her business. Montana could do whatever she liked. But did it have to be on her birthday?

She caught herself. It wasn't her birthday. She didn't have a birthday. This was exactly what she was afraid of. She was getting so used to being treated like a person she was starting to forget she wasn't one. Montana didn't owe her anything. Caswell was the one who got carried away, sowing foolish hopes in a barren field. She had earned this crushing sensation in her chest.

That didn't mean it hurt any less.

With a flourish of her cape, she flew back up the stairs, disappearing into her piano room. She started playing, overcome with vigor. This was better. This was what she needed to silence the emotions threatening to boil over in her.

She hit a sour note, wondering if Montana was home yet or still out with her date. It was late for a fling, but maybe it was more than a dinner date. She shook her head and tried to get back into the flow of the music.

Another mistake. How many nights did Caswell spend worrying that Montana had died when she was really off exploring another person's body? It was her own fault for worrying. Montana was not close to her and never pretended otherwise. She started playing again, slowly, taking it one note at a time.

Then her piano yelled like a human, and Caswell fell off her stool. She realized the yelling was not coming from her piano, but her entrance way. Recovering from her fright, she returned to the parlor to find Montana, panting like she'd run a marathon.

"I am so sorry," she gasped out, volume too loud considering they were in the same room. She spoke quickly. "I had to close up, so I was running a little late, and I wasn't paying attention, and this dude hit me with his car. He was going to call a hospital, and that was a good move because he really hit me, like, it was ugly, but obviously I can't go to a hospital or a vet probably, so I asked him to pay for my bike. That was when I could talk again. Like I said, he got me good, but anyway the bike place was closed, so he took me back to his place and gave me his bike because I think he thought I was like the devil testing mankind, and if he didn't appease me, I'd curse his bloodline for generations. Something like that. Also I stole these from his yard." She held up a fistful of smashed flowers. "Uh, for you. I know, they're ugly and they don't make up for it, but I really am sorry."

Caswell stared. Despite having to work late and getting hit by a car, Montana still came as fast as she could. She was unbelievable. Caswell couldn't hold it in anymore. She laughed.

"Shit, you must be really mad." Montana seemed mildly horrified. "I've never heard you laugh like that before."

"I'm not." Caswell waved her off, smiling at her for a moment with such adoration Montana was stunned silent. "You're just so ridiculous."

Montana smiled too, setting the crumpled flowers down on the nearest flat surface. "Really? You're the first person to ever tell me that." She turned back to the door. "Now come on, we gotta hurry. We've got a full night of stuff to do in like six hours."

Caswell followed her out into the yard where her new bicycle was. She had been in such a hurry, she hadn't put down the kickstand, letting it fall onto its side. Montana righted the bike. "Don't tell the kids I ride without a helmet. I don't wanna be a bad influence. Okay, sit on the handlebars. We'll be a little off balance, but I'll make it work." There was a bag next to the bike that she slung over her shoulder.

"Uh, no." Caswell quirked an eyebrow when she realized Montana was being serious. "I'm not doing that."

"After everything I've gone through to get here, you're really going to just say no?" Montana pouted. "Come on, Beatrice." Hearing her first name on Montana's lips felt borderline unreal. "That's mean, even for you."

"I am capable of flight. I'm not going to sit on your handlebars."

"Okay, well, I can't fly."

"You ride your bike. I'll fly next to you."

"That's…" Without arguing, Montana let her arms fall to her sides. "Yeah, that's fine."

Montana got onto her bike, and Caswell turned into a bat. They struggled a little to keep pace with each other. After a few minutes of quiet while they got the hang of it, Montana asked, "How come when you transform, you take your clothes with you, but when I transform, my clothes fall off?"

"Mine is magic, while yours is a curse." Caswell ignored how Montana snickered over her squeaky bat voice.

"But isn't a curse magical? Where do your clothes go when you change? It'd be really cute if you wore a tiny version of them."

"Thanks for the input." Caswell rolled her eyes. "Are you going to giggle like that every time I talk?"

"No," Montana said, but her voice still sounded like laughter. "What? I'm not doing anything."

"You're a terrible liar." Caswell would remind her that she was with a bloodthirsty and unholy monster, but she knew Montana would find that as adorable as her calling herself cute and fluffy. A drop of rain hit her and she missed a flap, having to speed up for a moment to regain her position.

Montana noticed the rain too. "You're kidding." She groaned. "The one night I wanted a clear sky." After a few more droplets hit, she stopped her bike. "Okay, hang on, time out."

Caswell flew back, hovering in front of her. "What?"

"I'm not gonna make you fly in the rain." She unzipped her tracksuit. "I'll get us there. You hide out in here."

"That's disgusting."

"Stop giving me trouble." Montana tried to sound annoyed but was unable to hide her laughter. She simply grabbed Caswell out of the air again. She was much too good at that. Caswell needed to work on her reflexes. "It'll just be for a little bit." She stuffed Caswell in by her chest and zipped back up, leaving the front still a little open. Not that it was necessary since Caswell couldn't suffocate. She figured Montana forgot.

Montana got back to pedaling. Caswell was too frazzled to do anything. Pressed against her like this, she could hear Montana's quickening heart rate. The consistent thumping was rather comforting. And she was very warm. Caswell wondered if that was how body heat was or if Montana radiated it like she radiated friendliness. It was warm and soft and undeniably nice. Caswell didn't know what was coming over her, but for once, she didn't fight it. She had spent most of the night emotionally distressed and most of her existence touch-starved, so she let herself have this. It wasn't like Montana could see her. Afterward, she could pretend it was horrible. For now, she could just listen to Montana's heartbeat.

Montana rode for another thirty minutes or so before coming to a stop, this time using the kickstand. She unzipped her tracksuit a little more. "Okay, we're here. I'm gonna...scoop you out of there I guess...You're kinda fuzzy...almost soft." Montana carefully lifted Caswell back into the night air. "See, that wasn't so bad."

Caswell flew from her hand and transformed back. "The rain has mostly cleared up," she said, neither denying nor agreeing with Montana's statement. She looked around. They were on top of a little cliff, surrounded by trees on most sides. Everything was still dripping from the rain, and all the critters who lived there were asleep or taking shelter. "Where are we?"

"Uh, middle of the woods. I'm gonna kill you. I'm a serial killer."

"You say that as if your body odor hasn't already done the job," Caswell shot back easily, much to Montana's delight.

She grinned. "Nah, actually, I was thinking you spend all day and night in the same stuffy house, and a change of scenery could do you some good. I know you're not into places with a lot of people, so I thought some place outside would be nice. And the view here is pretty great when the sky isn't overcast."

"I'll take your word for it." Caswell turned back to face her. "This was a nice gesture, thank you."

"I'm not done!" Montana reached into the bag she had brought with the bike. "I was hoping to give you this back in October or even November as thanks for talking to me and all, but turns out I'm a pretty slow learner. Also was hoping to make something a little nicer, but again, slow learner." She pulled out a mess of blue yarn and moved in close to wrap it around Caswell's neck. The movement brought their lips a breath apart, but she pulled away just as fast. "I know it doesn't really fit your goth aesthetic, but when I saw it I was like woah, that's exactly her eye color. And I like your eyes." There was a beat of silence. "Which isn't really the point of a gift. I'm really bad at this."

Caswell lightly ran her hand along the scarf. "It's very ugly."

Montana laughed. "Yeah, but it'll still do its job. Your hands are always so cold I thought you could use some warming up."

It was itchy and poorly constructed, and the color really didn't match her look at all. It didn't feel very warm either, but Caswell gave it a pass on that one, considering it was hard to compare anything to the body heat extravaganza she had experienced a moment ago. Still, despite all that, it made her warm on the inside. Montana had thought of her and spent months doing something she wasn't any good at...for her.

"You can finally get rid of that doughnut box." Montana smiled at her, and Caswell realized what this gift meant. Montana was thanking her for helping her and, by extension, ending any need for continued relations between them. They had both fulfilled their parts of the bargain. It could be over. Caswell could be alone again, left to her musical passions and dark work, never having to worry about another knock at the door until the end of time.

"I don't accept." Caswell said suddenly.

Montana blinked. "What?"

Caswell looked away, her logic childish at best. "You can't give me one lousy gift and expect it to cover both my birthday and a thank you gift. That's cheating."

"Didn't know you liked presents so much. All right, all right, keep the doughnut box. I'll come up with something else. Until then," Montana brushed her mess of hair out of her face so her eyes were on Caswell and only her, "Happy birthday, Beatrice."

"Thank you." She tried to say it dismissively, but she came across a little winded, as if Montana's gaze had knocked the air out of her.

Montana didn't seem to notice. "Let's get back. Sun'll be up in like two hours." She started walking back to her bike.

"Montana," Caswell said awkwardly, not entirely sure what she was planning on saying.

"You know, if I'm calling you Beatrice, you can call me Vic. You coulda called me Vic the whole time." She had tripped up on Caswell's name and tried a few more times, with differing inflections. "Bee-trice. Be-uh-trice. Be-at-trice. Bat..." Realizing what she had done, Montana's whole face lit up. "Batrice! Ha, that's funny. Because you turn into a bat. It sounds like your name, but it's got bat in it."

"I got it." Caswell scowled. "Never mind."

"Aw, come on, you know you love it."

"I do not. I don't know how anyone could be in a relationship with someone as annoying as you."

"Hey, you can't make fun of me for being single on Valentine's Day when you are too," Montana elbowed her playfully. "At least I've dated in the past century."

"I already told you my love life is none of your business." Caswell folded her arms across her chest, but she felt too light to play grumpy. The news that Montana wasn't seeing anyone affected her more than it should have.

Not that she had a chance. Not that she wanted a chance. But it was satisfying to imagine she was the only one who got to feel Montana's heartbeat. That little rhythm was a secret they could share, even if she didn't have one to match.

Chapter Eight

MAY ROLLED IN WITH an explosion of flowers and an overabundance of rain. Caswell used to be ambivalent toward weather patterns, but now she liked the rain. It made her think of her birthday. It made her think of Montana.

Montana was a topic she could think about for hours. That werewolf was made up of so many strange and captivating pieces that thinking of her felt like decryption, like solving a puzzle or a riddle. The more pieces she tried to put together, the farther she seemed from the finished picture.

And if she wasn't unraveling her mind, she was thinking about her physique. With the cold of winter finally waning, Montana would often lounge around in a tank top and sweatpants. She wore a tacky gold chain that Caswell would've made more snarky comments about if she wasn't so distracted. To think the sight of arms could distract her so.

Worse than that still was the way she watched Montana's mouth when she spoke. She wished she didn't, but Montana talked so much and it seemed as though she was trying to draw attention to her lips, like she couldn't keep that tongue of hers behind her teeth. Like Caswell wanted it behind her own.

She would have fought against the thought, but she was having similar ones so frequently it would be a waste of energy. There must be some horrible illness caused by spending so much time with what was supposed to be a rival species. If that was the case, she prayed it would stop taking its sweet time and just finish her off already. At this point it was being cruel.

She took to pacing the floor. The problem with spring, if you could set the general aesthetic aside, was that the nighttime was getting shorter. Getting visitors had put her on a schedule, and now she was waking up while the sun still wreaked its havoc on the world. That meant she was spending more waking hours alone, since no one wanted to accidentally murder her by letting the rays of light in with them. What an annoyance that sun was.

Though she couldn't stop herself from wondering what Montana looked like in the sunlight.

Finally, the creak of the door liberated her from her thoughts. June came in, setting down a bag on the floor. "Can I leave this here for now?" When Caswell did not object, she took that as confirmation. "Awesome. I'm never going shopping with Cameron again."

Cameron came in right after her, frowning, "It wouldn't have taken so long if the shoe display didn't fall on Dot. Or if the sprinklers hadn't gone off. Or if that lady hadn't managed to swap out her baby for a possum. That was out of all of our hands." Following her lead, he stacked his bags on top of her's.

"Glad she found her baby afterward," Dot chimed in, skipping after them. "Hi, Ms. Caswell! How has your night been?"

"Less eventful than yours, it sounds."

Montana brought up the rear. "Guess who I ran into on my way home today?" She motioned excitedly to the group. "Also, there was a lady with a baby possum."

"We already told her that," June said, slipping off her shoes. She got comfortable almost as easily as Montana did.

June and Montana actually got along swimmingly. Most of it was June daring her to do stupid things and Montana subjecting herself to it without hesitation.

"Also, you didn't tell me I shouldn't be eating chocolate, which was totally uncool." Montana's expression was nothing less than betrayed. "June said I wouldn't be able to eat a king-size Hershey's bar, and she was right." Case in point.

June nodded with pride. "Easiest five bucks I've ever made."

"It's not my fault you'd eat practically anything." Caswell was unapologetic.

"But chocolate is chocolate. I think it's safe to assume anyone would eat it." Cameron reasoned.

Dot pointed out, "Unless you have an allergy," and received some affirming murmurs.

Chocolate. Caswell knew that was something edible, and she was fairly certain it was some kind of confectionery. She tried to remember it. Had she eaten it? If she did, there'd be no way she could recall the taste after all this time. From the kids' reactions, she assumed they liked it.

"Do you even know what chocolate is?" Montana's ears flicked, noticing her pause.

June shook her head. "Unless she's been hiding under a rock since 1900 BC, she would know what chocolate is. It's possible her idea of chocolate is different from ours, though, seeing as it was a bitter drink until it reached Europe hundreds of years later. Even then it stayed rather bitter until the Industrial Revolution. It's a constantly evolving confectionery."

"So what type of chocolate have you had?" Dot asked.

"Her idea of chocolate shouldn't affect this," Cameron interrupted. "It's made of the same stuff. If it's not good for werewolves, it wouldn't have been at any point in time."

"Excellent point, Cameron. Are you trying to poison Vic?" June whipped her head back around to stare accusingly at Caswell.

"She would never!" Dot objected on her behalf, believing both in her friend and the power of true love. "She doesn't have the best werewolf resources, that's all."

"Can regular wolves eat chocolate?" Montana finally spoke up, apparently lost in thought over this.

"Since dogs can't, and werewolves can't, I'd imagine wolves can't either?" Cameron looked to his friends for support. Dot shrugged at him.

"She's not an orthodox werewolf," Caswell reminded the group. "At this point, I'm not sure what rules apply to her."

"If I were a meaner wolf, I'd be able to eat chocolate?" Montana pondered, as if she'd have any control over changing that.

"I don't know. I've never talked to a werewolf about their eating habits before." Caswell didn't know why she kept having to remind them of this.

"Ooh, that reminds me." Cameron brightened up. "Dot relayed to us that werewolves and vampires don't usually get along, so we were hoping you'd tell us how you met."

"First let's go sit down." Montana was nearly pushing them into the next room. "No reason to stand around like a buncha scarecrows."

"Have you guys ever seen a scarecrow explode?" Dot demonstrated what that looked like with her hands. "It's the coolest."

Caswell followed them, pulling over a chair so that Dot, Cameron, and Montana could sit on the couch. June opted to sit on the floor, cross-legged. "I can't imagine why our first meeting would be of any interest to you all," Caswell said.

"Well hang on. I think it's a pretty funny story." Montana said. "It was the same night I got bit."

"That's crazy." Cameron was in awe.

Montana shrugged. "Not really, seein' as I wouldn't have ended up here if it weren't for that bite. I was hurt, and this house was close. Thought she could call a hospital for me. She didn't, but it was okay. Probably better that I didn't end up somewhere else, since anyone in their right mind would've called a hospital, and then I would've been found out. Then I'd have probably ended up in a government lab or something."

"So by not saving you, she actually saved you?" June's lips quirked up into a half-smile.

Montana laughed. "Yeah, I guess that's true." She gave Caswell a dorky thumbs up. "Thanks, Beatrice."

"My intention was not to save you," Caswell grumbled. "I wanted you to go away."

"Well, I didn't," Montana said, in a "and we all lived happily ever after" tone.

"You left out too many details," Cameron whined. He hugged his knees to his chest. "Did you know what the other one was right away?"

"I didn't even know what I was," Montana admitted. "I don't think that would've made a difference though. I'm pretty much the same as I was then, just hairier. Even if she didn't hate my blood, I couldn't be scared of someone like her."

Caswell wanted to take offense to that, but the words were spoken with such an underlying fondness, she decided she'd ignore it, then overthink it later. "I, however, did know she was a werewolf. That's why I wanted her to leave me alone. The last thing I needed was wolf trouble." She bit her lip for a second, but gave in. "While she has proved troublesome, she's much easier to deal with than the average member of her kind."

That earned her a wink from Montana. It was meant to be silly, but it made her melt. Caswell cleared her throat, not going down without a fight, "It'd be nicer not to have to deal with a werewolf at all."

"A human girlfriend would be worse, though, wouldn't it?" June cocked her head, curls bouncing.

"Either you'd drink all her blood, or you'd eventually have to turn her," Cameron said solemnly.

"Don't sweat over that. She can't get any type of girlfriend." Montana chuckled, clearly not picking up on the implication that she was the current girlfriend.

"Still managed to get you." June pointed out. "Unless you're under her evil vampire curse."

"Get me?" Montana snorted. "You've got it backward. The only reason she hasn't kicked me out is because she's a lonely old bat. Heh, bat. Because—"

"I got it," Caswell assured her, in a not very assuring voice.

"They're not actually together," Dot finally stage-whispered to her friends. "Just friends."

June and Cameron exchanged a glance that made it clear they weren't buying that. June couldn't hide her skepticism. "Vic, are you in a romantic relationship with Caswell or not?"

Montana stared at them. Cameron hid his face in his hands, letting out a low, slow, "Oh my god."

"A romantic relationship?" Montana echoed. "That's..." she looked at Caswell, who wouldn't meet her eyes. She forced a laugh. "Oh man, that's so funny. We couldn't, not in a million billion years."

"We shouldn't have assumed." Cameron groaned.

"It's okay!" Montana tried to convince them. "Really, that was super cute of you guys. It's...it's not a possibility."

Caswell gripped her pant legs, staring down at her knuckles. She wanted to laugh it off like Montana did. But she was scared that her voice would waver and expose her.

June was going to say something but her phone buzzed. She pulled it out of her pocket. “Ahh, my dad wants to know if we’re still good to sleepover, Cameron.”

“Yeah.” He sat back up. “Actually, guys, we should head back. My mom was gonna order pizza while we were out.”

Montana let out a puff of air, and although Caswell thought she sounded relieved, it was possible she was projecting. “All right, nice seein’ you kids. Make sure you stay safe on your way home.” She ushered them back to the door, where they gathered up their shopping bags. She opened the door and looked up at the sky. “Ooh, it’s raining pretty heavily. Are you lot gonna be okay?”

“Yes ma’am!” Dot started pulling raincoats and umbrellas from her backpack. “I came prepared!”

“Sorry again for making things awkward.” Cameron’s face was still red.

Montana waved them off. “Don’t sweat it, kid. It’s been more awkward around here than that. Stay safe out there!”

A little chorus of goodbyes cued Montana to shut the door, and she returned to Caswell, who had watched them leave but hadn’t moved an inch. Montana made no effort to hide her affection for the friends. “Man, those kids are crazy.”

“No crazier than you.”

“Should I be insulted by that?” There was the distant rumble of thunder that only their advanced perceptions could detect, and Montana stiffened up. “Ugh, I hate the rain.”

“Why?”

Montana flopped back down onto the couch. “Not all rain. I know the plants need it and all. But storms like this...they make me anxious.”

Caswell stealthily moved from her seat to join Montana on the couch. She was honestly surprised. She didn’t think someone as laid back as Montana could get anxious. “And why is that?”

Montana laughed a little, but it was weak. “I think it’s a werewolf thing. I used to be fine with ’em. Now the thunder freaks me out. I know it’s stupid.”

Caswell didn’t call her stupid. She didn’t say anything at all. She rested her hand on top of Montana’s. Their fingers entwined. They sat in comfortable silence for a while. Caswell’s mind did not wander far, only paying attention to the size and warmth of the hand wrapped around hers. As the storm got closer, Montana's grip tightened.

After a particularly large bolt of thunder caused her to jump, Montana rested her head on Caswell's shoulder. "I'm glad you saved me, Beatrice," she whispered.

Caswell waited for the sound of thunder to cover her quiet, "So am I."

Chapter Nine

"IT'S SO HOT OUTSIDE, I'm going to melt," Montana complained loudly, as that was the only way she seemed to know how to complain. Caswell for once had no complaints, seeing as the hot weather meant that Montana was swapping out her usual garb for tanks and shorts. Most were still that hideous shade of orange she seemed to adore, but the color was hardly what was eye-catching. Her thick, strong legs were newly on display. With more body showing, her body-hair problem was a little more obvious. As she told Caswell in all too explicit detail, anything she shaved would grow back by the end of the day. "How are you not a puddle when you're dressed in all black like that?"

Caswell walked past her place on the couch, cape swishing with the motion. Even if the temperature affected her, she wouldn't give up the look that was an integral part of what she thought made a vampire. "I'm not alive. I don't do homeostasis."

Montana grinned. "You learned that word from June, didn't you?"

"Of course not," Caswell lied. She was caught off guard by how quickly Montana saw right through her, though she should be getting used to it by now. "You really think I've been around this long and haven't picked up any new words?"

"Yeah, that's exactly what I think." Montana fanned herself. "Even if you don't overheat, you gotta change up your wardrobe sometimes. You gotta..." She snickered, and it took her a few times to get out her next words. "You gotta revamp it. Vamp like, like vampire."

"I understood." Caswell rolled her eyes. She wished Montana would outgrow her love of stupid puns. "And what about you? You're always dressed in the same horrendous colors, and it's either a sweaty tracksuit or ill-fitting shorts."

"Hey, I already got my makeover. Remember?" Montana took out her phone, pulling up the picture Dot had sent her of a psyched-out Dot and puppy-Montana wearing sunglasses. "She said I was the coolest dog in the world."

"I'd say you can't wear sunglasses and nothing else, but I'm sure you've already considered it." Caswell thought for a moment before asking, "Why do you wear those sunglasses anyway? Isn't it dark enough without those on too?"

"Oh, I'm colorblind," Montana said casually, tapping the rim with a finger as she slipped her phone back into her pocket with her other hand.

Caswell blinked. That raised more questions than it answered. "Pardon?"

"Do you not know what that is?" Montana sounded a little surprised. "Well, uh, I was born with dumb eyes that don't register all the colors. These glasses make it so I can see the whole shebang."

"I see." Caswell couldn't hide how impressed she was by the concept. Modern technology truly was a marvel. "So...that scarf..."Montana had said it matched her eyes, and that's why she couldn't resist it. Caswell recalled the uncontrollable grin on her face.

Montana laughed. "Yeah, I guess I get a little excited when it comes to color stuff. Can you blame me? I thought brown and grey were like, the only options for most of my life."

So that's why she chose such tacky colored everything. There were so many things Caswell didn't know about Montana. The more she knew, the more she wanted to learn. She never dreamt she could've become so invested in another person. At that thought, she had to swallow down the fear that she was too invested. Montana was fascinating, but in a league of her own.

Montana's amusement faded as she remembered the temperature. "Ugh, can I put my hands on your cold body?"

"Absolutely not." Caswell mentally cursed herself for the quick reaction. Sure, it would've made her feel ridiculous, but it still would've been skin-to-skin contact, which should not be passed up so easily.

"You're the worst." Montana continued to complain, but it was halfhearted. She stuck her tongue out experimentally, curious to see if that would help with the heat.

"I can live with that." Seven months with Montana and she had picked up quite a few phrases. It didn't make any sense to say she could live with anything, but it was terminology that Montana understood. And that brought them a little bit closer, which was worth being inaccurate.

"I wonder when the middle school goes on summer break," Montana said abruptly. She had a habit of letting her mind wander and sharing out loud only some parts of it, creating confused and jumbled topics. "They'll be able to visit way more once they don't have homework and stuff. Or they could start coming earlier. We really need to get you a phone so we can set this stuff up."

"Or you could learn to plan more than one day at a time," Caswell countered. "I don't want a phone, nor do I need one."

"Whatever you say, man," Montana held up her hands in mock defense. "I'm just saying it'd be a lot easier if we had some lines of communication." Her ears twitched, and she sat up straighter. "I think somebody's at the door. Beatrice? There's totally somebody at the door."

Caswell groaned, already heading over to open it. "I'm on it. Calm down." She opened it, finding the kids outside. Cameron had his hand up like he was about to knock.

"Yo." June tilted her head in greeting. "Is Vic hanging with you?"

Caswell pointed to her right. "Uh, yes, she's in the other room."

"I told you," Dot said, practically jumping up and down. "Whenever Ms. Vic is over, they know we're here before we knock!"

"That's quite the observation, Dot." Caswell hadn't thought about it before, but it was most likely true. She couldn't tell if there was someone outside unless she was near the door, but Montana always knew, much to her own dismay since it drove her crazy.

"How does she do it? Can she smell us?" Cameron asked, mirroring Dot's astonishment. "Would she still be able to smell me if I put on a ton of cologne?"

"She'd probably be able to smell you more." June wrinkled her nose at the thought of it. "That's a good question though. Is there anything that could mask our smell?"

"Why don't you ask her yourselves?" Caswell motioned them inside. By now she had grown accustomed to redirecting their questions to her laid back partner whenever she found herself overwhelmed.

"Actually, we came because we have a question for you." As Dot talked, Cameron pulled a twig loose from her hair. "Thanks!"

"No problem. Think you're gonna be finding leaves in your hair and clothes for a week after that incident." Cameron mimicked the incident with his hands, but without context, it seemed totally nonsensical.

"These two are convinced our teacher is a vampire, even though he's nothing like you," June cut to the chase, kicking off her shoes and searching for Montana. Spotting her on the couch, she took a running start and elbow-dropped her square in the stomach as they both screamed.

"Nice to see you too," Montana wheezed. She moved over so June could sit next to her, then waved at Dot and Cameron as they followed June at a respectable distance.

"He's not exactly like you," Cameron admitted. "But he's got the telltale signs! He hates the sun. He's super pale and wears a cape. He's allergic to garlic, and he's got scary paintings of his ex-wife. His eyes are normal, but he could be wearing contact lenses! Am I forgetting anything?"

"We've never seen his reflection, and he sleeps in a coffin," Dot said.

June interjected, "We don't know that last one."

"Well, if he's a teacher, he's definitely better adjusted than this guy." Montana pointed conspicuously at Caswell.

"That's a nice way of saying he's conformed to human expectations," Caswell defended herself sharply. "I'm doing very well for a member of my kind, and it's not comparable to your standards."

"But another vampire in town." Montana whistled. "What are the odds?"

"So you haven't even met the guy and you're convinced too?" June made a skeptical face. Montana shrugged nonchalantly, and June said, "All the stuff he does has perfectly reasonable explanations. I wasn't convinced before meeting an actual vampire, and now I'm even more sure that he can't be one. They're basing everything off old horror movies. Drake looks way more human than Caswell, and he doesn't have that bite mark."

Caswell subconsciously wrapped her hand around that side of her neck, fingers breezing against her hair. Like Montana's scar, that was the one injury that wouldn't heal. She couldn't see it without access to a reflection, but she could feel it. She could always feel it.

"His name's Drake?" Montana looked at Caswell. "See, that's the kind of name I thought you'd have. Everything else about you is so classically vampire, and then your name is so...Caswell."

"Your name is a state," Cameron pointed out, unimpressed. "And not even a cool one."

"Have you all come here, into my home, just to bully me?" Montana complained.

"This isn't your home," Caswell said heartlessly.

Montana sighed dramatically, flinging an arm over her eyes. "Dot is the only one who respects my plight."

The others looked to Dot, whose loyalties seemed torn. Even when joking around, she tried not to let anyone down. "Maybe you should meet Mr. Drake. Would you recognize another vampire if you met one?"

"Of course," Caswell said, offended that anyone would doubt her skill. "Though that could hardly be a group outing. If he really is a vampire, he would not be the biggest fan of Montana."

The simply stated fact was met with stiff silence. Montana's arm was still over her face from her previous gag, and she certainly did not move it away then. June's eyes were focused on the rug like it was the most interesting thing she had ever seen. Cameron shifted his weight from foot to foot. Dot rubbed at her arm.

"I don't think..." Dot started. "I don't think Mr. Drake could...he's not..."

"He wouldn't." Cameron shook his head, but he sounded like he was trying to convince himself.

"We'll keep researching on our own then." June tried to play it off. "When we find out more, we'll let you know."

Caswell was not expecting such a reaction out of all of them. She thought the implication would have already been obvious. Certainly, if she knew other vampires, she wouldn't risk having Montana around. She'd rather lose the ability to see her anymore than the alternative.

"Dot, how are you not sweating to death in that sweater vest?" Montana's arm fell back to her side. Luckily, everyone else wanted to escape the tension equally as badly and followed her lead to a lighter mood.

"Oh, I've got some circulation trouble." Dot yanked at the fabric. "So I feel fine."

"Well, I'm dying," Cameron admitted. "I didn't know it was going to be so hot today, so I wore jeans."

"Wanna cut those into jorts?" Montana opened and closed her index and middle finger to represent scissors.

"Thanks, but my mom would kill me." Cameron waved her off.

"You should tie them around your waist like a hoodie," June suggested jokingly.

"A denim hoodie would suck," Dot said, pondering this deeply.

"Ew." June shuddered. "All denim sucks."

"But you can't bite through denim," Montana argued, "so it'd keep you safe in a zombie apocalypse. Beatrice, if you were a zombie, would you eat my brain?"

Caswell sighed, finding the question pointless. But it did manage to distract her. "I suppose I would, Montana, since that's what zombies do."

Cameron gave her a disapproving look. Montana faked hurt. "I thought you liked me."

"What else was I supposed to say?" Caswell got flustered. "I wouldn't be able to control it!"

"But you wouldn't fight it?" Dot asked her in disbelief, and it felt like they were all in on some big joke, as if they were all expecting the same answer out of her over such a ludicrous question.

"I would fight it," Montana said, as if that were the obvious answer. "I don't want to eat your brain."

"It seems like you'd be safe after all, since you don't have any brain I could eat." Caswell snarked, which caused Montana to break character and snort.

"She'd have to get through all your hair too." June reached over and grabbed her ear. "It'd probably be gross."

Montana swatted her hand away playfully. "I think your hair would be way grosser. And you've got so much more than I do."

As the conversation ran its course and the manor was filled with laughter, Caswell had a sinking feeling that if she ever found herself in a position where she'd have to send Montana away, it'd be a lot harder than it should be.

Chapter Ten

"YOU'RE LATE," CASWELL SAID as Montana finally entered. She didn't really mind. She knew Montana had her responsibilities, but the conversation had to start somewhere.

"Sorry, I was kinda distracted." Montana walked past her and leaned against the wall. It was strange she didn't find a seat. Obviously, she wasn't planning on staying long. Caswell wondered where they were going.

"I'll forgive it." Caswell sighed deeply.

As predicted, her dramatics earned a giggle from Montana. "What generosity."

Caswell allowed herself a small smile. "So what's distracting you?"

"Well, someone sent me a letter today." Montana reached into her shorts pocket. "I didn't know people even did that anymore. Anyway, it was this weird invitation, and I would've been pumped because hey that's fun, but it smells funny and I need a second opinion."

When she finally fished it out, Caswell covered her nose and mouth with a hand. She was all but used to Montana's stench at this point, but the smell of other werewolves was still disarming. "You received a letter from werewolves?"

"Werewolf! Okay yeah, that's what I was thinking. I guess that makes sense. Do you not like how that smells?" Montana sniffed it again. "I didn't think it was a bad smell. It's like, familiar."

"I imagine it must be." Caswell stepped closer and looked over Montana's shoulder to read aloud, *Grown into that new skin yet? We'd like to meet you.* Sounds barbaric."

"So what do you think?" Montana crimped the edges of the paper as she talked. If Caswell didn't know better, she'd think it was a nervous habit. "Should I go?"

"Go where?"

Montana waved the letter. "Wherever this smell leads me."

"I thought you weren't interested in being a proper werewolf." Caswell was slightly offended that Montana was only disinterested when it was Caswell teaching. She supposed it was par for the course. Vampires and werewolves didn't get along, after all.

Vampires and werewolves don't get along.

If Montana was hoping to find her pack, did that mean she was sick of Caswell? Did she feel stuck with her? When they held hands during stormy nights, did Montana grit her teeth because she wished she could be with anyone else? Was their whole relationship built off circumstances she couldn't avoid as opposed to ones she'd willingly put herself in?

"Yeah, but my friends are kinda alienating, and you don't like me a whole lot, and the kids are great, but they're kids, y'know?" Montana's voice snapped Caswell out of her spiraling. "It'd be nice to belong somewhere."

"I don't...not like you." Caswell said.

"Thanks." Montana laughed lightly. "I think I wanna check it out though."

Caswell stared for a moment, trying to think of what she should say. She had no real reason to stop her from going. The only danger was the selfish one of Caswell losing her. And she couldn't say that. "Right." She breathed. "You'd better get going."

Montana looked up at her with an expectant half-smile. "Are you...not coming with?"

"Me?" Caswell sputtered.

"Well, yeah," Montana said, as if it were the most obvious thing in the world. "That's why I was asking you."

"I thought...I thought you were confused." Caswell admitted, somewhat sheepishly.

"Come on, man. I'm not a complete idiot," Montana brushed it off. "So are you coming or not?"

"I..." Caswell looked away, getting quieter. "I don't think I should. There's no way they'll accept you if you're seen with someone like me."

"I'm not trying to join a cult, I just wanna see what's going on." Montana paused for a moment, then pointed to her shorts. "If you're so worried about that, why don't you transform and hang out in my pocket? No one will see you. That way I've still got your moral support. And if they turn out to be really cool, then you can change back and say hi."

"Only if you promise not to laugh at my voice." Caswell crossed her arms. Her newfound affection for Montana still had limits.

"I don't think I can make that promise." Montana gave her puppy-dog eyes. A subjugating asset. Vampiric magic didn't even hold a candle to them. "Please come?"

"Fine." Caswell was powerless to say no to that face. Plus, she really was curious to see what would happen. She knew very little about werewolves. "But don't grab me. Your hands are always sweaty." She turned into a bat, and they struggled with getting her situated for a few minutes. Finally, they got it right so she could peek out without being noticed.

"God, that's adorable," Montana said before focusing. "Okay, I'm gonna try and track this."

As Montana headed outside, Caswell thought about how she used to never think about shapeshifting. It was something she could do and did often enough, but she never really paid it any mind. Now it was like some parlor trick. Montana and the kids found it so amusing, and it served to highlight how different her life was from what used to be normal.

There she went again, calling it a life. Spending so much time with them made her feel impossible things, like she was alive, like her differences weren't so different. She didn't breathe, but Cameron was double jointed in his right arm, and Dot was literally cursed. Everyone was a little strange, so why couldn't she be strange? Why shouldn't she get to live?

Montana reached the local park, and Caswell was overwhelmed by the smell. Images flashed in her mind, memories she had buried. She shoved them back down quickly, but they left behind an instinct, urging her to disappear. She was...afraid. She'd forgotten werewolves were capable of making her feel fear. She did her best to ignore it.

There were at least twelve of them, scattered almost casually around the place. "Hey, you guys know the playground closes at sunset, right?" Montana called out to them. "You're gonna get in trouble."

One jumped up from his seat on the swings. He was muscular and tall, and his slicked-back, dark hair left his ears more noticeable. He grinned sharply. “You planning on calling the cops, hot stuff?” He made his way over, his confident stride better resembling a jungle cat’s than a wolf’s. “Glad to see you survived this long.”

Once he reached Montana, he grabbed her face firmly, dragging his tongue up the side of her cheek. Caswell would’ve been jealous if it wasn’t so bizarre. She felt Montana tense. “Woah, weird!” Montana laughed.

“Name’s Brick.” The man pulled away, licking his lips. “Now, it’s custom to wait a few months before welcoming a newcomer to the pack because we all start a little pissy, and we don’t want to encourage that type of behavior, you know?” Brick paused for confirmation from Montana, who nodded uncertainly. “Right. But it’s been nearly a year, and for that we’re sorry. We would’ve called for you sooner, but we thought a vampire got you in first.”

“And you thought she’d kill me?” Montana asked slowly, her tone unreadable. The situation still seemed to be sinking in.

“You’ve met one, so you tell me,” Brick said, and a few of the others snickered. Most watched Montana quietly, sizing her up. “You still stink of it, and it was what? Six months ago? Forgotten what a shower was, buddy?” Brick slapped her arm playfully. Montana laughed with him after a brief second of awkwardness. “But yeah, we thought we had lost you already! No offense, but you don’t look very tough. Didn’t think you’d be the one to make it out with your head attached.”

“Yeah well, I’m alive.” Montana’s face wasn’t visible to Caswell from where she was, but she could hear the forced smile.

“So you are!” Brick bowed his head with mock respect, flourishing his arms. “And I know I couldn’t be happier. You’re home now, uh…what was it, Dakota?”

“Montana. But I hadn’t told you my name.”

“No, you haven’t told us anything yet.” Brick said it like it was a shame. “But we had to get to you in some way. Sorry for the letter, must’ve seemed creepy. We didn’t have your number.” Everything he said felt lined with a harshness, but Caswell wondered if she only felt that way because of what she was. She imagined there was a bit of culture shock for Montana, but she wasn't in danger here.

"So do you guys do anything other than hang out where you're not supposed to?" Montana shifted her weight slightly. Caswell didn't know what that meant. She didn't understand Montana. These guys did.

"You're so cute, I want to eat you up." Brick flashed another view his teeth. "But to answer your question, yes. We do all sorts of things. We're like a family. We're better than a family." His expression became sympathetic. "I know it must've been hard, all that time you were forced to be alone. But you don't have to worry about that anymore. You never have to be alone again."

"Sounds nice." Montana said, but her words were a little off. They were almost hollow, and Caswell wondered if it was still the shock. "Yeah, I like the way that sounds a lot."

"Your struggles are over, Montana," Brick promised her, stepping closer so their feet nearly touched. "Can I see it?"

"It?" Montana leaned back a little. Brick was a good head and shoulders taller than her.

"The bite." Brick reached his hand up under her shirt. Montana seemed surprised but not miffed. She let him carry on. "I wanna see how bad I got you."

"You." Montana said, and that was all.

After lifting her shirt Brick laughed, almost barking, as he stepped back again. "Yeah, that's a good one. Mm, I remember the way you tasted. I bet you remember that night pretty damn well too, huh?"

"So you're the son of a bitch who ruined my life."

Brick laughed again. "Son of a bitch, that's a good one." His laughter was cut short by Montana's fist.

As Montana lurched forward, Caswell fell backward out of her pocket and took to the air. She didn't think before flying away. She could not think. In the confusion below her, the only thing she noticed was how Montana's whole body was shaking.

Caswell flew several blocks away, turning back into her regular form, knees nearly buckling beneath her. The sensation of a werewolf fight would not leave her mind. She could remember it so clearly now. She wished she couldn't.

She had forgotten what it meant to be scared. The memory was powerful. She had given into the fear so quickly, she had left Montana. She had left Montana with those monsters. She was so useless. Moral support, Montana had asked of her. Just be there. And she couldn't even do that much. The one time she needed her, and Caswell vanished. There wasn't a single thing she could do for Montana. Useless, useless, useless.

She had to go back. But she couldn't move. Her feet were glued to the pavement. Her legs did not listen to her brain. Her brain did not listen to her heart.

So you're the son of a bitch who ruined my life. Caswell's racing mind suddenly dropped all other thoughts. Becoming a werewolf was the worst thing that had ever happened to Montana. Of course it was. It ruined her life. Caswell thought that was how she wanted Montana to think. It was normal, traditional, the truth. But it hurt. It wasn't supposed to hurt.

Montana's life was over the moment she stepped into Caswell's home. Every second they spent together, Montana would've given up if it meant she could go back. She only made the best out of the situation because that's what she always did. That was the sort of woman she was. But she wasn't happy. She was never happy. She couldn't be happy. She had a life before, and now it was gone. She had lost everything.

It would be better if Caswell disappeared.

There wasn't time for this. She had to make sure Montana was alive. Her feet started to move again, and suddenly she was running. She ran all the way back to the playground, now still and empty, as if the night had only been a bad dream. There was no sign that the wolves had ever been there. Except for the smell of blood.

They left Montana on the roundabout. It didn't look much like Montana anymore. Her expression was blank, frozen. Her eyes were glazed over. It was hard to tell if she was conscious or not. It would be for the better if she wasn't. But there were no burns, which meant no silver. They weren't trying to kill her. They were sending a message.

Caswell was crying. She hadn't felt it at first. When she did, she didn't immediately recognize it as crying. She hadn't cried in so long. She didn't remember she could even do that.

"I'm sorry," she said, gasping out the words. "I'm sorry. I'm sorry for everything."

Caswell wanted to pick her up, gently, but firmly gather her up. She wanted to hold her in her arms and promise her she'd be all right. Tell her she had a home. Their home. She wanted to bring her back there. Sit with her as she healed, keep her safe. Be a better friend.

But that's not what Montana needed. It's not what she wanted.

She spotted Montana's sunglasses, strewn a couple yards away. They were broken, shards of colored glass everywhere. Caswell picked up a shard. "I'll take this," Caswell said aloud. She could not stop the tears from streaming down her face. "Instead of the doughnut box. You don't owe me anymore."

She walked back over to Montana. It was hard to look at her. That was good. Otherwise, she might never leave. She hesitated for a moment before pressing her lips gently against her forehead. She could not avoid the taste of her blood, but she didn't pull away.

"Goodbye, Vic."

Chapter Eleven

BY THE MORNING, MONTANA could move again.

She sat up slowly, rediscovering how her body moved. She wasn't burning with rage anymore. Whatever fury had possessed her last night had drained out with the blood. Now she just ached.

She looked down at her hands. They were trembling. She was trembling all over, and she couldn't stop. She felt like she had been kicked over the line that separated the living and the dead, then stomped to a pulp on the other side. Her body was mostly reformed on the outside, but she still felt like a living smoothie.

They had been vicious, not stopping when she was down. Not even stopping when she couldn't move anymore. She supposed, since they were in the same boat she was, they knew what was going to hurt the most and what would take the longest to heal. But she knew why they did it. She had attacked one of their own. She'd been angry enough in the moment to feel justified, until she realized she had put Caswell in danger too. She didn't know at what point she had lost her, but she was glad Caswell wasn't there for the fight.

She thought she had heard Caswell at some point. She could've sworn she saw her face. But in her memory, Caswell was crying, and that couldn't be right. Caswell wasn't a crier. Montana wasn't even sure vampires could cry.

She stumbled to her feet, the roundabout creaking as it turned ever so slightly with her movement. She grimaced at the bloodstain. She felt sympathy for whoever had to clean the place up, but she couldn't stick around to help. She gathered up the remains of her glasses and threw them in the trash bin, knowing that was the least she could do. She stopped with her hands pressing down on the lid, her breathing ragged. She still wasn't fully reformed, and all the movement certainly didn't do her any favors.

"Get it together, Vic," she muttered to herself through her teeth. "You're better than this."

Her argument wasn't very convincing, but she couldn't stand there all day. She started walking again, a zombie-like stagger, heading in the direction of her apartment. She could do this. And even if she couldn't, she had to.

"Vic?" She froze in place. She recognized the voice instantly, but part of her wished she was mistaken. She didn't need to see her like this. "Jesus Christ, what happened to you? Did you wrestle with a woodchipper?"

"Hi, Ali." Montana turned to face her with a weary smile. Ali had stopped her car on the street next to her and was rolling down her window, as if that gave her a better look. A pang of guilt hit Montana as she noticed Ali's makeup and realized she was probably on her way to work. It was clear from her expression she would not be going until she told her everything. "Do I look bad? I feel bad."

Ali glanced her over. "Well, you're limping around in broad daylight and covered in blood that I can only hope isn't what's left of your most recent victim. Your tracksuit is literally in tatters, and you look like you slept in the woods. Is that how you feel?"

"More or less." She laughed a little, but that sent a sharp pain through her ribs. "Don't worry. It's my blood."

"Don't say that like it's a good thing." Ali whipped her phone out of her purse, typing a million words a second. She must've been canceling some arrangements, which made Montana feel lousier. "Okay, I'm getting you back to your place. Get in."

"Could you drive me to work instead?" The face Ali gave her made it clear that was not an option. Montana had already suspected that would be the case, but it was worth a shot. "Come on, even a werewolf's gotta make a living."

It was Alison she had been protecting the night she was bitten, and it was Alison she always told her secrets to, ever since the third grade. Ali had accepted her half-dog status like she accepted everything about Montana, not fully understanding, but still supportive. Montana rambled about her nights to Ali whenever she had the chance, but it most likely never made a lot of sense.

Alison sighed. "I thought you were taking today off anyway." She only got a blank stare in response. She clarified, pointing at the sky with a manicured finger, "Because of the moon?"

"That's tonight?" Montana ran a hand through her hair. She had completely lost track of time.

Alison reached over and opened the side door from the inside. "Get in already. Someone's going to call the cops on you if you keep creeping around looking like that."

Too tired to argue, Montana got in the passenger seat. She stifled a groan as her body protested the change in position. "Blood should be dried," she offered up, motioning weakly. "Won't make a mess."

"So many of your bodily fluids have already spilled in this car, it doesn't even matter," Alison responded halfheartedly, her mind preoccupied with something else. She didn't say anything yet, driving to Montana's apartment in silence. She tried to help Montana out of the car, but Montana waved her off.

"I'm fine. Healing by the second." Montana fumbled for her key before letting them both in. Her place was on the small side, but it was comfortable. It looked a little more dismal without her glasses. She flopped face down onto her couch.

"Obviously not fast enough." Alison closed the door behind them and flicked on a light. She hesitated for a moment before asking the question Montana knew she'd been holding back. "You said that was all your blood, right? You're sure?"

Montana gave her a thumbs up. Her voice was muffled by the cushion, "Maybe a little bit is this one bastard, but it's definitely mostly mine."

"So what the hell happened?" There was that tone. She knew that tone. She didn't respond. "Was it a fight? Was it that vampire?"

"Why does everyone think that?" Montana forced a laugh, but she didn't find it very funny. "It's not like that. I'm fine, Ali. I'm still breathin', aren't I?

"I need you to talk to me, Vic. Do you know how terrifying it was to see you like that?" Her silence was heavy with guilt. "I haven't said anything about you running off every other night, exhausting yourself and breaking your heart. I haven't said a single word, because I trusted you to make the right choices. I know stuff's crazy and you're still adjusting, but I can't trust you unless you do the same for me." She crossed her arms over her chest, but it looked more like an attempt at comfort than a show of her displeasure. "Can you do that for me?"

"Yeah. Yeah, I'm sorry," Montana finally croaked out. She found herself swallowing quickly, trying to will away the tears pricking the corners of her eyes. "I don't want to hurt you."

"Then stop hurting yourself." Alison was nearly pleading. "We've already had this conversation."

"I'm trying," Montana admitted, sounding as small as she felt.

Alison sighed. "I need you to try a little harder." She walked past the couch to Montana's little kitchen. "How about you go take a shower and get into some actual clothes? I've got a meeting I can't miss in an hour, but I'll make you breakfast first and steal some coffee. You don't have to tell me anything yet, but I'll stop by later and give you a ride to that creepy place you like to spend full moons at. Okay?"

"You're the light of my life, Alison."

"I know."

When evening rolled around, Alison kept her promise and honked to let Montana know she was outside. "Gimme a sec!" she yelled, giving her hair one final pat down before rushing out. She was basically back to normal now, and it was obvious in the way she moved. She joined her in the car. "You really don't have to do this. I feel great."

"It's on my way," Alison lied. She was good at that, but Montana could always see right through her.

"How were the meetings?" Montana asked, as they pulled out of the parking lot. "Boring?"

"Boring," Ali agreed. "I don't know who said men could run a business, but I'd like to have a word with them. Somehow, I still managed to stay productive." She glanced out the window. "Is that the place?"

"Yep." Montana unbuckled her seatbelt. Traffic hadn't been great, but they still had a good few minutes before sunset. She hoped she'd be able to get a word in with Caswell first. "Thanks for the ride." She got out of the car, closing the door behind her and practically running up the lawn. She reached the door, but when she tried to turn the handle, it wouldn't budge. She tried again, to no avail.

"Uh, Beatrice?" She called out, trying to pretend it was a coincidence. "Is something blocking the door? Is it locked? I can't..." her voice lost a little of its vigor. "I can't get in." She tried knocking.

"Beatrice? Are you mad at me? Can we talk?" She waited for a few moments. "Beatrice, I'm sorry, but locking me out isn't going to help. Let's talk. Let's figure something out. We're both adults." She turned back to Alison, trying to wave her away, but she would not drive off until she knew Montana was inside. She turned back to the door. "Are you nervous 'cause of my friend? She drove me here. That's all. I could ask her to leave."

Montana wished there was at least a window she could look through. There was only one on the entire house, and it was so high up she assumed it looked into the attic. She had never been in the attic, but that was not at the forefront of her mind. She knocked again, a little more desperate. "Are you hurt? Did you fall and can't get back up? Should I try to break down the door?" She was grasping for straws. She turned back around, pressing her back against the door and sinking to the ground. "Listen, I know I was a jerk yesterday. I shouldn't have endangered you. But you know I'd never hurt you on purpose, right? I was being stupid. I was mad! But you shouldn't have to suffer for that. I'm sorry."

Montana was greeted with nothing but silence. She hugged her knees to her chest. "You're making me look bad in front of my friend, dude. Please let me in." She felt like she was going to cry again. "Please don't let my stupid mistake be what ruins this."

Alison watched her stages of desperation from the car. The longer it went on, the more pissed off at this vampire lady she became. Who did she think she was? Montana was a sweet girl, but she was a pushover, and she needed Alison in her life to make sure she didn't get stepped all over.

She fixed her hair and cracked her knuckles, making up her mind. She wasn't going to sit and watch any longer. But when she looked again, Montana was gone. She blinked. She brushed her bangs from her face so she could get a better look.

She got out of the car, hurrying over to the doorstep. There were Montana's clothes, and there was a little puppy who looked like the picture Montana had sent her a while back. The puppy didn't seem to notice her. She was just sitting there, staring up at the door and whining. Alison wasn't a dog person, but that pulled at her heartstrings a little.

"Okay, that's enough." She patted her thighs, talking in a baby voice. "Here, puppy! Come here! Come here! Who's my good little guy?"

Distracted from waiting for the door, puppy-Montana wagged her tail and hopped over to Ali, who scooped her up. "There we go. I've got you." As an afterthought, she shifted so she was hugging her to her chest with one arm, then gathered up Montana's clothes with the other. She then slammed her shoulder into the door. "Is this how you treat everyone who cares about you?! Vic tells me about what you put her through, and she might be willing to put up with your shit, but I sure as hell won't! If you don't stop playing these stupid games with her, then you've booked an appointment with my fists!"

Montana whined at her. Alison had never had a dog before, so she wasn't sure how to handle her. She treated her like a fluffy baby and bounced her a little. Truthfully, she would've been more at a loss with a baby than a dog. "Hey, it's okay. You're coming home with me." She shot one last dirty look to the house, as if the owner would somehow be able to feel her intended offense.

If it was up to her, Montana would stop hanging around this place. If she needed a supernatural resource, they could find her someone who treated her better. Someone who didn't take her devotion for granted. But it wasn't Ali's life, and it was Montana who had taught her she couldn't always be in control. There was really no help for her bad decisions.

After all, Montana was in love.

Chapter Twelve

THE CEILING LOOKED THE same as it always did, but that did not stop Caswell from staring at it like it might change at any second. She was lying on the floor, bracing herself for what she could only imagine would be another night of some of the worst suffering she'd ever known.

Caswell thought that leaving Montana would be like tearing off a Band-Aid, vividly painful, but once she got over the initial sting it would be over. It wasn't over. Montana did not seem to get the message that she did not want to see her anymore. Each night she'd stand outside the door and yell until her throat got hoarse, then she'd either knock or sit there until the sun came up. Caswell nearly opened the door on twenty occasions, but she'd managed to stay strong every time. If you could call locking yourself in the bathroom and trying to twist your arm off every time you'd want to give up strong.

The worst part of it was Montana had convinced herself that Caswell was mad at her. Caswell was dying to tell her otherwise, but she couldn't take that risk. Her final goodbye had to be that, final.

And if that meant she had to let Montana hate her, then she'd have to keep acting detestable.

But this night wore on without any appearance from Montana. Caswell breathed a sigh of relief. Maybe she had finally given up on her. The idea of Montana never showing up again was more than a little heartbreaking, but it was for the better. Caswell had survived all those horrible nights which seemed to stretch on for much longer than a week. She could turn her focus to moving on, consoled by the knowledge that she was finally able to do something right.

She hadn't been feeding as often as she used to, with all the visitors she'd had coming through, and the craving was starting to get to her. Now she was free to take care of that. She unlocked the door and slipped out. In case Montana was only running late, Caswell went farther from the manor and deeper into the town than she usually did.

It was almost three in the morning, so there weren't a lot of people out. She found a man in a parking lot, searching through his trunk for some lost item. Caswell silently snuck up behind him. Now this...this was what she was good at. This was what she was meant to do. Not acting as half of a comedy duo or some kind of eccentric aunt. She was a hunter, a monster.

The man closed his trunk, having found whatever trinket he was looking for. Caswell followed him a few yards before clasping one hand over his mouth and the other on his shoulder, yanking his shirt collar aside to get to the bare skin. Just as she was about to bite into his neck, there was a shout from behind. "Hey! Get ready to run!"

Caswell twisted to see Montana standing there, and the sight of her would've been enough to make anyone's heart skip a beat. She had a grocery bag slung in the crook of her elbow, and her hair was tied back in a messy ponytail. They met each other's eyes. She still hadn't gotten a replacement for her sunglasses. There was something passionate in them Caswell hadn't noticed when they were obstructed by the tinted glass. She found it hard to look directly at that wild kind of beauty. Caswell was so enthralled, she forgot their entire situation.

Montana made a little cross with her fingers, making Caswell flinch and lose her grip on the guy, who scrambled off. Caswell could've chased after him, but she was too offended by the move. Plus, Montana might follow her around all night if she didn't acknowledge her. All of Caswell's victims would be scared off before she had the chance to bite. "That's right! You're free now!" Montana called out to the guy.

Caswell didn't know what to say. There was a lot she should say. But first, in regard to what had happened with her dinner, she chose to say, "What the hell?"

"I should be asking you that," Montana said, laughing in disbelief. "You keep your door locked for a week with no warning, then you show up at my apartment building trying to eat one of my neighbors? What kind of message does that send?"

"This is your building?" Caswell blinked. She didn't know what kind of odds those were, but she had a feeling there had been some mischievous divine intervention involved. "It's nice."

"It's not—not the whole building—it doesn't matter." Montana sighed, pinching the bridge of her nose. "What were you thinking? If you're mad, that's fine, but you...I needed something. You can't barricade the door and hope for the best. And what if it wasn't me at the door? The kids are out camping for the week with their parents, but you wouldn't know that. You don't talk to them, and you don't talk to me."

"I couldn't!" Caswell protested, finding herself on the defensive. "I can't expect you to understand it, but I couldn't! I shouldn't even be talking to you right now!"

Montana's ears flicked and her face scrunched up with frustration. She seemed to be trying to figure out some sort of compromise, or at least something to say. "Fifteen minutes," she finally settled on. "Give me fifteen minutes." Not waiting for an answer, Montana pushed past Caswell and went to one of the doors, opening it up and going inside. She left the door open behind her.

Caswell's logical mind told her she should leave. If she stayed and explained herself, it could ruin the bad blood between them. And if Montana started looking at her with that fondness again, it would be so much harder to try and separate. On the other hand, she felt like she owed Montana this much. She could handle fifteen minutes.

Caswell stood in the doorframe, watching Montana quietly. Montana walked over to her kitchenette to set her grocery bag down. She pulled the scrunchie out, and her hair instantly fluffed back up. She ran a hand through it in a halfhearted attempt to smooth it down and gather herself. She turned toward Caswell. They stared at each other for a moment. "Are you just gonna stand there?"

Caswell wrung her hands together. "I, uh, I need explicit permission. Leaving the door open doesn't count as an invitation."

Montana looked away as she tried to stop herself from laughing. The gesture flooded Caswell with unexpected emotion. She had missed this. She had missed her. "What exactly do you need? Do I gotta use my full name?"

"A simple come in will work perfectly." As soon as she said it, she regretted passing up the opportunity to find out what Vic was short for.

"Then come on in," Montana said with a sweeping gesture. "Make yourself at home. I'd offer you food, but you don't eat, and everything I've got is empty carbs. And beef jerky, but I'm gonna eat that like, right now." As promised, she tore open a bag and shoved a handful in her mouth. "I'm gonna end up eating raw meat one of these days, but I'm trying to keep things moderate. Not that I know what that word means in relation to food. Always been a stress eater, and life's always stressful."

"Right." Caswell said, not knowing what else to say and distracted by finally seeing where Montana lived. The whole place smelled like her. Caswell hadn't realized she missed that smell. She positioned herself so she could lean against the back of the couch, as Montana did a little hop up to sit on the counter. "So."

"So," Montana echoed as she watched her, tail swishing lazily.

The awkwardness was overwhelming. Caswell didn't know how to begin. She forced a smile, hoping her nervousness didn't show. "You look better! Less, uh…"

"Like a dumpster fire?" Montana finished for her. "So you did see me."

Caswell blinked. "You didn't hear me when I said goodbye?"

"I don't know what I heard." Montana looked away, biting into more jerky, treating it like an excuse to not have to talk. But then Caswell did not speak up either, so she had no choice. "Look, I came by every night since then. I don't know if you heard me, but I was being pretty loud. I scared a lot of birds."

"No, I heard you. I heard the birds too."

"And I tried to apologize," Montana placed a hand over her chest. "I know I was being selfish and I put you at risk, but I need you to forgive me or…not. I was gonna give you a little space, but then you showed up here."

"There's no reason for you to apologize." Caswell had to admit, it felt good to finally say that, even if having this conversation was the wrong choice. "You didn't do anything wrong."

"Then why are you so mad?" There was an edge of hopelessness in Montana's tone. Her lack of sleep was becoming more apparent on her face.

"I'm not mad! I was never mad at you, Montana," Caswell said, trying to sound supportive. "I just...I realized how angry you were. How angry you've always deserved to be over this whole situation. You can never be human again, but you can still salvage...something. One night out of the month you'll want to be in a room with a locked door, but that's not so bad, is it? You're not that different. You can still be okay. You can still go back to what you had...before me."

Montana stared at her for a moment. She put the bag down, crinkling it as she chewed slowly. Finally she spoke. "Why would I wanna do that?"

"Because that Brick guy ruined your life. You said it yourself." Caswell faltered slightly.

"And you think that means I wanna stop hanging out with you?" Montana slid off the counter and walked over to Caswell, cupping gentle hands around her cheeks. Caswell could not move if she wanted to. Montana shook her head slightly. "Are you really that dumb? Beatrice, you're the best thing that came out of this whole mess."

"I am?" She could not manage any better than a squeak.

"Oh my god, yes." Montana moved her hands to Caswell's shoulders and pressed the top of her head against Caswell's chest. There was that warmth of hers. Oh, how she had missed that warmth. "I can't believe that was what this was all about. I thought you hated me or something."

"I..." Caswell looked down at her. She smiled, speaking softly, "I don't think I could ever hate you."

"That's the best news I've gotten all week." Montana's tail started wagging, picking up speed exponentially. "And for the record, my life isn't ruined. I was still angry at him for attacking me and my friend, that's all. I've been having a pretty decent time, all things considered."

Caswell realized she had no idea where to put her hands. She considered hugging her, but that might be too forward. "Am I forgiven for my stupidity, or should I go outside and yell for a couple days?"

"I think I did enough of that for the both of us." Montana paused but couldn't keep her laughter in. "Was that a good acceptance of your apology, or do you need a formal one?"

Caswell shrugged, playing along. It felt good to do that again. "You'll have to consult the vampire high council on that." As she talked, her hands seemed to decide where they wanted to be and landed on Montana's head before she gave them permission.

"Are you...petting me?" Montana asked, sounding even more amused.

"No," Caswell lied, rather pointlessly. There was no other explanation for what she was doing. But, at the very least, Montana did not seem completely weirded out. In fact, she appeared to like it.

"All right, then you can keep not petting me on the couch and I could not throw on a movie?" Montana offered. Or not offered.

"Sounds terrible." Caswell agreed and sat beside her. Their legs pressed together, and it was casual but almost more intimate than Caswell could handle.

Montana flipped through the channels before finding something she liked. "Oh, I love this movie. We missed the first thirty minutes, but that's okay. If you're confused, I can explain what's going on." She shuffled closer to Caswell, head on her shoulder for easy petting. "I know you say we're supposed to fight like, all the time, but fighting with you sucks. How about instead of trying to be a werewolf and a vampire, we just be Vic and Beatrice?"

"I think that's what we're best at." Caswell hummed, as she went back to stroking her ears.

And for the few hours before the morning, they were just Vic and Beatrice. And for the first time in a long time, everything felt like it was going to be all right.

Chapter Thirteen

CASWELL WOKE UP TO Montana poking her in the eye. She didn't remember going to sleep, but she swatted her finger away. "Would you stop that?" she grumbled.

"You sleep so much, dude. Is that normal for a vampire or are you like, exhausted?" Montana was pressed up against her, and Caswell realized that's how she fell asleep. Montana droning on over that ridiculous movie, warm and soft against her. She wondered how long Montana had waited to wake her. She quickly realized how that could be a problem.

"What time is it?"

"That's the problem." Montana offered her a semi-apologetic smile. "I didn't notice you were asleep, then I didn't want to wake you, and I totally lost track of time, so you're probably gonna have to stay here for the day."

Montana got up and disappeared into an adjacent room. She said, loud enough so Caswell could hear her, "I've got good light-blocking curtains in here, so you can hang out in my bedroom since I gotta use the door in the front room. Because like, I have a job. You know how it is. Actually, I guess you don't. But still."

Montana's bedroom. That felt forbidden. But she didn't have many other options. Although a quick and horrible death due to the sunlight would be less awkward.

"Get in here," Montana yelled again. Caswell obeyed reluctantly, trying not to look at anything. "Sorry it's a mess. I haven't had company for a while. Except for Alison, but we've been friends long enough where she doesn't expect anything more of me. But yeah, you can just..." Montana awkwardly smoothed out the blanket on her unmade bed. "Sleep here, and you won't even have to worry about splinters like in your coffin. If you're missing your coffin, you could just...uh..."

Montana lay down on the bed, grabbing the blanket and rolling so she could cocoon herself in it. She nearly rolled right off the bed but caught herself at the last moment. “Like this! Just like home, right?”

“Don’t you have to go be stupid somewhere else?”

“Shit, you’re right.” Montana unrolled herself as fast as she had done the reverse. She then threw off her tank top.

“What are you doing?” Caswell sputtered, mind straying to the movie they’d watched. When the spy girl invited the man into her bedroom, it had gone similarly to this, sans blanket burritos.

“I’m not going to wear the same clothes two days in a row. That’s gross.” Montana went over to her dresser, shuffling around. “I mean, I’ve totally done it before, but that was when I was clinically depressed. Now I have energy!”

Caswell covered her eyes. “Whatever. Hurry up. Couldn’t you have done this while I was in the other room?”

“I’m not a psychic, Beatrice. I can’t think that far ahead. Okay, I’m dressed. How do you say it? I’m mediocre?”

“Decent.” Caswell corrected her, removing her hands. If she hadn’t watched part of the changing process, she wouldn’t believe Montana was actually wearing new clothes. They were identical to her last outfit. “You say, I’m decent.”

“Okay, so you hang out here.” Montana grabbed her arms and gently walked her over to the bed, pushing slightly until Caswell got the memo and sat down. “Uh, if you need anything, you can call my cell from the landline. It’s labeled *me*, because it’s my phone.” She paused. “Do you know how to use a phone?”

“Yes,” Caswell lied. It couldn’t be that hard to figure out.

“Awesome.” Montana absentmindedly patted her arms before letting go. “Stay in here, but I’ll knock before entering in case you’re wandering around. Obviously, yell if I can’t come in yet. No one else should come by because they know I’m at work. If you hear knocking that isn’t me, don’t respond and they’ll go away. Okay, I think that’s it. Is that it?”

Caswell had no idea how Montana thought she would know who was knocking, but she played along. “I think that’s it.”

“Great! Awesome.” Montana was walking out of the room. “Okay! Bye. Love ya.”

She left, as if that statement was a reasonable thing to leave Caswell with.

Instead of sleeping, Caswell ruminated for hours. Not only was she staying the night (her equivalent, at least) in Montana's bedroom, but Montana told her she loved her. It wasn't an I love you. It wasn't even a love you. She distinctly said, "Love ya." That was too casual for a confession, but then again, Montana was very casual. Maybe that was how she rolled.

But Montana was a platonically affectionate woman. Was she the sort of person who told her friends she loved them? That would make sense. But she had never said it to Caswell before. Maybe it was an occasional thing. Every once in a while, she might send her friends on an emotional rollercoaster for kicks.

Or maybe it was a new custom that Caswell didn't know about. Maybe whenever you leave your house, you're supposed to profess your love to your guests. Just the general love you're capable of feeling. It's not directed at anyone specifically. It's probably for luck. But Montana wasn't the type of woman who practiced customs.

It had to be platonic. But maybe it was romantic. If it was platonic, why hadn't she ever said it before? But if it was romantic, why now? Right after making up from a fight and right before going to work? That was hardly the optimal time for that sort of thing.

Suddenly, a ringing sound pervaded the apartment. Caswell was pretty sure it was the phone. She headed over to it and confirmed her suspicions. She knew what phones did, broadly, and she had seen people use them plenty of times. She never had a use for one herself, so she mostly ignored them. That lack of curiosity felt silly now that she needed to learn. She picked it up and held it gingerly to her ear.

"Hello?" she asked. The phone continued to ring at her. "Hello? Is someone there?" She held it out and looked at it, getting the sense she was doing something wrong. This was different from the phones that Dot and her friends had, and Caswell was pretty sure Montana had called them cells. Hopefully, that meant it was supposed to look different. There were lots of numbers, and she compulsively counted the buttons. Vampires had a thing for counting, which Montana luckily hadn't figured out yet. Two buttons stuck out, so she chose the one with the green drawing of a phone, because green was preferred over red by most humans. “Hello?” She repeated, still holding it almost at arm’s length.

“Beatrice?” The phone responded. She didn’t know who it was or how they knew her name.

“Who’s asking?” She narrowed her eyes.

She heard laughter on the other end. “It’s me, Vic! Uh, Vic Montana. Do I really sound that different over the phone? Everybody tells me that.”

“Everybody is right.” Caswell was able to relax knowing it was only Montana. But she became stressed again when she remembered what Montana had said, leaving her in anguish for hours. “What do you want?”

“I thought I should let you know I’m gonna be late tonight. I'm closing, then I need to pick up my new glasses. I won’t be home until after dark, so you don’t have to wait up for me.” She heard something crash in the background, but Montana was unfazed. “Unless you don’t think you’ll be able to tell when the sun is down. Then you can totally wait.”

“I’ll be fine,” Caswell said quickly, more pressing matters on her mind. “Montana, before you left, you had said something peculiar, and I was hoping you’d shine some light on it.”

“Oh, I was hoping you didn’t hear me.” Although the voice didn’t sound like Montana, it definitely sounded regretful. “I slipped up, man, like, when you’re at the airport and the lady is all, have a nice flight, and you say you too, then you have to live with that! I’ve told at least eight cashiers I love them at eight stores I can never return to ever again.”

So that was it then. A silly mistake. Knowing Montana, Caswell should have figured it out on her own. It definitely took a weight off her chest. “All right.”

There was silence on the line. “Okay…” Montana dragged out the syllables. “If that’s all, I’ve got to go…so…bye?”

“Goodbye.”

“I love you.” Montana paused. “That was a joke because earlier…”

“Oh! Yes, all right. Good one.” There was a clicking sound.

"Montana?" No response. Caswell was pretty sure that meant the phone was off, so she put it back down. She was proud of herself for her first successful phone call.

Now that she no longer had to agonize over Montana's word choice, she could do whatever she liked as she waited. As she considered the possibilities, she stepped on a discarded wrapper. She picked it up and tossed it into the garbage bin, then soon found herself tidying up the place. It also gave her an excuse to look around that felt less like spying.

She ended up sorting everything into three piles. Some things seemed obvious to throw away, others to be put away. The third pile collected things that she could not easily categorize as garbage or not. She put away the tank top Montana had so carelessly thrown on the ground earlier. As she did that, she started looking through her clothes, mostly curious to see how many pairs of the same shirt she owned. She found a red sweater in the far back and tried to pull it out, but it snagged on something. In a lapse of proper judgment, Caswell tugged harder and ripped off an entire sleeve.

She stared at her handiwork for a minute, in shock at her own stupidity. She didn't know what to do, but maybe it wasn't that big of a deal anyway. The sweater looked like it had been too small for Montana. It was probably very old and Montana had probably completely forgotten about it.

She slipped the one-sleeved mistake on over her clothes, deciding it would be better to take the evidence away with her. It had a rather unfortunate looking snowman stitched on the chest. She threw away the lone sleeve, then tried to straighten out her cape from underneath the rather nice souvenir. It smelled like Montana, and it was warm like Montana. Not quite as warm, but it was still nice. Anyway, she was pretty sure Montana had stolen one of her capes a while back for comedic purposes. This was getting even, albeit accidentally.

That was, decidedly, enough snooping around. She checked the clock, and figured the sun had to have set. She experimented by opening the curtains a little. As no light poured in, she kept opening them until she could see outside. There was the moon, waning down to a half. The lunar cycles had always been strangely captivating to Caswell. The moon had been her only company for years, after all.

That line of personifying was dangerously Montana-like, so she scrapped it and made her way outside. It was nice to get some fresh air after being in the muskiness of that apartment for almost twenty-four hours. There were still quite a few people bustling around. Not wanting to make a scene, she kept her head down, hoping no one would notice her.

She was so busy trying to avoid eye contact, she smacked right into someone. They both fell to the ground, and she was mildly surprised a person had enough strength to knock her down.

"Sorry about that," a thickly accented tongue spoke with a bit of a laugh. The person stood and offered his hand. "My head was in the clouds!"

Caswell looked up at him but quickly looked away. The man did not react to her eyes, so Caswell took his hand and stood up. "Thank you," she muttered.

He did not let go of her hand, but was too friendly to be threatening. "Why haven't we met yet?" There was wonder in his voice. "Are you new in town?"

"Hardly." Caswell couldn't hide her confusion. She took in the man's appearance. He was dressed like a goth, though he seemed too old for that kind of subculture. He had a very prominent widow's peak and dark hair that matched his eyes.

"I guess I simply don't get out enough at night!" The man confessed, then shook her hand heartily. "I'm Gregory Drake."

"As in the teacher?" Caswell asked before she could think.

Drake smiled. His teeth were sharp, but he didn't smell like a vampire. He didn't smell like a human either. "Yes! I take it you've met some of my students?"

"Yes, I have. Dot, Cameron, and June." Knowing no one would ever know she said it, she said, "They're very good kids."

"Ah, I'll have to agree with you there." He let go of her hand, noticing the way Caswell stared at him. "Sorry, am I keeping you?"

"No, just..." Caswell cocked her head and asked rather bluntly, "What are you?"

Drake looked around, grimacing slightly when he saw people. "Do you mind if we go somewhere more private for this conversation?"

Caswell was fairly certain she could take him in a fight, so she agreed. "All right."

They walked a few blocks, then into the wooded area where Montana had taken Caswell for her birthday. They didn't go nearly as far into the trees, but it still brought back the memory. A nice memory. That was a pleasant sensation she wasn't used to.

"I wish Dot had told me she had met a vampire," Drake started, confirming Caswell's suspicion that he knew exactly what she was and making her wish the feeling was mutual. She racked her brains. Drake was too human and too vampire at the same time. It didn't make any sense. "It seems like the sort of news she'd want to share right away. I'm surprised she didn't suspect you and I were in some kind of a coven."

"That's unimportant." Caswell had a feeling Dot did not tell because she was worried about Montana's safety. She wondered if Montana was going to tell them about the werewolf attack. Probably not. She wouldn't want to worry them. "I asked you a question."

"And I'm going to give you an answer," Drake responded, still light and playful. "But it is a secret. I need you to promise me you won't tell the kids."

"Depends on the secret." Caswell furrowed her eyebrows. "If they are in danger, they will not be the only people I tell."

"I was right. She'd love you." Drake said cryptically, with a hint of fondness to hid voice. "I assure you no one is in any danger. Most humans react poorly to learning about us, and I'd hate for word to get out to the more judgmental parents. I love my job and the kids, and I'd hate to lose that."

"You're not human then, of course." Caswell frowned, trying to piece it together. "But you're not a vampire either. Clearly not a werewolf."

"And you'd know that." Drake's eyes were on her sweater, and as a knowing smile quirked on his lips, Caswell suddenly realized she was not the only one who could smell Montana on the garment.

"It's...it's not like that," Caswell stuttered, obviously flustered and not very convincing.

"I am the last person who could judge you." Drake put up his hands in defense. "And that's why I knew you'd be the last person who could judge me. I'm a dhampir."

"...A what?"

"It means I'm half and half," he explained simply. "My mother was human, and my father was a vampire. As such, I am neither vampire nor human, and yet, I am both. Interspecies love is taboo, as I'm sure you know." His eyes were on the sweater again. "So that's why you've never heard of it. It's a bit of a struggle to balance, but I manage."

"I see." Caswell never even considered that there could be such a thing. She felt unusually young, like life was opening up to her. Suddenly, the world was very big, and by comparison, she was very small. She had never felt quite like this before. The feeling left her breathless, equally terrified and exhilarated. "That's...I'm sorry, I'm a little speechless."

"Understandably. I need to head back. I've got a quiz to grade, but here's my number." He took out a scrap of paper from his jacket and scribbled down his digits. "If you have any questions or need support, feel free to hit me up."

Caswell accepted the note, glancing it over before slipping it into her own pocket. "I will," Caswell said, and it wasn't a lie.

"Are you going to tell on me?" Drake was, for the first time that night, uncertain. "I know June and Cameron and Dot would be excited to know, as would most of my other students, but I can't risk it."

"Your secret is safe with me." Caswell tried to brush it off coolly, but her voice had lost its protective steel. She could not hide her sincerity. He had stripped her bare so easily.

"But if you feel the need to tell your significant other, I won't mind." Drake smiled with such kindness, Caswell almost didn't want to correct him. That, and because there was something intoxicating about being mistaken for Montana's girlfriend.

She didn't say anything. She just nodded and waved as they parted ways. Caswell walked with a little spring to her step, surprised by how impacted she was at the knowledge that monsters out there were going against the grain and chasing their happiness. If they could do that, why couldn't she?

Chapter Fourteen

JULY ROLLED IN WITH the shortest nights of the year. Montana and Caswell still found time for each other, but perhaps it was too much time. The space between them was quickly diminishing, both metaphorically and literally. It had gotten so bad they could finish each other's sentences. The less infuriating Caswell found Montana, the more infuriated she became with herself. Montana seemed either unaware or unaffected by the change.

"Hey, Beatrice," she called out as she entered the piano room. "The kids were hoping we could build a fire."

"Why would they want to do that?" Caswell frowned as Montana joined her, knowing instinctively which room she'd be in. It was becoming routine.

"Because it's summer. They wanna make s'mores and tell ghost stories and stuff. Dot isn't allowed to do it any closer to town than this. It'll be good for bonding." Montana was clearly in favor of their plan, even if her voice remained monotone. She adjusted her sunglasses, which she had successfully replaced with a pair that looked the same as the original.

"That sounds like a horrible idea." Fire with Dot's curse was bound to make an absolutely terrible combination. If Montana fell in, she'd survive. The others would not. Caswell didn't want to lose her fragile friends for the sake of summertime bonding.

"Oh, come on," Montana whined. "You're no fun. Wait, that reminds me. When you were over at my apartment, did you mess with my stuff at all?"

"The entire place was disgusting. I didn't touch anything," Caswell lied quickly. Luckily, it was convincing. Or Montana was too trusting.

"All right." She scratched the back of her head, trying to think. "Damn..."

"Why? Did you lose something?" Caswell asked, mustering up as much innocence as she could.

"Yeah, my old sweater. It barely fit anymore but I was pretty sentimental about it and whatever." Montana looked pretty bummed. "I could've sworn I hadn't moved it at all from the back of my dresser, but I couldn't find it."

Of course. She had reorganized the whole place, cleaning up all the garbage and putting things back where they belonged, but the most notable thing she did was the one thing she messed up. "I'm sure you'll find it," Caswell said dismissively. "So when are we setting things on fire?"

"We can do it?" Montana instantly brightened up. "Awesome! We'll just wait for them to show up. Dot said they're getting a ride from her mom. Let's go outside and wait for them."

Montana grabbed her arm and was dragging her out onto the lawn. "Slow down, Montana." Caswell made a halfhearted attempt to pull away. "I don't want to meet her mother. That's going to be weird."

Montana did not relent. "Everything's weird with you around. I wanna meet her!"

"You can meet her on your own," Caswell said, but the minivan had already pulled to the curb. June and Cameron hopped out of the back, thanking the driver. Dot kissed her cheek before climbing out of the passenger seat. Seeing the two standing on the lawn, the mother got out to greet them.

"Prepare yourself!" June distracted Montana by charging at her and trying to tackle her to the ground. Montana did not fall. She spun June around and set her back down.

"Stop attacking me. I'm trying to make a good impression with Dot's mom!" Montana pleaded with her.

"You have to prove yourself to her by trial of combat." June politely called over, "Mrs. Liang, do you mind if Ms. Montana proves herself to you by trial of combat?"

"Go easy on her, June." Mrs. Liang said. As June began her attack, Mrs. Liang turned her attention to Caswell, holding out her hand. Mrs. Liang hand kind eyes and deep smile lines. Her bob was much more neatly groomed than her daughter's. She looked a decade or so older than Montana. "Hi, I'm Dot's mother. You can call me Wendy. You're

Ms. Caswell, I take it? Dot has told me so much about you. It's nice to finally meet you."

Dot must've told her mother about their respective conditions because she made no mention about their appearances. It was strange to be greeted like another human. Caswell shook her hand. "The pleasure is all mine."

"Ooh! So cold! And so polite." Mrs. Liang let go of her, clasping her hands together. "I'll be back to pick them up at nine tomorrow. Is that all right?"

"One moment." Caswell smiled at her before shooting a glare at Montana. "Did you tell them they could stay the night?"

Montana was trying to wrestle June off her. "Uh, yeah. It's not like you have plans. I was gonna stay all night."

"Hey, June, if you bite her, do you think she'll turn back into a human?" Dot piped up, watching the fight.

"I don't think it works like that." Cameron shook his head.

"I'm not gonna bite her. She's super hairy." June tried to get her into a headlock. Montana flipped her over her back, making sure she was gentle and that she landed on her feet. June spun back around to face her, hair all in her face. She pushed it aside so she could look up at Montana, eyes shining with awe. "Do that again!"

"In a minute! I wanna talk with the adults." Montana smoothed out her shirt and ran over to Caswell and Mrs. Liang. She rested her elbow on Caswell's shoulder and lifted her hand in greeting. "Wassup."

Caswell made a face at her. "Montana, we didn't prepare for them to sleep over."

"Don't worry about that," Mrs. Liang cut in. "They've all got sleeping bags. I'm also only a call away, so I can bring more sleeping bags if something goes wrong." She winked. "This isn't my first sleepover."

Montana grinned at her. "See? They'll be fine. Thanks, ma'am. We've got the little rascals from here."

"I should be the one thanking you. But if you'll excuse me, I've got plans with my husband, and he can be so impatient. It was very nice meeting you ladies." Mrs. Liang waved goodbye and made her way back to the car. A giant branch fell on the hood, but she didn't so much as blink.

"Mom, can we have that?" Dot asked as she ran over, as if her mother had grown attached to the branch in the few seconds between when it fell and when she noticed it. Dot was already grabbing it.

"Of course, dear. Be careful." Mrs. Liang ruffled her hair. "I'll see you tomorrow. Call me if you need anything. Or you could call your dad, or the ER."

"I will!" Dot promised and blew her a kiss, as she dragged the branch back to her friends. "I love you!"

"Love you too. You kids be good!" Mrs. Liang got back in the minivan, waving one last time before driving off.

"Fire! Fire! Fire!" The kids started chanting, following Dot into the backyard while she waved the branch around.

"Good socializing." Montana fist-bumped her. "I think she liked us."

"At least enough to leave her chaos child with us," Caswell agreed. "Let's go make sure they don't kill themselves."

They headed to the backyard, where the kids were already gathering sticks. Montana nodded to herself. "Okay, I'm gonna dig a little hole over here so we don't catch the grass on fire." She began kicking loose clumps of dirt.

"Hey, Vic?" June shouted from across the yard. She held up a stick. "Do you think you could catch this in your mouth?"

"Only one way to find out!" Montana immediately dropped what she was doing. Caswell rolled her eyes. Montana was such a child. But it wasn't a terrible thing, since everyone always had a good time around her. She could light up a whole room. Caswell did not fight these affectionate thoughts.

June handed the stick to Cameron, suddenly unsure of her throwing abilities. Cameron tossed it, and Montana caught it, but when she bit down it splintered into a thousand pieces, most going in her mouth.

"Oh no." She coughed, spitting out bits of wood. "My teeth were so much stronger than that stick."

"You're an idiot," Caswell informed her.

"Hey, have you guys seen Dot?" Cameron called over to them. "I can't believe she missed that."

Dot reappeared from the side of the house. "Sorry! I found a really good stick, but I guess a woodchuck wanted it more than I did. I didn't know they were still awake so late at night!"

"Dot, Vic caught a stick in her mouth and exploded it," June filled her in gleefully. "It was awesome."

Cameron picked up another stick, poking its pointy end with a finger. He yelled, "Caswell? If I stabbed you with this, would you die?"

"You're not strong enough to drive it through my chest."

"That...that kind of feels like a challenge, but I'm not super comfortable taking it," Cameron admitted. He walked over, dropping the stick into the pile. Now at a distance from Dot and June, he asked Caswell, "Can we go inside for a second? I need...uh...water. Yeah, that's it. I need water. I'm so thirsty."

"You don't need my permission," Caswell pointed to the house. "You know how to get in."

Cameron glanced at the house, then back at her. "No, I need you to come with."

"I don't see why." Caswell's eyebrows furrowed. "The sink is right in there, but if you want a bottle, you'll have to ask Montana. She hides all sorts of food around the place."

Cameron groaned. "I need to talk to you in private."

"Oh! Oh, all right. Let's get you that water then." She winked and gave him a discreet thumbs up. It might not have been as discreet as she hoped, seeing as Cameron cringed.

Once inside, Cameron sat down on the floor with his back against the wall. "Here, sit with me." Cameron motioned to the other side of the hall. Caswell sat down so they were facing each other. "Okay, let's talk about feelings."

"Oh, no." Caswell tried to get back up, but Cameron ushered her back into a sitting position. "Really, I'm no good at this sort of thing. You'd be better off speaking to Montana about whatever it is."

"Hear me out, please." Cameron did not ask for a lot from, well, anyone. The least Caswell could do was listen to what he needed to say, even if she wouldn't be much help. Caswell remained seated. "Okay. So to start this off, let me say Dot and June are also rooting for you. They may not always show it in the best way, but it's the truth. They just don't get it."

"And you do?" Caswell quirked an eyebrow, ready to brush him off. "Child, I have lived your lifetime dozens of times. A decade doesn't even feel like a minute anymore."

"Except when you're with her, right?" Cameron smiled softly.

Caswell was taken aback. He was right. It hadn't even been a year yet, but every moment she spent with Montana felt like an eternity. A special little forever where it was only them and infinity. She used to not notice the passing of seasons. Now she kept track of the hours.

Cameron shrugged. "I may not be crazy old like you, but man, love is love. It's always been the same, and it's always going to be the same. The way you look at her isn't anything new."

Caswell slumped forward until her forehead was on the floor. She began to groan, which slowly devolved into a frustrated wordless scream. She sat back up at breakneck speed. "Fine! You've found me out! My horrible little secret is revealed! I'm in love and it's terrible! Are you happy now, Cameron? Did you come here to torment me?"

"No! That's not it at all!" Cameron said frantically. "I came to help!"

Caswell paused her angry fit. "Why?"

"Because you're my friend," Cameron said, as if it were the simplest thing in the world. "And one time I was in Vic's shoes. I didn't realize her feelings. I had no idea what I was putting her through, and I still feel guilty because my friend was suffering all that time and I...I never even knew. And I didn't feel the way she did, but I did care about her so much, and that was the last thing I could've wanted for her. I'm sure Vic doesn't want you to suffer either."

"I don't want her to know," Caswell said suddenly, panic seizing her. "She said I was her friend. She said I was the best thing that happened to her since she turned. If she finds out how I feel, she will think I've been taking advantage of her this whole time. She'll hate me."

"She's not going to hate you!" Cameron promised. "I will do everything in my power to make sure you two don't end up like me and Maxine did. And you won't! I know you won't. Because I'm going to help you tell her, so she doesn't find out on her own when it's too late. And one other thing."

"What's the other thing?" Caswell asked after waiting a beat.

"Sorry, I was pausing for dramatic effect," Cameron conceded sheepishly. "Anyway, there's one other thing. And it's that your crush isn't unrequited."

"You don't know that." Caswell tried to shut it down, but her heart betrayed her. The thought that Montana was feeling all the things she was feeling was so impossible but so wonderful. She hadn't allowed the thought before, because she wouldn't have been able to handle that much foolish hope.

"There's only one way to find out." Cameron snapped out of his self-induced daydreaming as if he'd remembered something. "Oh, and I won't tell June and Dot what we're up to if you don't want them to interfere. I didn't tell them beforehand, because I thought that kind of stuff should be up to you."

"No, I'm going to need all the help I can get," Caswell admitted miserably. "I haven't done this sort of thing since I was human."

"Wow." Cameron could not hide his horror. "Not even once?"

"I've been a little busy, seeing how I'm undead and all." Caswell rolled her eyes. "Dating is tough when you exist as a constant reminder of the futility and cruelness of life."

Cameron nodded slowly, trying to process as little of that as he could. "That kind of talk is gonna be a little off-putting, even to Ms. Perfect." He reached out his leg and tapped Caswell's shoe with his, a move that felt surprisingly supportive and comforting. "But we'll figure it out. Dot and June and I will come up with some really great plans. We've survived all sorts of stuff with our quick thinking. Romance isn't that much harder than dangling off a cliff."

They were interrupted by the door slamming open. June, Dot, and Montana ran in, laughing so hard they were wheezing. They were also drenched.

"I mean, I knew it was gonna go bad," Montana managed to gasp. "But I thought..."

"Yeah, yeah." June wiped at her eyes. "Me too!"

"You never know!" Dot was clutching Montana's arm like it was the only thing that was keeping her upright. She looked up and saw

Cameron and Caswell, who had quickly stood up and were prepared to pretend their talk had never happened. "You missed it, Cameron." Dot pointed outside, but couldn't get words out through her laughing. She buried her face in Montana's arm instead, as if the world itself was too funny to look at. "You smell like wet dog!"

This brought on a new wave of laughter. "You guys are nuts." Cameron shook his head, sending one more smile Caswell's way. Caswell smiled back. "I take it no fire?"

More laughter. "Stop, you're gonna kill us!" Montana begged through her laughing. Unable to take it anymore, she fell to her knees and dragged the other two down with her.

June and Dot finally managed to collect themselves enough to push Montana off them, still smiling and chattering playfully. Montana flopped onto her stomach and rolled over onto her back. Her hair was strewn about wildly, yet it managed to frame her face perfectly. She grinned up at Caswell, still breathless from her giggle fit. "Hey, Bea." Her voice rasped, and there was no denying it.

Caswell was in love.

Chapter Fifteen

MONTANA WAS BEING FOLLOWED.

She knew that, but she pretended she didn't. It had been going on for about twenty minutes. She was in a store, and it was the middle of the afternoon, so a lot of people were around. She didn't want to risk making a scene. She didn't know what her pursuer was willing to do, but she wasn't about to test them with innocent bystanders.

Her heart thumped painfully hard in her chest at the thought of people getting hurt or worse because some sicko wouldn't leave her alone. When did her life turn into that? It was a stupid question. She knew the exact moment her life became like this. She still had the scar to remind her.

"Hey!"

Montana's heart froze. Of course Dot had to be there. It was the kid's rotten luck, after all.

"Yo, kid." Montana threw up a peace sign, keeping her poker face. "I'm a little busy right now. Got a lotta errands to run."

"Oh, okay! I'll give you space." Dot grinned at her. She was such a good kid. "I'll see you later!"

"Yeah, all right, I'll see ya." Montana didn't even look up as they passed each other, much less pat her shoulder or any other gesture that would betray their closeness. She was friendly with her because she was friendly with everyone, that's all. That's what she wanted her pursuer to see.

Dot's presence caused a display of cans to knock over and fall on the guy, and Montana couldn't completely cover her snicker.

"Oh my goodness, are you all right?" Dot called to him. Before she could inspect him any closer, her mom called her from across the store, and she had to run off. Montana swallowed a sigh of relief. That was almost disastrous. God bless Mama Liang for keeping her girl safe even when she didn't know it.

"You gonna stop creeping around, Brick?" Montana approached him, her amusement gone. She watched him get back to his feet without offering a hand.

Brick flashed her a smile. "You're the one who's been leading me around for half of an hour. If I didn't know better, I'd say you're enjoying yourself."

"Do you want something? I'm a little busy."

"I wanted to talk." Brick moved like a predator. Something in the way he carried himself could've triggered a flight or fight response in anyone, but Montana's seemed to be broken. She just stood there. "You replaced those cute little shades of yours. I'm so happy. It really crushed me when they broke in our scuffle."

At the reminder of that night, Montana had to clench her fists to stop herself from trembling, digging her nails into her palms. "Thanks. Bye."

"That's not what I wanted to talk about." Brick chuckled, as if they were playing, "You tease!"

"Then spit it out." Montana started picking up the cans that had been knocked over. Any excuse not to have to look at him.

"I'm trying to be friendly. I do want to be your friend, Montana," Brick said, although he better resembled a scorpion than a wolf. "I've been thinking. Thinking about you. And somehow, I still can't see you as a killer."

"Thanks." Montana gave him a look. "Means a lot, coming from you."

Brick's lips quirked up into a vicious kind of grin. It felt more like he was baring his teeth. "So what I'm thinking is, you didn't actually kill that vampire. I can't see it."

Montana said nothing, returning the last can to its place, but her blood ran cold. She couldn't panic now, even if she wanted to. Oh, she really wanted to. But she didn't know how much he knew, so she couldn't slip up and give him more.

"Not to mention that smell on you hasn't gone away. It kinda seems like it's getting stronger. I'd give you the benefit of the doubt and say you haven't gotten rid of the body yet, maybe keeping it as a trophy, but I've never known a vampire that didn't turn to ash when their time had come. So if I can smell her, it follows that she's still alive. And I can't imagine a positive reaction from the pack if they found out a vampire was on the loose. Yes, I'd imagine we'd do away with the old bat before she even knew what hit her." Brick circled around her as he spoke.

Montana felt sick to her stomach. She tried to think rationally. She knew that if Brick wanted to go after Caswell, he would. But he hadn't, so he must be missing something. It couldn't be a weak spot. Brick wouldn't need any shortcuts. Scratch that, he wouldn't want one. He loved the thrill of the hunt. Maybe it was Montana who was missing something.

Brick continued. "Now, that's hardly fair, don't you think? That's what I think. If this was our territory, that'd be a different story, but technically we're the ones trespassing. This dreary little town isn't our home. We were passing through, picking up some new friends. But the others aren't as reasonable as me. You've seen them. If they think they're in danger, they'll bite back. It's survival. I can't deny them survival, you know?"

Finally, it started to make sense to Montana. Brick wanted her to come with the pack. He was providing her with an ultimatum. If she joined them, the vampire would be left in peace. But Brick, despite his illusion of confidence, was unsure. He knew Caswell was alive, but he didn't know *why*. And Montana was still new enough to the werewolf business where there could've been quite a few reasons she didn't want to kill Caswell. It was even possible she couldn't and had barely escaped with her life.

She scoffed. "Are you trying to blackmail me, Brick? I'm not scared of you."

Brick stopped moving, his expression changing in a subtle way Montana didn't understand. "I know. You're not the first to attack me, but no one's ever stood their ground when I shoved back. You're not scared of me. After everything, you can still say that to me and mean it. I'm the leader of the pack. It's disrespectful not to fear me. And yet...it's enchanted me."

"You're kidding."

"I know we got off to a rocky start, Montana, but it only feels that way because you're not used to it. You need to learn how to play rough. You can't stay a puppy forever."

"Do you mean that like, physically or…?"

rick's face scrunched in confusion, his charisma disappearing. "I meant mentally, Montana. I meant you're acting like a child. Why would I mean physically?"

"You're not ready for that conversation if you have to ask." Montana shrugged. "Sorry, didn't mean to interrupt. Keep going with your creepy spiel."

"Laugh it up, Montana., I don't mind. Playing hard to get doesn't lose you any favors. But once you're done joking around, you really should look at things realistically. Who else is gonna have you?" Brick sneered. "A human? You're not one of them anymore. There's no place for you with them."

"Can I go now?"

Brick stepped aside, holding up his hands in mock defense. "You can do whatever you want." He licked his lips. "But don't think word won't get back to me."

"Cool." Montana casually picked up an orange from a nearby stand and tossed it behind Brick.

"That's not—It's not gonna—" He tried to fight the urge but ended up running after it.

"Go buy some ChapStick while you're at it! You shouldn't lick your lips that much," Montana called after him before heading off in her own direction. She was a little surprised that had worked, but she was glad she wasn't the only one who chased random objects.

It would be nice to have someone who understood what she was going through.

She shook off the thought. She didn't want anything to do with those creeps. Even if Caswell and the kids didn't always understand what she did or why she did it, they were always there for her. She didn't need to be understood.

As if on cue, her phone buzzed. She checked it, seeing a text from Dot.

*Hey! How are the errands going? ^u^*

She sent back, *just finished*, to which Dot replied, *omw!* Montana didn't know whether that was a typo or an acronym. Before she could ask, Dot came barreling around the corner toward her.

"I told June and Cameron I ran into you, and they were all like perfect let's get started, and I was all like no she's busy, but they told me to keep messaging you until you were done because they're all ready to get started," Dot spoke a thousand words a second.

"Slow down, kid," Montana said. "What are they getting ready for?" Instead of an answer, Dot responded by grabbing her hand and practically dragging her across the tiles. She brought her over to her mom, who was still checking out. Montana waved with her free hand. "Uh hi, Mrs. Liang."

"Hi, dear." She smiled at Montana before turning her attention to Dot. "If you finish up before six, tell June and Cameron they can come over for dinner. It's taco night." It seemed like everyone was in on this plan except Montana. Mrs. Liang looked back up at her. "And you're welcome to join us, of course, as long as you relay any dietary constrictions. I'm afraid I'm not a big fan of scary movies, so I don't know much about...you know." She motioned to her ears.

Montana was a little dumbstruck by the offer. She wondered if the whole Liang family was this kind, or if Dot took after her mom. "Um, thanks, ma'am."

Dot gave her hand a little tug. "I'll ask her on the way. We need to hurry!"

"All right, see you two later," Mrs. Liang waved to them.

They waved back as Dot sped up, pulling her out of the store. Montana looked back. "I think I'm a little bit in love with your mom, dude."

"Please never say those words to me ever again."

Montana snorted. "All right, all right, I'm kidding." She let Dot lead her into a different store, some kind of clothing boutique she had never been in before. Montana bought most of her clothes in bulk at thrift shops. Those were the comfiest and, in her own mind, looked the best.

"There you two are," June cried as they made their way over. It looked like she and Cameron were in the middle of an argument. They were both wearing silly hats with the price tags still on, but that seemed unrelated. "I need your help. Cameron's being ridiculous."

"She's the one being ridiculous." Cameron adjusted his sun hat so it titled the other way, then crossed his arms over his chest. "Vic, you know her better than anyone. Do you think Caswell would prefer something classy or something *funky?*" The distaste he said the latter with made it clear where he stood. June shot him a glare. He shrugged. "Your description, not mine."

"That's a biased question," June interrupted. "We were helping her redefine her look because everything she wears is scary or old or both, and she said she liked my skirt. My skirt is casual and fun. We're trying to help her look less stuffy, not just stuffy in a new era!"

"Elegance isn't stuffiness," Cameron argued. "She likes the concept of skirts, not yours in particular."

"Show us the options," Dot shouted to be heard, jittering with excitement.

Cameron revealed a mass of black fabric that was longer than he was. It was an evening dress with a neckline so low Montana felt like she shouldn't be looking at it even while it was empty. June showed off something pink and orange that had no discernible shape or openings.

Dot motioned for Montana to lean in, then whispered in her ear, "Are you thinking what I'm thinking?" Her breath tickled Montana's fur.

"Depends," Montana whispered back. "What are we thinking?"

"We cut them in half and sew them into one super dress." Dot got too excited and stopped whispering. Montana straightened back up to save her hearing.

"Great idea, definitely." Montana offered her a smile, turning to the other two. "They're both great! I think Beatrice would love them. It's just...well..."

"What is it?" Cameron and June asked in tandem.

"Her favorite color is green, so I was thinking she'd probably love something that's green," Montana said, as if she were admitting some great secret.

June and Cameron hung their chosen outfits back up on hangers, reunited with a new goal. "Let's go see what they've got in green!" Dot cheered, and Montana watched them race off to a different clothing rack. She chuckled, following lazily.

Brick had been wrong about a lot of things, but his biggest mistake was thinking Montana didn't have a home right where she was.

Chapter Sixteen

CASWELL WAS NERVOUS. THE thought of attempting to romance Montana sent her head spinning. Why had she agreed to this? So many things could go wrong. And with Dot around, they probably would go wrong. Caswell didn't know why she was taking advice from middle schoolers in the first place. Montana was immature, but surely, she wasn't that bad.

"Okay." June clapped her hands together. "Dot is out with Vic right now. We told her to distract her for twenty minutes, but since it's Dot, we should have a good hour to work with."

"Realistically, an hour and half, but we don't want to overestimate in case it's a light day," Cameron said, setting down the bag he was carrying and digging through it.

"Why do we need time?" Caswell scrunched up her nose.

June and Cameron exchanged a look. June said bluntly, "Because you look like a nightmare."

"Oh! Thank you."

"It's...it's not a good thing." Cameron shook his head. "That might be like, your thing and I respect that, but it's not ideal for dating. Vic is used only to seeing humans as possible romantic partners, so we gotta show her that you fit into that group too. Then you can go back to being creepy. For now, we've gotta make you a little more...accessible."

June pushed a bag into her arms. "Go try this on! We'll get ready for you out here."

Caswell took the bag and disappeared into her room. She let out a sigh. They might be children, but they were giving their all for her. She had to try her best too. Even if all she wanted to do was flee up north, farther than humans could comfortably live, and make a new start in the great polar expanse.

Caswell didn't make a break for it. She stripped down and dumped the contents of the bag out on the floor, then slipped on the forest-green dress with ease. A black ribbon around the middle was tied in a bow at the hip. She liked the way it looked with the hemline down to her knees. The only issue was the off-shoulder cut, which left her neck and shoulders totally vulnerable. She put her cape back on over the dress.

She went back to find Cameron and June, who made a face. "Come on, cape off."

"Absolutely not."

The kids were obviously displeased but did not press her on the nonnegotiable choice. Cameron pulled over a chair. "Okay, sit here."

"Aren't we done?" Caswell sat in the offered seat.

"Not even close." June reached into the bag that Cameron was carrying earlier, and pulled out a box. "You're in luck. I have a full set of this stuff because my aunt got it for me as a birthday present. I've only used it twice, for Halloween."

She clicked open a lock on the box and revealed it was full of makeup. Cameron pulled out a brush, covering it in powder. "I'm gonna try and make you look less like, uh..." He glanced to June for support.

"A demon-infested corpse?" she offered.

"A demon-infested corpse," he repeated with a nod. He started brushing the powder on Caswell's face. "I've been doing theater for years now. I've picked up a lot of tricks."

"So we couldn't find any contacts to fix your eyes," June said, watching Cameron work his magic.

"Montana likes my eyes," Caswell blurted out. Now she felt like she was the schoolchild, saying embarrassing stuff like that.

"Well, that takes care of that," June said, sounding pleased. "Guess we won't need plan c after all."

"Good, I hated plan c." Cameron reached for a different brush.

"You're really digging into that blush, huh?" June questioned.

"Her face is so lifeless, it needs it." Cameron glanced at Caswell. "Uh, sorry, dude. No offense."

"None taken." Caswell didn't realize being alive was such a beauty standard. She really hadn't put any time or thought into trying to make herself attractive. There had never been anyone she wanted to see her that way, at least as far back as she could remember.

"I'm gonna get the kitchen set up." June grabbed her bag.

"Okay, remember we agreed on one candle," Cameron called over his shoulder. "Lowers the risks."

"I know." June scoffed, but discreetly took two candles out of the bag. She walked to the other room with a skip in her step, excited to put all their planning into action.

Cameron instructed Caswell, "Close your eyes for a second."

Caswell obliged. She fidgeted with her hands as she waited. "Do you really think any of this is going to work? Fixing my face isn't going to fix me. There's still the chance she won't be very smitten at all."

"Hey, hey, woah." Concern laced Cameron's voice. "Nothing about you needs fixing, okay? You shouldn't think stuff like that."

Caswell was surprised by the adverse response. She had barely even registered the words coming out of her own mouth. It was just anxious muttering. "Sorry?"

Cameron sighed. "You remind me too much of Dot sometimes." Another surprise. Dot was so optimistic and likable that the comparison didn't really make sense to her. "She says the most concerning stuff like it's nothing. It's like, she can't even see how awesome she is."

"You should tell her that."

"Hey, I'm the one giving you the dating advice, remember? Not that...it's not like I want to date her, or...You know what? You're done. You can open your eyes." Cameron smiled a little at his handiwork. "You look good! I wish I had some way to show you."

Caswell lightly felt her cheek with her fingertips. She could feel the powder, but it wasn't a terrible sensation. "I'll take your word for it. Thank you, Cameron."

"No problem, man. I'm gonna text Dot and see if they're still alive, then you can go help June in the kitchen." Cameron was already taking out his phone.

"Do you think having one of those is useful?"

Cameron glanced up. "Uh, you mean my phone? Yeah, it's pretty great. You thinking about getting one?"

Caswell paused. "No." She was not a terrific liar, and she went to join June before more questions came up.

In the kitchen, June had laid out a white cloth over the table. She had also arranged a handful of flowers in a cup, which was fighting the single candle for centerpiece.

"Looks pretty romantic, right?" June grinned at her.

It was strange seeing her table without the doughnut box on it. She almost asked June if she had moved it, but she remembered disposing of it when she was trying to distance herself from Montana. What a terrible time that was. "It's lovely, June, thank you."

"I wonder when Dot's getting back. We're totally ready for them," June said. "HEY, CAMERON, HAVE YOU TEXTED DOT YET?"

Caswell jumped nearly a foot in the air.

"YEAH, I DID," Cameron yelled back.

June rolled her eyes, giving Caswell a look she wrongfully assumed she'd understand. "AND WHAT'D SHE SAY?"

Cameron paused for a second, presumably checking his phone. "SHE'S ON HER WAY."

"GREAT!" She turned back to Caswell. "Okay, you just sit here, and we'll let them in. It's gonna be amazing."

Caswell took the indicated seat at the table. June rushed out of the room, and Caswell found herself waiting alone. She drummed her fingers on the table, doing her best not to imagine how much of a mistake this whole night was going to be. But there wasn't much else to think about. She stewed, letting it tear her up a little. She was going to ruin their whole friendship, and Montana was going to hate her and never talk to her again by the end of the night.

"Yo, Beatrice!"

Caswell immediately straightened herself up. June, Cameron, and Dot followed Montana into the room, Dot waving a little hello. Montana set down a takeout box on the table and gave Caswell a smile. "Hey, that looks great on you! Give me a twirl."

"I beg your pardon." Caswell narrowed her eyes. She wasn't sure what that was slang for, but she was ready to get pissed about it.

"Uh, y'know." Montana spun around. "Like that?"

Caswell couldn't hide her embarrassment. "Oh. Right." She stood up and made a modest twirl before quickly returning to her seat.

Montana clapped, sitting down across from her. "Yeah, that looks awesome! I'm glad it fit. I only had that one cape to go off for size."

"I knew you stole one! Wait, did you...?"

"Oh, yeah, I helped these knuckleheads pick it out. Thought you'd like the color." Montana patted the box she brought with her. "Speaking of, you gonna eat this, Dot? Thought you were starving."

On cue, Dot straightened up. "I feel fine now!" Even her friends gave her a look for that excuse. "Maybe you and Ms. Caswell should share it," Dot suggested.

"That's a nice offer, kid, but you know she doesn't eat. Remember the jelly doughnut thing? She spat it out like it was on fire." She twisted around to look at the other two. "June? Cameron? You guys hungry? We got...spaghetti. Why'd we get spaghetti, Dot?"

Cameron and June both politely turned down the offer of late-night pasta. Dot was faltering. She shrugged, smiling nervously. "It seemed like a good idea at the time. Sometimes you crave those noodles. And then it passes."

"Guess so." Montana turned in her chair, so she was facing Caswell again, who was screaming internally. She knew exactly why Dot was instructed to ask for spaghetti. They were trying to reenact a romantic movie June had made them watch, *Lady and the Tramp*. If Montana had any clue about the plan, Caswell was sure she would've been delighted by the reference to dogs in love.

"Not gonna let it go to waste," Montana said. "You got me in the mood for it now." She started eating the spaghetti, completely unaware of the awkward silence in the room as four people watched her eat. She eventually caught Caswell in the act. When she didn't look away, Montana paused. "Did you...want some?"

"Swallow before you talk." Caswell frowned instinctively, then kicked herself for the reaction. Criticizing Montana was not exactly fostering that romantic atmosphere she was trying for. "And no. I don't want some."

The kids were all mouthing things behind Montana's back, clearly disproving of Caswell's choice, but she was remorseless. It wasn't her fault human food had to taste like that.

"Hey, did you do something with your face?" Montana did not speak through a mouthful of food this time. She motioned lazily with her fork. "Looks different."

Caswell sat up a little straighter. "Do you like it?"

"Uh, yeah. Sorry, no, I totally like it. It's just..." She laughed. "I don't know, I guess I've gotten used to your weird pastiness. It brings out your eyes and stuff."

Cameron was rendered useless by that attack on his emotions, but Dot and June were frantically trying to pantomime that now was the perfect time to go in for that spaghetti kiss. They all froze when Montana turned around to look at them. "Hey, can you kiddos see all right? Need the light on? Or we could light this candle." She gestured to the candle on the table. "Has that always been there?"

"We're good!" June forced a smile.

"Uh, I'm not." Cameron raised his hand. "I can barely see Dot, and her heavy breathing is kinda freaking me out in the dark."

"I can't see either. I'll get the lights!" Dot hopped over to the light switch.

"Wait, Dot, no!" June tried, but it was too late. Dot flicked on the light, and the contraption June had set up dumped a couple buckets worth of confetti on the monster pair. It knocked over the cup of flowers. "Not yet." June groaned.

Montana was laughing very hard. "What's happening? What is all of this? Confetti? Spaghetti? It sorta rhymes. Is that the joke? I still kinda wanna eat it."

Caswell was brushing the confetti off herself. "Don't eat it. It's paper."

"But it's colorful."

"So are marbles."

"And they look delicious," Montana said with a tone that suggested they were agreeing. "But seriously, can someone explain this to me? What's going on?"

"I'll tell you what's going on," Cameron said abruptly. "It's too quiet in here is what's going on! Dot, wouldn't you agree?"

"That I would, Cameron!" Dot finger-gunned him and fished her phone out of her pocket. "Good thing we've got the miracle of technology!...And...my phone is dead."

"I'll pull it up." June took out her phone. "Hang on, there's an ad. I can't skip it."

"Refresh the page," Cameron said quietly.

June shook her head. "That'll change it to a different ad."

As they waited for the music in silence, Montana hacked up some confetti. Caswell made a face. "Did you seriously put that spaghetti back in your mouth?"

"It didn't taste as good as it looked, but I was in too deep to stop," Montana admitted, almost shameful. Emphasis on almost.

"I got it!" June cheered, tuning up her volume all the way on a seventies jam, with a slower Bruce Springsteen song that was sure to reel Montana in.

Her tail started wagging. "Hey, I love this song!" The trap was set.

"Dot, will you..." June started, but reconsidered. "Cameron, will you hold this for me?"

"Of course," Cameron took her phone, and she ran over to Caswell.

"May I have this dance?" June asked sweetly, holding out her hand. Caswell lightly took her hand. June jolted from the cold touch but didn't pull away. They looked absolutely ridiculous together. They'd barely taken one step, when June cried out, "Ah! I've sprained my ankle!" She clutched Caswell's waist, leaning against her dramatically. "I can't go on. Vic, take over for me. But first, carry me over to the table, for I am wounded."

Montana stood up, actually falling for the terrible act. "Yeah, here, nice and slow." She lifted June off her feet. "Do you need an ice pack?"

"Dot's got me covered," June said, and that was actually the truth. If anyone was injured, Dot would be prepared. "Just set me down over there and"—She grabbed Montana's face, squishing her cheeks together—"dance, you fool."

Montana sat her down on the table. June kept hold of Montana's face for a few more seconds, slowly pulling her hands away. She maintained eye contact that whole time. "For me, Vic," June said solemnly. "For my sacrifice."

Montana ran a hand through her hair, turning back to face Caswell. "I guess that means it's me and you now, dude."

"You and me," Caswell corrected her, stepping closer. Her brain started freezing up, and she forgot how to control her arms. So it was Montana who grabbed her hand, and Montana who placed a hand on her hip. It was Montana who led, and surprisingly, it was Montana who didn't trip over her feet. "You can dance," Caswell said, stupidly.

"Yeah, I learned how to slow dance in high school. Thought it'd impress girls." Montana narrowly avoided getting stomped on by Caswell for the fifth time. "Kinda looks like you can't though."

"I never learned." Caswell admitted, embarrassed but too entranced by Montana's movements to get flustered. "No one would want to dance with me anyway. I'm all knees and elbows."

Montana laughed. "Well, you're doing fine." As they moved, Caswell was starting to feel the music, humming a little before Montana began singing along. Caswell couldn't focus on the words. Montana had a good singing voice, rumbly and deep like a river that Caswell would be happy to drown herself in. Drown herself in Montana. That sounded pretty good right about now. She started to lean in. Montana murmured along with lyrics about hungry hearts and looked up at her through half-lidded eyes, like she was caught in some kind of dream state. She rose up onto her toes, something more like intrigue than surprise in her expression. Her breath was warm and steady. Caswell wanted to steal it away.

The music came to a sudden stop. Montana instantly dropped back to the balls of her feet, letting go of Caswell's hip so she could turn to look at Cameron and Dot.

"Sorry, sorry, her phone crashed," Dot apologized quickly, but the damage was already done.

"It's cool," Montana assured her. "It's getting pretty late anyway. You guys should hit the sack."

"The sack isn't the only thing I'm gonna hit," June grumbled, sliding off the table and ushering Dot and Cameron into the other room, most likely to complain that they had one job and let her amazing acting go to waste.

Montana started to follow them, stopping when she realized she was still attached to something. She was still holding Caswell's hand. She looked back, her lips parted in an expression so full of wanting it seemed like she must be aching. But she didn't say anything, and Caswell returned the favor, too dumbstruck to struggle with words. Montana gave her hand a squeeze and let go.

Caswell let her walk away.

Chapter Seventeen

JUNE WAS THE FIRST to wake up. She stepped over Dot and Cameron in their sleeping bags and discovered Montana had fallen asleep with them at some point in the night, sprawled across the floor. As much as she wanted to wake her, June had a feeling she was needed elsewhere.

She found Caswell in the kitchen, picking apart one of the flowers. June wondered if it was an absentminded action, or if she was doing a "loves me, loves me not" sort of thing. "All things considered, I think it went all right." June offered a smile.

Caswell noticed her and set down what was left of the poor, mangled flower. "Good morning."

"Morning." June pushed her hair out of her face, only for it to spring back to where it was. "Don't look so bummed out. Nobody falls in love in one night. We've got more plans. Come on, high five." She held her hand out, getting a reluctant high five in return. "Do I have permission for a hell yeah?"

"Why are you asking me that?"

"Uh, 'cause you're the only adult in the room." June rolled her eyes, as if it was the most obvious thing in the world.

Caswell considered this briefly. Although some of the kids' antics were strange to her, they did always manage to cheer her up, or at least momentarily distract her from her looming despair. "You have full permission."

"Hell yeah!" June whisper-shouted victoriously. "Seriously, things will work out. You just gotta give it time."

"I will." Caswell sighed, tapping her temple. "Sometimes I wish I could get inside that head of hers."

Caswell should've learned by then that any and all wishes were bad ideas.

That night only Montana showed up. She was acting almost normally, as if the night before hadn't happened, but she kept herself at a weird distance. She smiled at Caswell but wouldn't touch her. An invisible wall existed between them. Caswell desperately wanted to tear it down but had no idea how to even start.

On top of that, Montana seemed restless. She was wandering around instead of hanging in a single spot like she usually did. She hadn't explored the place like this since her second visit. She eventually stayed put when she found an old bookshelf and was entertaining herself by shuffling through its contents. Caswell didn't even remember she had half the titles Montana was calling out.

"And this one," Montana pulled out a book, flipping through the yellowing pages, "is about witchcraft? Are you a witch too? A vampire witch?"

"No." Caswell slipped the book out of her hands, checking it over herself. "It's research material. I like to be informed."

"That's a super boring answer," Montana complained. "I thought you could do like, magic or something."

"I can do magic. Minor arcana. It comes with the vampire package."

Montana stared at her, mouth agape. Apparently forgetting the invisible wall she had constructed, she grabbed Caswell's shoulders. "How could you wait this long to tell me. Please show me."

"Of course." Caswell cleared her throat to try to hide the giddy pride she was feeling. Here was something impressive she could do that Montana wouldn't be able to laugh at. She glanced over a page in the book. It had been a while since she had done anything like this, so she was feeling a little rusty. With Montana's hands still on her shoulders, Caswell raised a hand between them, mentally rehearsing the wrist flicks she'd need to perform. As she parted her lips to cast, Montana stepped back. The movement caused Caswell to lose her focus and mess up rather horrendously.

Whatever she had done, it was *loud*. It sounded like everything was happening at once right on top of her, and it wanted to crush her into dust. As if the sound wasn't bad enough, she could suddenly smell almost as many things as she could hear. The world was a cacophony for all of her senses.

"What the hell." She groaned, but it was not her own voice. She stared at her hands. They were not her hands. Now that she was getting a handle on her increased hearing, she noticed a sound that should not be there under any circumstances. She heard a pulse.

A woman in her clothes stood across from her. Caswell realized, in horror, they had switched bodies. Montana was grinning with sheer delight. "You kept your accent! Ooh, I kept mine too!"

"Is that really what I look like?" Caswell asked, knowing it was a dumb question, but their situation was dumb enough where she was allowed a couple of those.

There she was. She knew she was tall and slender, and she knew the sclera of the eye, meant to be white, was black in her eyes. The eyes and the fangs were the most obvious signs of vampirism. She knew these parts of herself, but she didn't recognize her own face. The dramatic arch of her brows, her high cheekbones, thin lips. She didn't remember any of that. What was the most striking to her, however, was how young she looked. A little shy of Montana's age.

Montana. She was inside Montana, quite literally. Her face went red at the thought. The lack of blood in her true body had protected her from looking as embarrassed as she felt on numerous occasions, but now she no longer had that luxury.

"I feel so powerful!" It was weird to see her own face, but it was weirder to see it smiling like a kid in a candy shop. "But also tired! And kind of icky! Is this what it's like to be undead? I'm pretty sure I've physically died before, but this is like...different. Crunchy death." Montana moved her arms and legs purposelessly, simply delighted by the fact she had control over them. "This is a really cool trick, dude. If I knew you were a magician, I wouldn't have teased you about how you dress so much."

"This isn't what I was trying to do," Caswell growled in frustration, which was so much more satisfying with Montana's deeper voice. "And I'm not a magician."

"Does that mean you wanna switch back? Ow! I bit my lip. Your lip? Someone's lip." Montana held out the book for Caswell to take.

"It's not in there." Caswell had messed up what she thought would be a straightforward mind-reading spell and created a new spell instead. She still didn't understand how Montana's brain worked, even while inside Montana's body. That probably made sense because Montana's brain was now in Caswell's body.

"You sure? There's a lot of pages." Montana tried to look through it but ripped the book in half. Her eyes widened. "Dude, why are you so strong?"

"I'm a vampire," Caswell condescendingly reminded her, then a wave of dreadful realization hit. "Actually, I'm a werewolf. You're the vampire. You have the magic right now."

Montana was brushing her new bangs with her fingers. "You definitely said that like it was a bad thing."

"It is." Caswell pulled on the neckline of her tank top. Now she was sweaty. When one was alive, one's body was constantly doing way too much. "You're going to have to figure out how to change us back."

Montana laughed. "Aw, you have such a nice laugh, you have to show it off more," she said, briefly distracted. "Anyway, my mom tried to teach me to do magic tricks when I was seven. I ended up losing like, nine dollars' worth of quarters and three sets of cards. That wasn't magical. I just had trouble keeping track of stuff. She would tell me I'm very good at making things disappear, but I needed to figure out how to bring them back. So I'm not going to be much help."

"You have to try." Caswell folded her arms over her chest. "It's easy. Easier than this breathing thing, which is very annoying, I should like to add."

Montana set the book halves on the bookcase. "I'll try, I'll try, but don't get your hopes up." She cracked her knuckles, making a horrible sound that no body part should make, like hay being snapped in half. "Oh my god. I'm gonna ignore that. Okay, what do I do?"

Caswell opened her mouth. Then she closed it again. "It's…it's sort of like…" she racked her brain. "It's hard to explain, you just…do it."

"Wow, that clears that up. Can I take off your cape? I feel like it's strangling me."

"Would you like it if I took off your shorts?" Caswell sputtered, turning red once again. This surplus of blood was a curse.

Montana thought for a moment and shrugged. "I don't think I'd mind." She was totally unbelievable. As always.

"Fix this!"

"Okay!" Montana held up her hands in defense. "Are there magic words or something? Can you give me literally anything to work with?"

Caswell shrugged, at least having the decency to look guilty about her lack of helpfulness. "It's like...like a muscle memory. Could you explain how to walk? It's like that."

"Uh, yeah, you put one foot in front of the other."

"Just...try to picture how you feel before you transform on full moons. That's magic, but you're not in control of it, and you black out before it really gets started. So it's a little different. But it's somewhere to start, right?"

"That's all I asked for, a jumpin' off place." Montana tried to think back to her last full moon. It worked, but not in the way they were hoping for. She turned into a bat and fell unceremoniously onto the floor with a little thump. She groaned. "Why wasn't flying intuitive?"

"At least this proves that you're capable of figuring it out. Okay, so now picture when you turn back after the full moon."

"I'm not conscious for that part."

Caswell crouched down, poking Montana experimentally in her tummy. "Oh. Right. Then...picture your transformation in reverse?"

"Beatrice, I swear to god."

"Sorry. We should get outside help." Caswell finally gave in. This clearly wasn't going to go anywhere. "I suppose Drake might be able to do it. Even if he can't, he's an instructor, so he'd at least be able to explain it more eloquently than I."

Montana continued to lie there in adorable defeat. "Wait, you mean that teacher the kids think is a vampire?"

"I've made his acquaintance. He's not a vampire, at least, not a full one. He's half human." Caswell clasped her hands over her mouth. She really needed to learn how to keep it shut. "I wasn't supposed to tell anyone. Please don't tell anyone. Even Dot."

"I was gonna say Cameron told me Drake is on vacation, visiting his family in Transylvania, which Cameron thought was more proof." She paused. "So like, he can't help us. He's in Transylvania. I was gonna tell you that."

"I got it." Caswell's hands migrated from her mouth to cover her whole face. "I told you his secret for literally no reason."

Montana laughed at her, an odd, but cute, squeaking. "Nice going, dude. How about we go see Alison? Her grandmother used to do witch stuff, and in college she dabbled in dark magic. Tried to summon demons and stuff. I think I made out with a ghost because of her, but I was wasted when it happened, so it might've just been that pale kid from across campus."

"It's not like we'll have better luck here." Caswell conceded, although she was a little afraid to meet Montana's friend face-to-face. Their only interaction had been Alison yelling threats at her through a door. Caswell awkwardly scooped Montana off the floor, who was still refusing to move on her own, then grabbed a few books she thought could help and tucked them under her other arm.

Montana gave her directions, and they eventually managed to get to Alison's house. Montana had sent Caswell around a couple of wrong turns, but the streets looked different when you're less than ten times your usual size and it was dark. Caswell let it slide with minor complaining, and when they finally got there, knocked on the door.

Alison opened the door a little, rubbing the sleep from her eyes. "Vic…? What are you doing here?"

Caswell forced a smile. "Uh, hello, Alison. I hope I didn't wake you."

Alison stared at her for a moment, then closed her eyes and took a deep breath. She spoke slowly. "Listen, Vic, I love you, and you're my best friend. But if you ever, and I mean ever, show up to my home again at three a.m. doing a terrible British accent, I will melt down all of my silver jewelry and make you drink it."

"Her accent isn't that bad," Montana piped up. "Also, that's not me. You know that vampire I've been telling you about? We accidentally switched bodies."

Alison stared for a long moment at the talking bat. She looked at Caswell, opened her mouth, and closed it again. She glanced at Montana once more before closing her eyes and taking an even deeper breath. "This might as well be happening." Alison sighed, opening the door all the way. "Get in here."

Caswell brought them in, finding herself oddly pleased with the notion that she could've entered even if Alison didn't invite them in.

"We don't mean to intrude, but Montana said you've had some practice with—"

"Hang on a second," Alison interrupted and plucked Montana out of Caswell's hand by a wing. Holding the bat in front of her face and giving her a disapproving look, Alison scolded, "Is this what you do now? Turn into little fluffy things, then get in trouble with your on-again, off-again girlfriend?"

"Ali, she's not my girlfriend!"

"And you don't even let me meet the gal until you need something! You think I don't want to meet the person you're losing sleep over? I still want to be a part of your life, even the weird bits." Alison said, continuing to chew her out.

"Beatrice, could you give her a hug for me?" Montana asked. "Even if I knew how to use these, she's got the grip of a kung fu master." She flapped her free wing pitifully,

Not having many other options, Caswell put down her stack of books and awkwardly wrapped her arms around Alison. She did not hug back, but neither did she push Caswell off.

"Aw, you guys are so cute," Montana squeaked. "Okay, Beatrice, let her go. I'll do introductions."

Caswell took a couple of steps back, grabbing the books again so her hands wouldn't be empty.

Montana motioned to her as best she could while she was dangling. "Alison, this is Beatrice Caswell. She doesn't usually look like my reflection. She's a grumpy silver fox, and she drinks blood, but she's secretly a softie. She's the one I've been hanging out with at night. She's my favorite vampire."

Alison ran a hand through her hair, fighting off a frown, obviously working to process everything being thrown at her. "Right. Okay. It's, uh, it's nice to meet you. Montana has told me quite a bit about you too."

"Let me do this officially," Montana said, stopping her. "Beatrice, this is Alison Carlisle. I know it's crazy, but I do have a friend my own age, and she's basically the best human to ever grace the earth. She's got her whole life figured out, except for me, which I guess is part of my charm. Now you know each other."

"Works for me." Alison glanced at Caswell. "Do you want her, or should I put her down somewhere? If she gets too annoying, I've got plenty of mason jars we could put her in."

"You're so mean! And my wing is getting sore!" Montana protested with a squeak.

"Uh, I'll take her." Caswell held out a hand, and Alison handed her over. "So Montana told me you have some experience with magic, and we were hoping you'd be able to reverse this. I brought some books that might be able to help."

"It's been a while," Alison admitted, grabbing a hair tie and pulling her hair off her face and into a ponytail. "But learning how to undo a curse was probably the most important thing I figured out, so I haven't forgotten it yet. Hold your breath for a second, Beatrice."

Caswell did as instructed and watched Alison wave her hands around, scrunching her face in concentration and muttering under her breath. Caswell felt a rush like a sudden breeze and closed her eyes without meaning to.

Everything was quiet again.

Caswell was back in her original body and heard Montana say, "Thank god!" If that expressed relief was anything to go off of, she was back too. Caswell fluttered out of her hand and transformed back to her normal form. It felt good to be back where she belonged. Alison sized her up, nodding to herself.

"Hey, if you can undo curses, why can't you get rid of my werewolf thing?" Montana only now realized this discrepancy. She set down the books on Alison's coffee table.

"Different kind of curse," Alison and Caswell said at the same time. Alison flashed her a smile before continuing. "The only thing they have in common is that they're designed to harm the target in some way, which is what gets them the label of curse. It's an umbrella term. I can reverse simple stuff, like spoken word incantations, but that's it. The werewolf curse is super old. I'm pretty sure the only way to get rid of it would be to kill the alpha, right?" She glanced to Caswell for confirmation.

"I suppose so," Caswell offered. "I've never seen anything about it before, but that makes sense."

Alison yawned. “All right, it was nice meeting you, but you’d better get back to your place before the sun comes up. Don’t be a stranger, okay? As Vic’s friend, you are my friend by association. And I’m never too busy for a friend. Plus, I’ve got embarrassing stories about her I’d love to share.” She patted Caswell on the back.

“I’m sure we’ll be seeing each other again.” Caswell smiled lightly. Montana was already heading out the door, so Caswell gathered up her books and followed. “She was very nice. I’m glad you have a friend like that. Someone who knows you and can help you get back on your feet when you fall. It’s nice.”

Montana did not look back at her. “Hey Beatrice?”

She perked up. “Yes?”

“She was right. You oughta head back before the sun’s up. I gotta get home.”

Caswell was a little surprised Montana wasn’t going to at least walk her back. Fifteen extra minutes to say goodbye was something she would normally spare. But Caswell didn’t want to push it. If Montana needed a little space after all that, she would give her some. “All right then, see you soon. I hope my body didn’t treat you too terribly.” She didn’t even get a chuckle for that. Their paths diverged, and suddenly Montana was walking away. Caswell called out to her, “Stay safe.”

She didn’t hear an answer.

Chapter Eighteen

THE KIDS HAD PLANNED another date the next night, but Montana did not answer her phone. It was probably for the best since a swarm of late-night seagulls stole away all their preparations, the likes of which none of them had ever seen (except for Dot, who claimed this was the seventh time this sort of thing happened to her). Dot let Caswell know Montana had texted back, apologizing and saying she had been feeling sick and went to bed early.

Caswell did not tell Dot werewolves didn't get sick.

She wondered if she had messed up somehow. She was giving Montana the space she seemed to require, but maybe she was misinterpreting Montana's actions. Maybe Montana was the kind of person who took a step back when she wanted the other person to step forward. And here Caswell was, stepping in all the wrong places, the same as when they were dancing. But if Montana could forgive her for that, hopefully she could forgive her for this too.

It was a few more days before Montana showed up again. She looked tired. "Sorry it's been a while." Montana gave her a weary smile, not bothering to make up any excuses. She lay down on the couch, reaching underneath it to grab the worn out tennis ball Dot had gifted them with. She bounced it against the floor. It hit the wall and came right back to her hand. She continued the volley as she spoke, "So how have things been?"

"Normal." Caswell said. But things hadn't been normal. Nothing felt normal when Montana wasn't around. She chewed at her lip. She had to say something. "You've been acting worrisome though."

"Yeah, sorry, I've just been thinking." She kept her eyes on the ball. "Can I ask you a question?"

"Of course."

"You ever kill somebody, Beatrice?"

Caswell stood a few steps away from the couch, and she couldn't see Montana's face from that angle. "I have not."

The only sound in the room was the thump of the ball. The floor, the wall, her hand. The floor, the wall, her hand. "You ever wanted to?"

"Where is this coming from, Montana?" Caswell could no longer hide her concern. "This isn't like you," she said hesitantly, wishing she didn't sound quite as pitiful as she felt. "Did I do something wrong?"

Montana caught the ball and did not throw it again. She twisted around to look at Caswell, then cringed with apparent guilt as she saw her face. "Oh, Bea, I'm sorry. I didn't mean to make you upset. God no, that's not what I wanted." Montana ran her free hand through her hair, a gesture she often made when trying to sort her thoughts into words. "It's just...remember what Alison said about making me human again?"

Caswell's eyes widened when she remembered, and she spoke frantically. "We don't know if that would even work. You don't want to be human enough to kill someone, even if that someone is as bad as that guy, right?"

"I'm not considering it!" Montana put her fears to rest quickly. "I couldn't do that kind of shit, man. That's heavy. It's making me think. He's hurting people. He's killing people. He's turning people into killers. And if they wanna stop? They gotta kill him. It's just...it's heavy." Montana looked away and made a strange sound Caswell did not recognize.

"Are you all right?" Caswell allowed herself to get a little closer.

Montana noticed her shifting around and sat up, making room for her. Caswell accepted the nonverbal invitation and sat next to her. Montana started gnawing on the tennis ball, which Caswell supposed was a comfort thing. "It scares me a lot. I hate thinking about it, so I don't. But when she said that...I gotta face reality. I'm part of that violent circle whether I like it or not. I can't keep pretending that I'm the same as humans."

So Montana had not been asking about her experiences to know if Caswell were capable of killing, but because she was only now letting herself see Caswell as a monster. Montana had never asked if Caswell ever killed a victim before, or if a werewolf fight ever went that far. Caswell had chalked it up to her usual disinterest in most things, especially nonhuman things. But it wasn't that. Montana didn't want to know the answer.

"You're not like the others, Montana. You have so little bloodlust in you that you don't even turn into a wolf." Caswell knew she should do something comforting, but she was at a loss. The closest thing she'd seen to this vulnerability in Montana was during the thunderstorm, and that wasn't even close to this. Caswell gently placed her hand over Montana's. "There's a lot of hurting in the world, but that's not your burden to bear."

Montana pulled her hand away, and Caswell returned the favor, not surprised but hoping Montana wouldn't hate her too much for the uninvited intimacy.

Suddenly, Montana vaulted on top of her. Caswell found herself wrapped in a tight hug. Montana made that weird sound again, and Caswell realized she was sniffling. "I'm sorry," Montana mumbled against her shoulder. "This isn't your problem."

Caswell rubbed her back gently. "Don't be ridiculous. I don't want to stand by while you quietly torture yourself."

Montana's claws were digging into her back, but Caswell didn't squirm. She could sit still and deal with it for a little bit. She could handle that much for her.

Montana's breath hitched. "I don't want to hurt anyone."

"You won't." Caswell could promise her this wholeheartedly. Even if Montana was in a position where she needed to, she wouldn't hurt anyone. It was who she was. Caswell looked down at the mess of hair and fur pressed against her like she was Montana's lifeline. In that moment, Caswell knew that even if Montana couldn't hurt someone to save herself, she could do it for her. Caswell wouldn't let anything stand in the way of Montana's happiness. "Do you want to be human again?"

Montana sat up, slowly pulling away from Caswell in a way that was so strangely tender it didn't feel like they were being separated. She wiped at her eyes with her wrists, still clutching the tennis ball in one hand. "I only asked Alison because I thought, if it would be that easy, she should've at least offered."

"I see." Caswell was not convinced, and that came through in her voice.

Montana laughed, the sound a little shaky after the tears. "I'm serious! The big changes aren't even because of that. I've just been seeing a different side of the world. And even that hasn't been all bad." Montana met her gaze, then looked away with another chuckle. "Dating's a different story. Even people who like this much hair aren't gonna be fans of how I turn into a puffball every once in a while."

"I think it's cute." Caswell offered, too busy looking at her to even realize what she had admitted. Montana was visibly caught off guard but quickly regained her cool.

"Well thanks, Beatrice, that's sweet." For once, she sounded genuine. There was no joking edge to her voice, and her touch was gently when she cupped Caswell's cheek with her free hand. "You know what? I think, underneath your grumpy persona, you're the sweetest girl I've ever met."

"I...I think you're..."

Montana let the ball fall to the floor. It bounced once, twice, three times, and once more before it rolled away. Montana got on her knees, now eye level with Caswell. That meant their lips were also at the same level. Caswell didn't think there was a term for that, which was ridiculous, seeing as it was so much more important than being at eye level. In fact, the position of Montana's lips in relation to her own was the most important thing in the world to her.

"What do you think I am?" Montana whispered, a wry smile finding its way onto her features. Now both her hands were on Caswell's face.

Caswell swallowed. "Kissable?"

She couldn't see it, but she could hear the air swishing from Montana's tail wagging. She could only imagine the top speeds it was reaching. "That works for me," Montana said.

Caswell leaned in, closing the little gap between them. Right as their lips were about to touch, Montana leapt back a good foot, as if she had been electrocuted. She covered her mouth with her hands, and Caswell was equal parts confused and concerned, with a little disappointment mixed in.

"I had pizza like, two hours ago," Montana explained, wide-eyed. "There was garlic on that. I'm gonna go rinse out my mouth." She leapt off the couch, her socks making her slip on the floor and fall flat on her face. Before Caswell could ask if she was all right, she got back up on her feet with a little less vigor and continued her journey to the bathroom, leaving Caswell to deal with that.

They had almost kissed. They hadn't even been a full second away from kissing. Montana wanted to do that. When Montana came back, she might want to finish doing that. That thought was enough to short-circuit Caswell's brain.

"Okay!" Caswell was snapped out of it by Montana's shouting. She didn't know how long she had been sitting there, staring into space like an idiot. Montana wiped her mouth with her forearm. "Okay, we should be good now." Her face was flushed. "Do you, uh, do you wanna pick up where we left off?"

Caswell stood up to join her. "I would like that very much."

A sudden thought struck her, and Caswell sat back down. "Actually, I don't think we should."

Montana blinked and sat down next to her. "Why not?"

Caswell folded her hands in her lap and stared down at them so she wouldn't have to look at Montana. "You've been emotionally unbalanced for a couple of days now, and you finally got to let some of that negativity out, so you're still riding that rush. You probably feel like you can do anything, and I'd hate for that anything to be something you're going to regret." Caswell's anxiety refused to let her have this moment. "On top of that, I'm bound to be a terrible kisser. It's been literal lifetimes since I've done it last."

"Then let me remind you how." Montana gave her a dorky grin. She peeled one of Caswell's hands away from her lap, squeezing it in her own. "I appreciate the worry, but I'm not gonna regret this. Actually, since day one, I've"—she went rigid, head whipping toward the door—"there's someone here."

"I've got it." Caswell was torn between desperately wanting an escape and never wanting to leave the couch, so she took off before she could reconsider. She opened the door to find Dot.

"Hey! I hope this isn't a bad time, but June lost her bracelet and wanted me to look here." Her clothes were dirty enough to suggest to Caswell that this was not the first place she'd checked.

"This bracelet?" Montana had snuck up behind Caswell, jangling the little piece of jewelry. "I don't know how she coulda dropped it."

Dot took it from her, slipping it into her shorts pocket. “Thank you! You’re looking well. Are you feeling better? My dad said to recommend extra sleep and soup.”

Montana laughed, charmed by her concern. Caswell was trying to avoid looking at her, for she still wanted nothing more than to kiss Montana, and seeing her face would make it worse. Montana told Dot, “Thanks kid, I’m all right. Feelin’ a lot better.”

“That’s good.” Dot looked up at the night sky, as if it could tell her what time it was. Knowing her collection of odd skills, it probably could. “I’ll see you guys later. I can’t stay tonight. I’ve got to get up early tomorrow!”

Montana glanced out at the street behind her. “Are you here alone? Not even with your bike?” She shook her head when Dot said yes. “Okay, let me walk you home. It’s too late for you to be walking by yourself.”

“Thanks for the offer, but I’ll be fine.”

But Montana knew her weak spots. “If you let me walk you home, I’ll try to talk to your dog.”

Dot lit up at the concept. “Okay!” Even this late at night, she still had so much energy, nearly skipping away from the door. Montana followed after her, and Caswell was left watching them go.

After a second or two, Montana came running back and grabbed a fistful of Caswell’s cape, yanking her down and accidentally smashing their noses together. Not allowing herself enough time to even recover from that, Montana tried again and managed lip to lip contact. Caswell was being partially strangled, and her nose stung from the impact. It was perfect.

Montana pulled away almost as quickly as she’d swooped in, cheeks dusted with pink. “I’ll, uh, I’ll see you tomorrow…champ.” She slugged her in the arm, then ran after Dot, who hadn’t noticed she wasn’t still being followed.

Caswell felt like she was floating and nearly tripped over something by the door. She realized it was, bizarrely, Montana’s shoes and glanced down the sidewalk to see Montana traipsing along, too preoccupied to realize she wearing only her socks. Caswell picked up the shoes but didn’t know what she’d even say if she caught up with them. Instead, she threw them at Montana from the door. The first shoe missed but the second got her square in the back of the head. Caswell had thrown it a little harder than she meant to, and Montana was, once again, face down on the ground.

Dot looked around, mildly perturbed, mostly curious to see where the shoe came from. She waved enthusiastically at Caswell when she spotted her watching from the house. "She's alive!" Dot yelled to her, giving her a thumbs up.

Caswell returned the thumbs up. She retreated back into the manor, decidedly having interacted enough with Montana for one evening. Once she had closed the door, she let herself sink to the floor with unadulterated glee. She couldn't contain the butterflies the kiss filled her with. It was like the kiss had brought her back to life. Most surprisingly of all, it felt nice to be back.

Chapter Nineteen

IT WAS AUGUST NOW. The kids were trying to squeeze in as much last-minute summer fun as they could and didn't have much time to spend with them. Dot had told Cameron and June about the kiss, and they were happy for her, although Cameron was a little bitter over the fact that their romantic plans had gone to waste. June reminded him that one kiss wasn't endgame, and there would be more dates to organize in the future.

Meanwhile, Caswell had thought the next time she'd see Montana, it would be awkward. She expected the kiss to have changed Montana's life as much as it had changed her own. She thought there'd be skipping heartbeats and quick glances and all of those things she tried to forget when she tried to give up on love.

But Montana was the same.

She wasn't pretending it didn't happen, she just didn't seem to care. It had been short and sudden, but it was still their first kiss. That should mean something. Caswell wanted it to mean something to her.

The fear that she was only a distraction for Montana began to gnaw at her. After so many years spent alone, she didn't want to open her heart up only to become a plaything.

Caswell felt silly to be getting so worked up over something Montana wouldn't bat an eye at. She was feeling foolish, and that made her act defensively. She was sharper-tongued and more critical of everything, but it was the only way she knew how to protect herself.

Montana was lying on her stomach in the kitchen, making her way through a bag of chips. Caswell grimaced at her. "I'm under the impression it's labeled *family-sized* for a reason."

"I live alone. I'm my own family."

Caswell poked Montana's side with her foot. "If you insist on making a mess, can you at least go sit in a chair like a regular person?"

Montana grunted but did not move. "It's hot. The tiles are cool." Realizing she was out of chips, she licked the dust off her fingers.

"That's disgusting." Caswell huffed. "Are you really incapable of being anything other than a slob?"

Montana glanced up at her. "Dude, can you get off my back for like, five seconds? You've been giving me such a hard time for everything lately."

"Well, well you..." Caswell stumbled over her words, a mess of emotions fighting each other for dominance. Whatever won was something dreadfully childish. "You haven't been giving me any attention!"

Montana lifted herself partially off the floor, shifting so she could sit cross-legged. She was making a face somewhere between disbelief and disgust. "Are you serious? This is the third day I've visited you this week. Do you want me to stop sleeping?"

"That's not what I mean." Caswell crossed her arms over her chest to deter herself from wavering. "I mean you haven't said a word about..." One of her hands wandered up to her face, hovering over her mouth. "That."

Montana slumped a little, relaxing her body. "Oh, is that all?"

"Is that all?!" She made angry air quotes. "We kissed! On the lips! It was a big deal, and you don't even care!"

"What are you talking about? Of course I care."

"You don't act like it."

"What do you think I'm gonna do? Read you Shakespeare?" Montana gave her an uncertain half-smile.

There it was again, the creeping sensation that Montana was only playing. It made Caswell feel like her mouth was full of tar. "I thought you would stop treating my feelings like a joke." Caswell spat, glaring at her. "But I should've known better. Everything's a big joke to you. If you can't be serious, go home." She stormed off.

"Beatrice, wait!" Montana chased after her. "I care! I care a lot! I didn't wanna pressure you!" Montana caught up, but that was because Caswell had slowed to a stop. "I thought it was kinda sudden, and you seem like one of those classy girls who take things like a snail, so I was gonna let you start it next time you were ready." She laughed, and there was a strange helpless quality to the sound. "You still call me Montana! Not even my boss calls me that!"

Caswell turned around to look at her, annoyance quickly fading into curiosity. “Is it really any different than when you call me man or dude?”

“Those are more, uh, verbal tics than anything else. When I wanna talk about you, I call you Beatrice.” Montana paused a beat. “Which you said you were okay with, but...”

“No,” Caswell said before she could finish her thought. “I don’t mind it.” That was a strange way of saying *my knees get weak every time you do it*. “So you’d like me to call you Vic, then?”

“Since day one, dude. Uh, Beatrice. Since day one, Beatrice.” Montana corrected herself. “That’s gonna take a while to stop.”

The fact that Montana was immediately ready to switch up her speaking patterns for Caswell’s sake caused the corners of her mouth to splinter into a smile. “Dude is more than fine, Vic. But...I need you to be frank with me.”

Montana grinned. “How can I be Frank if I’m Vic?”

“That’s exactly what we need to talk about.” Caswell sighed. “What...What is this to you, Vic? What am I to you?”

The amusement in Montana’s expression totally vanished. She cocked her head slightly. “What do you mean?”

Caswell swallowed. She was having trouble keeping eye contact. “Are we playing? Every time I think something meaningful happens, you go right back to joking around. I didn’t mean to snap at you earlier, but I did mean what I said. You don’t take anything seriously. And I was hoping...” her voice wavered, “I was hoping I meant more to you than that.”

They were silent for a moment. Slowly, Montana pointed up at the ceiling. “Is there a way up onto your roof?”

Like always, Montana managed to be completely unpredictable. Caswell raised an eyebrow. “I beg your pardon?”

“Is there?”

Caswell nodded hesitantly. “I don’t see what that has to do with our conversation.”

“Perfect.” Montana grabbed Caswell’s hand. “Lead the way.”

Curious to see what Montana was planning, Caswell led her up to the roof. Once in the night air, Montana stifled a groan against the muggy heat. She squeezed Caswell’s hand and brought her to the edge of the roof. They looked out over the town, seeing a few flickers of lights in windows, but mostly darkness. Montana took a deep breath. She cupped her free hand over her mouth and shouted with everything she had, "I KISSED BEATRICE CASWELL!"

Caswell jumped a little. "What are you doing?"

"SHE MEANS A LOT TO ME, AND I'M NOT SCARED TO ADMIT IT! I'M NOT ASHAMED OF HER, AND I DON'T THINK SHE'S A JOKE! AND I'LL SHOUT IT FROM EVERY ROOFTOP IN TOWN IF THAT'S WHAT SHE WANTS!"

For once, it was Montana being genuine and Caswell laughing.

"AND IF I'M BEING HONEST, I'VE DATED A LOT OF PEOPLE BUT I'VE NEVER BEEN ANY GOOD AT BEING ROMANTIC! I WISH THAT I COULD DO SOMETHING REALLY COOL FOR HER, BUT I DON'T KNOW HOW, SO I'VE BEEN SITTING AROUND LIKE A CHUMP!"

"You're not a chump." Caswell did not try to stop herself from laughing. It felt good. "And you might say you're not romantic, but you're the only woman who's ever yelled from a rooftop for me."

Montana smiled at her, voice a little raspy from shouting, "What? You're kidding." In the summer haze and starlight, she seemed to glow. Caswell could see the tips of her teeth through her parted lips, still hung open in a dorky grin. The image left her with a craving she had all but forgotten.

"Can I kiss you?" Caswell, despite not having screamed, sounded a little out of breath. Their lips hadn't even touched yet, and Montana managed to steal her voice away.

"That'd be nice." Montana leaned in and Caswell met her halfway. Warmth flooded Caswell's mouth. This time, they lingered. Montana kept trying to pull her in closer, and Caswell found herself adoring the idea that she was what Montana was hungry for.

Caswell realized she was leaning a little too heavily into Montana, when she knocked her off the roof.

There was a rather unfortunate crunch when she hit the ground. Caswell peered over the edge, seeing her sprawled on the lawn, her right leg bent the wrong way. "Are you all right?" she asked anyway. It was the polite thing to do.

"Yep." Montana gasped, eyes still wide with pain. "I'm great."

Caswell waited a moment, but it didn't seem like Montana was getting up any time soon. "Do you want me to jump down too or...?"

"Nah, it's all right. Give me a minute." Montana sat up, wincing. She grabbed her leg and tried to twist it back to where it was supposed to be, letting out a string of curses as she did.

Caswell felt kind of awkward standing there, so she decided to jump down anyway. Before Montana could even call out to her, she had floated down, landing gracefully on her feet. Now that she was closer, she could see the little scrapes on Montana disappearing almost as quickly as they had formed. Montana stared at her. "How did you do that?"

"How many times do I have to tell you I'm a vampire before you actually believe it?" Caswell sat down next to her. "Was the kiss okay?"

"It was more than okay." Montana laughed, albeit a little weakly. Werewolves didn't feel pain as strongly as humans did, but they still felt it. "The fangs are new to me, but I'm learnin' to love it. Ugh, it's awful out here. Can I take off my shirt? I'm gonna take off my shirt." She peeled her tank top off and dropped it in the grass, revealing her simple, worn bra. She wrapped her hands back around her hurt leg and sighed with relief. "Yeah, that's better."

Caswell tried not to stare at Montana's exposed midsection, but Montana clearly had no problem with being admired. She looked so soft and touchable. Caswell would've done anything to hold her, but she became distracted by the scar. Almost a full year later, it still looked painful. There was an aching in her fangs. This wasn't the first time she had felt this primal stirring inside her. Some inhuman rage threatened to pour out of her. She felt it every time she remembered Montana at the playground, a bloody heap of torn fabric and lifeless eyes. Caswell hadn't been there for Montana then, but now she could be. She could get it right this time.

"Beatrice?" Montana snapped her out of it. "Did you hear what I said?"

"My apologies. Could you repeat it?"

Montana stared at her, and Caswell was afraid she somehow saw right through her. "I forgot what I was saying," Montana admitted. She lay back, injured knee still precariously bent. “I’ll remember eventually.”

Caswell followed suit and lay down next to her. “Vic?”

“Mhm?” Montana was staring up at the sky, and the stars were reflected in her dark eyes. How could every part of her be so pretty?

“Will you hold my hand again?”

“You don’t gotta ask.” Montana sighed and took her hand. “But it’s sweet that you do. Oh! I remember what I was saying! I was telling you that you shouldn’t ever change. You’re super just how you are.”

Caswell thought about who she was before she met Montana. Cold and lonely and having tricked herself into thinking she was better off that way. “No,” she finally said. “I’m going to keep changing.”

“Okay,” Montana relented, looking confused but clearly admiring her conviction. “As long as you promise me you won’t change your mind about wanting to hold my hand.”

“Now that I could promise as many times as you’d like.”

Chapter Twenty

"GUESS WHO'S GOING OUT tonight?" Montana sang as she entered the manor. Caswell assumed the question was rhetorical, but Montana spoke plainly after a pause. "You. You're going out tonight. Well, so am I. We're going out together. Tonight."

"I got it," Caswell rolled her eyes. "Where are we going and why?"

"Well, earlier, while I was out, my hair caught on fire. It grows back so fast, you can't even tell it got scorched this morning. Look at that." Montana pointed to a chunk of her hair. "Anyway, I was like, 'yo Dot,' because it must've been because of Dot, yeah? But it wasn't! I mean, he kinda looked like Dot, but his scars were in different places, and he was missing a finger. Also, he was like forty years old and a dude."

"Fascinating."

"Okay, so it was actually Dot's dad, and so we started talking, but he kept sneezing, and was all 'Sorry I'm allergic to dogs,' and we said a lot more, but long story short, he invited us out to get drinks or something. Apparently, we're not Dot's only babysitters, because he's bringing the wifey too."

Caswell made a face. "Why would you agree to something like that?"

"Because we are well-adjusted adults who can handle a double date."

Caswell wondered whether the words registered any significance in Montana's brain. Well, she couldn't take them back now. "Are you asking me out on a date?" Dread and excitement mixed in a terrible concoction in the pit of Caswell's stomach.

"I, uh, guess I am."

Caswell paused for a dramatic stretch of time, pretending she had to really consider this. Her voice betrayed her with a giddy crack. "I accept."

"Awesome! Let's go." Montana grabbed her hand and started walking, being yanked to a stop when Caswell didn't move.

"Don't tell me you're going to wear that." Caswell sized her up disapprovingly. While the garish creamsicle-colored shorts and stained tank top were surprisingly alluring to Caswell, they were not proper date-night clothes. Really, she shouldn't dress like that outside at all. A person should only wear such a disheveled outfit in their home. Though, Montana wasn't technically at home in Caswell's place. It was strange how Caswell nearly forgot that fact.

"Don't throw stones in a glass house, Beatrice. You're dressed like it's 1875 and you're gonna rob a grave." Montana eyed Caswell's outfit in return. "We don't have time to go back to my place, so I couldn't change if I wanted to."

"You could borrow some of my clothes." Caswell motioned vaguely in the general direction of her room.

"I don't think you realize how tempting that is." Montana started bouncing on the balls of her feet. "Okay, I need to find the ugliest thing you have and put it on my body. Wait here." She took off running.

"My clothes are not ugly." Caswell grumbled. She looked down at herself. Her clothes weren't *that* odd. Maybe it was the cape. She slowly unhooked the collar, letting yards of fabric fall to the floor. She absentmindedly traced her fingers over the bite mark on her neck.

"Okay, I'm—Hey, you took off your cape!"

Startled when Montana ran up behind her, Caswell quickly popped her collar to cover the mark before she turned to look at her.

Montana's grin faded. "Are you crying?"

Caswell hadn't noticed it, but her eyes had welled up with tears. She wiped at them and blinked furiously, trying to erase any sign of feelings. "No, sorry, I was just thinking about...It was a long time ago. Why don't you tell me about what you're wearing?"

"Sure." Graciously, Montana allowed her to drop the topic. "Well, I found this horrible maroon and lime shirt that I wanted, but I hated the texture. So I grabbed this purple one with the yellow strings on the shoulders because look at it. Did people really wear stuff like this? Then I found these bell-bottom pants? Why do you have these?"

Caswell smiled at her confusion. "I do occasionally get new clothes, you know. I just prefer the ones I prefer."

"Well I think you should dress more like this. I also grabbed a cape for the mysterious allure." Montana spun in a little circle to show off. Montana's eyes fluttered to the cape on the floor, then back up to Caswell's shoulders. "Are you sure you'll be comfortable...I dunno, showing that much neck?"

"You're right. One moment." Caswell left the room, practically gliding. She returned with the scarf Montana made her wrapped around her neck. "Much better."

Montana lit up. "Is that the only scarf you own or something?"

"No, but it's the ugliest." Caswell got a hearty laugh for that. She curled and uncurled her fingers before extending her hand for Montana. "Now I'm ready to go."

They walked together, making pleasant conversation, as Montana swung their hands. Holding her hand became incrementally less daunting each day. It was starting to feel natural, like that was where their hands belonged and had always belonged. Her hand was starting to feel empty when Montana's wasn't in it.

They finally met up with the Liang parents, who welcomed them warmly outside of the bar. Montana nudged Caswell with her elbow, winking, "Don't worry. I've got this." She turned to the front doors and shouted, "Hey, are you guys open?"

An employee inside opened the door. "Yeah, come on in."

Montana gave her a goofy smile. "The whole way over I was trying to figure out how to get you invited in."

Caswell tried to hide how impressed she was by the trick. Mrs. and Mr. Liang led them in and over to a table. They slid into opposite sides of the booth. "So Dot's been telling me a lot about you," Mr. Liang said, which made his wife laugh.

"All the time! She thinks you're both very cool," Mrs. Liang said in agreement. "We're happy there are some adults in town she can trust, who aren't afraid of her."

"So you both believe in this curse thing?" Caswell asked. She had noticed strange happenings, but she still wasn't sure if she believed a curse was on the family or if that was the way Dot processed the world around her.

"I didn't believe it for a very long time," Mrs. Liang said. "I was never a very superstitious person. But I always knew he was the one for me, curse or no curse. Now, well, now I believe in all sorts of things I didn't think were possible. I certainly never thought I'd be here with a werewolf and vampire. The world is full of strange things, but that makes it exciting."

"Afraid of her." Montana snorted in disbelief, still a few sentences behind. "Man, I guess I get other kids getting freaked out by all the mishaps, but adults? It's not that hard to get used to. It's just, like, probability." She was interrupted by Mr. Liang sneezing. "So like, anything that happens might've happened anyway."

"It's easy for us to say that. We're nearly immortal," Caswell pointed out. "But Dot is such a good kid, I'm surprised she hasn't won over more folks."

Mrs. Liang sent her husband a private smile that seemed to speak volumes between them.

"So what do you do for a living?" Montana asked. "The only things we know about the two of you are what Dot's shared, and you know she's got selective interests."

"Well, I'm a safety inspector." Mr. Liang laughed lightly when Montana snorted. "I know, I know, it seems ironic, buh-buh-pardon me." He sneezed and Mrs. Liang handed him a tissue, which he accepted gratefully. He said, sniffling, "But my condition actually helps me make sure things are in tip-top condition."

Mrs. Liang nodded along with his words. "And I do a little bit of everything. Currently I'm on a web-design project, which is all new to me. But when opportunity knocks, I'll always give it a fair chance."

Mr. Liang wrapped his arm around her waist. "Yes, she's very ambitious. I'm lucky I could slow her down long enough to marry me."

"I wouldn't have missed it for the world," She pecked his cheek, turning back to Montana. "And what about you, dear?"

"My job's way less exciting than those." She jerked a thumb at Caswell. "And she doesn't work at all." A waiter passed by carrying drinks, and Montana sat up a little straighter. "Beatrice, can I get drunk?"

"I'm not your keeper, Do whatever you want."

"No, I mean physically." Montana looked down at herself, placing a hand over her chest. "I heal so fast, can I even get intoxicated? And what about you?"

"I'm not going to put anything in my mouth," Caswell said, her refusal instant. While she was an avid hater of eating and drinking, it wasn't like there was anything stopping her from doing it. Only blood could sustain her, but ingesting food and drink wouldn't harm her. She just didn't enjoy it.

"Are you backing down from a challenge? Are you too chicken?" Montana heckled her, prodding her repeatedly in the arm.

Caswell swatted her hand away. "Of course not. I'll do it."

"You lovely folks getting wasted tonight?" Montana glanced at the Liangs.

"I don't drink." Mr. Liang shook his head. He sneezed a few times in a row. Apparently, Montana was shedding.

"And I do the driving," Mrs. Liang declined as well.

"If that's the case, can you keep track of who drinks more?" Montana smiled pleasantly, then turned to Caswell. "I'm going to count throwing up as forfeiting." Montana waved down a waiter, asking for whatever held the highest alcohol concentration.

An hour into chit chat and five drinks in, Montana was feeling a regrettable amount of nothing. It was like she had been drinking fruit juice all evening. "Yeah, I don't think this is working. Thanks for being a good sport anyway, Beatrice." She patted Caswell's back, then pointed at Mrs. Liang. "And thank you for keeping track of how many drinks we've chugged."

"No problem, dear." Mrs. Liang cleared the numbers off her notes app and put her phone away.

"It's hot in here, Vic," Caswell complained. The temperature usually didn't affect her, but sometimes it felt like she'd take any opportunity to complain.

"You're telling me. This is way too many layers of clothing for August," Montana said with a chuckle. Caswell reached over and grabbed Montana's cape, fumbling with the clasp. "Use your words, dude. You want it back already?"

"It's too hot for you," Caswell slurred. "You gotta…gotta get these clothes off."

Montana blinked at her, grabbing her hands and returning them to her lap without much of a fight. "Wait, are you actually drunk?"

"No. No! I'm not drunk." She scoffed but wobbled a little. "Can I wear your glasses? I wanna see more colors."

"Does she usually drink that much?" Mrs. Liang quirked an eyebrow.

Montana's mistakes were beginning to dawn on her. "No, we should've taken that slower. At least she can't get like, alcohol poisoning. I think? I wonder what the science behind this is."

Caswell had erupted into giggles. "Funny. You're sooo funny. I wanna kiss your funny mouth."

"Yeah okay, I should get her home. We'll have to do this again sometime."

"I don't wanna go home! It's too early!" Caswell whined. "I wanna…" She looked up at Mrs. and Mr. Liang across the table, then moved in closer and cupped her hand over Montana's ear. Unfortunately, she didn't speak any quieter. "I wanna take off your clothes, and I wanna get you in the bathroom, and I wanna have sex with you."

Mrs. Liang slapped Mr. Liang's hand when he started snickering.

Montana's face turned red. "I'm gonna hafta pass."

"You wanna know if I can do it, right? I can do it. I can do anything if I believe in myself!" Caswell lost her balance, draping her arms around Montana's shoulders and resting her head on her chest. "Aww, there's your heartbeat! Hi, Vic's heart. Thanks for giving her air. I love you."

Montana moved Caswell around so she could hoist her over her shoulder. "Had a great time, really. Tell Dot we send our love."

Caswell lightly kicked Montana's face, as she floated out of her arms, feet aimed for the ceiling. "Would you stop that?"

"Are you going to need help with her?" Mrs. Liang asked, concerned but still amused.

"Thank you for the offer, but I've got her, even if she's a bit of a handful." As if on cue, Caswell simply vanished. Montana stared at the empty space with wide eyes. “No, no, no, that’s not what I meant. You can be a handful. It’s fine, please don’t vaporize.”

A scream erupted from the other side of the bar, so Montana ran that way. After a second, she came back, hurriedly putting down the money she owed. Mr. Liang smiled at Mrs. Liang. “Reminds me of our fourth date.”

She smiled back, fond of the memory. “Ah, to be young and in love. But old and in love isn’t so bad either.” She laughed, as she brought his face in for a kiss.

Montana smiled at how cute they were, but she ran off again when she saw Caswell had rematerialized on another person’s table, downing their drink. “Beatrice! Oh my god, I am so sorry, ma’am.” Montana dug out her wallet. “It’s been a long night,” she said and gave the shocked woman enough to cover the drink. Giving Caswell a pointed look, Montana scolded, “What are you doing, man? That doesn’t belong to you.”

Caswell giggled. “You were right, Vic, it’s so good. I love this stuff! Humans know how to party!”

“We can discuss this later.” Montana helped her down from the table, slinging an arm over her shoulders to give her more support. “If you walk out of here with me like a normal person, I’ll give you a surprise.”

Caswell seemed to consider the offer. “What kinda surprise?”

“If I told you, it wouldn’t be a surprise.” This worked pretty well, and Montana managed to get her outside without further incident, only some odd looks from strangers. They made it a decent distance from the restaurant before Caswell started talking again.

“Is…is my surprise blood?” Caswell stumbled, trying to whisper again. “Because I need some.”

“Uh, are you just saying that, or do you actually?” Montana grimaced. She had no idea how this whole thing worked. She had avoided asking about how Caswell fed because it kind of grossed her out, but now she wished she knew. “Shit, I can’t have you biting anyone like this, that can’t be safe.”

“I’m hungry, Vic,” Caswell said. “I need it.”

“Okay, okay…” Montana racked her brains. “Shit. Okay.” She unclipped her cape, pulling her shirt collar aside and tilting her head.

"You can bite me, okay? I know I don't taste the best, but blood is blood, right?"

Caswell looked at her for what felt like a very long time. In the dark, her eyes seemed to glow. They were piercing, like she was staring right through Montana's skin and bone. It made her feel weirdly self-conscious. She wondered if Caswell liked what she saw.

Finally, Caswell leaned down, her lips brushing up against Montana's collarbone as she clumsily aimed. "I love you," Caswell mumbled against her flesh.

"I bet you say that to all your dinners." Montana tried not to let her fear show. Not that Caswell would notice one way or the other in her current state. It was the principle of the matter. "Pick a vein already."

Sharp, hot pain flooded Montana's shoulder. She bit back a whimper. It was a pain unlike anything else. She wanted to run only as much as she never wanted to leave this position.

Her knees began to wobble, and her vision started coming and going. How much could she possibly take?

Caswell pulled away too abruptly, tearing her skin as she went. She turned away from Montana, then started heaving up the blood onto the sidewalk. There was so much of it. Or maybe time was slowing down around Montana. The bite stung red and angry, but everything else had gone hazy.

In hindsight, this may not have been her best plan.

"I guess blood is not blood," she muttered, as she started to fall backward. She couldn't straighten back up. Oh well, she'd survive cracking her head open on the cement.

She didn't hit the ground.

"Vic?" Caswell's voice.

Is she holding me? Was my blood so foul that it sobered her up?

"Are you all right?"

"I dunno," Montana said. She was pretty sure she said it. Maybe she thought it very loudly. As she considered trying to say it again, she slipped fully from consciousness.

Chapter Twenty-One

"BEATRICE…?" MONTANA STIRRED, SHIFTING and falling right off the couch. She was fine, and Caswell could not hide a sigh of relief. Montana looked up at her, eyebrows scrunching with concern. "Dude, you look terrible."

"Glad to see you're all right too." Caswell couldn't blame her for the remark. Her skin had gone from paper white to ashy gray, and many of her veins were now visible beneath her skin, all dark and reasonably upsetting. Her joints refused to bend overly far, but that did not stop her from hobbling over to sit beside Montana. Her legs stuck out rather oddly, but that hardly mattered.

"What happened?" Montana was rubbing her neck, and Caswell looked away as guilt shot through her again. That cringe of pain was her fault. The mark was gone, healed through werewolf regeneration, but it didn't erase what she'd done.

"I was hoping you could answer that for me," Caswell admitted. "My memory got fuzzy after the second drink."

"I'm not surprised. You were super wasted. Uh, you were getting really flirty, and I was a little worried about the impression we were making 'cause of that, but they were cool. Oh!" Montana's tone became accusatory. "Then you disappeared! Like, straight up stopped existing for a little bit! You were in my arms, and then you weren't! What the hell was that? Don't tell me it's 'cause you're a vampire. I got that part. I don't need the how, I need the what. Did you teleport?"

"No, that's preposterous." What a silly notion. Montana had the wildest imagination. "I just turned into mist."

Montana seemed more pissed off by the answer than her question. "Mist! That's not a living thing."

"Neither am I." Caswell countered defensively. "I'd show you right now, but I'm a little worse for wear as it is."

Montana shook her head, as if that would dispel her distractions. "Right, we'll deal with that later. So I was getting you out of there and getting you home, but then you said you needed blood. You were still a mess, and I didn't want you sucking on anyone while you were like that."

"Do you have to phrase it like that?"

"Let me finish. I was worried you wouldn't have the best self-control and might do something you'd really regret. Then I thought that if you took too much of my blood I'd still be okay, and maybe the taste would be able to deter you from going that far." Montana's hand flopped down from her neck to her lap. "And then I'm not sure what happened."

"Right. I've got it from here. I feel like I must've told you this, but perhaps it slipped my mind. The greatest defense a werewolf has against vampires is their poisonous blood."

"Poisonous?" Montana's shoulders slumped. "Yeah, no, I think I'd remember if you told me my body was filled with poison."

"Yes, well, it's a rather effective paralyzing agent. Fortunately, I was so ridiculously intoxicated that my bodily functions were slowed to the point where it did not instantly affect me, and I was able to expel the majority of it."

"So if it wasn't for dumb luck, you would've been paralyzed out on the sidewalk, and I would've been unconscious, so no one would've helped you, and...the sun..." Horror was evident in her voice. "Oh my god, I almost killed you..."

"Oh come on, there's no reason for that tone. You couldn't really kill me. I've already been killed!" That did little to cheer her up. Caswell tried again. "And anyway, I nearly killed you too. If you were human, that much blood loss would've probably resulted in death. You were unconscious all through the night. So we're even."

Montana was quiet for a minute. "Wait, I was knocked out for the rest of the night? It's day?"

"I imagine it's hard for you to tell when there's no windows, but yes, I believe it's early morning."

"If it's been a few hours, what's happening with you right now? I thought you said you got rid of most of my blood?"

"I did, but most is not the same thing as all. It's still enough to make me feel my age." Caswell was hoping that would make Montana laugh, but she just looked nervous.

"What can I do to help?" Montana slipped her hand under Caswell's, coiling her fingers to make up for Caswell's lack of mobility.

"I need a little time, that's all. It'll leave my system on its own. The only thing that could speed this up would be blood." Caswell glanced at Montana. "Human blood, not your blood."

"Okay, so I'll get some blood. Do you think Drake would have some? If not, he'd know where to get some, yeah?" Montana tried to get up, but Caswell tightened her grip on her hand the best she could.

"I'll be fine, don't..." She lost her confidence and looked away, speaking so quietly she was almost inaudible. "Don't leave me alone..."

Montana did not need to be told twice. She instantly returned to Caswell's. "Okay, I'll call Alison, tell her to ask Drake, then she—"

"You're not supposed to know about him. You can't tell her too."

"Okay, so what am I supposed to do?"

"I'll process it eventually, so all I need you to do is..." she trailed off, but her desire for company was evident.

"Right. I can do that." Montana sat quietly with her for a while. It was nice.

Montana kept glancing at her as though she wanted to say something.

"What's on your mind?"

Montana looked down at their interlocked hands, speaking softly, "Do you remember it?"

"Do I remember what?"

"Dying," Montana clarified. "You kinda, uh, bring it up a lot."

"Do I?" Caswell focused on the warmth of Montana's hand. On the faint repetition of her pulse. One, two, one, two, one, two. She answered slowly, "Yes. I remember it."

She couldn't remember much from back then, but that memory never went away, just as the bite would never heal.

"You wanna talk about it?" Montana's ears twitched.

"There's not a lot to say," Caswell admitted. "What exactly did you want to know?"

Montana was pressing against her shoulder, and Caswell realized she was subconsciously protecting her neck. "Is it…did the bite kill you?"

"No, it doesn't work quite like that." For once, Caswell did not condescend. "To become a vampire, they drink your blood, you drink theirs, then you have to die. It doesn't work without the permission of the vampire, though, so if someone were to force me into turning them, they'd just…"

"Right." Montana could connect the dots. "If you wanted it, would I be able to become a vampire? I know you said I couldn't turn you, but does that go both ways?"

"I'd imagine you could be turned, but once you die you wouldn't still have the werewolf curse. If I'm being honest, I don't know for sure." She looked down at Montana. She couldn't see her face from this angle. "And I never will. I wouldn't…I couldn't do that to a person."

"Do you hate it?"

When Caswell didn't respond, Montana pressed, "Do you wish you weren't a vampire?"

"I can't really remember being anything else, so I don't have any measure of comparison." Caswell hummed. "I am glad I've existed long enough to meet you."

"Me too. That's such a sappy thing to say."

Caswell could hear the smile in Montana's voice. "You can't agree with it, then turn around and call me sappy." Caswell huffed. "That's not fair."

"Say." Montana looked up at her, eyes twinkling mischievously. "You can't move much right now, but you can still feel, right?"

"That's right. Why?"

"I wanna repay you for some of that sappiness." Montana smiled, bringing her face up to kiss her.

As the kissing went on, Montana lowered her down gently, so she didn't even make a sound as she was sprawled across the floor. With a knee on each side of Caswell's torso, Montana moved like a predator, kissing hungrily at her lips and jawline. Her hands traveled up beneath her shirt. She was needy, Caswell was needed, and everything was wonderful.

"V-Vic," Caswell said with a gasp, pushing her away gently.

Montana backed off immediately, sitting on her stomach. "Is something wrong?"

"No, no, it's just..." She didn't know how to put it. "I wanted to ask you, what...what are we?"

"Well, you're a dork on the floor, and I'm a cool person sitting in your lap," Montana said with a little affirmative nod to herself. "I think that covers it."

"No, I meant...together. Not what are you and I, but what are...we."

"Oh! Uh, I don't know. What are we?" Montana reached over and plucked the scarf from around her neck, which had still hung there loosely from last night. She began absentmindedly playing with it.

"That's what I'm asking you."

"Well what would you like us to be?" Montana gave her that silly, crooked smile she seemed to love to blind Caswell with.

She paused, considering this. Caswell wasn't expecting it to be up to her. The pressure of deciding upon something turned out to be too much. "I'm not entirely sure."

"Then we don't have to be anything," Montana said simply, as if any of this was simple. "If you think of something, we can be that. But for now, we're just us."

Caswell tried to come up with an argument, but it was no use. She sighed. "I hate how smart you are."

"You know, you're very good at giving compliments that sound like insults." Montana rolled off her. "I'm gonna grab a snack, but I'll keep screaming the whole time so you know I'm still in the house, then we can get back to chilling. Oh, and I could bring you back up to your room in case you get sleepy. It's getting late for you."

"Go get your food, but don't scream. Your oppressive smell will remind me you're still here. Go on." Caswell shooed her away, watching her go. She found it was strangely comforting to see her leave and know she would be back. Montana was silly, but she was warm and alive and loving. More than that, she was warmth and life and love. And Caswell didn't ever want to lose that again.

Chapter Twenty-Two

CASWELL EVENTUALLY RECOVERED ENOUGH to go out and feed, just like she said she would. But Montana did not stop staying through the day. Sometimes she hung around for a couple of days in a row, leaving only to work or to take care of other responsibilities. Empty chip bags and forgotten socks turned into an extra toothbrush by the sink and Montana's preferred soap brand on the shower ledge. Neither of them commented on these things.

"Dude, I know you've been feeding me on full moons." Montana walked into her room, sitting on her coffin as if she owned the place.

"I am not." She was given a look, so she conceded, "It's not my fault! You make such terribly sad sounds. There's no reason to avoid eating anyway. That's the purpose of full moons, bringing out the werewolf's true hunger. The craving of the soul."

"I'd like to think my soul doesn't hunger for snack foods." Montana wrinkled up her nose. "Is that why werewolves are supposed to be violent? Inherent bloodlust?"

"They're not supposed to be, they are." Caswell pinched her cheek as she walked by, "You are the exception."

Montana rubbed her cheek. "You make it sound like there's something wrong with that."

"Not at all. You should try to become a trendsetter. If all of your kind were lapdogs, it'd be so much simpler to deal with you."

"All right, well, I wanted to ask you not to give me food this time. I feel so sick after all the transforming, you're lucky I haven't puked on your carpet 'cause of it. Yet." Montana rubbed the sleep from her eyes. She was more tired these days than when they met. The transformations took a toll, physically and mentally.

"On the topic of the moon, I'm going to be busy tomorrow night. You should stay at your own home." Caswell pretended to busy herself with arranging her clothes. She couldn't look in Montana's eyes, not now. She wasn't a good liar, but she was going to have to do everything she could to keep this truth hidden.

"Whaaat?" Montana complained. "You're ditching me the night after the full moon? You never have anything going on! What is this new event that you like so much more than you like me?"

Caswell folded the same shirt four times. She should make it six, six was a good number. Numbers divisible by three were good numbers. She kept her mind busy with that. "It's a surprise."

"A lousy surprise," Montana grumbled, lying back too quickly and making a smack sound as her head hit the wood. "Hey, isn't it kinda dangerous for vampires to sleep in wooden coffins?"

Internally, Caswell sighed with relief. Bless Montana and her easily distracted nature. "Have you ever seen a coffin made of anything else?" As Montana thought about that, Caswell put the shirt back in its place.

Montana would try to stop her if she knew, but she'd be happy in the end. Yes, no matter the cost, Caswell would make sure Montana was happy.

Even if she had to get a little blood on her hands to do it.

After the full moon, Montana had dragged herself home, mumbling about how Caswell was a traitor a few more times before she finally left. Alone, Caswell went up to the attic. The latch was always locked and there was no ladder, so it was the one place that no nosy children or Montanas could get into. When she brought Montana up to the roof the other night, they had climbed the lattice. Unsafe, perhaps, but this was no more of a comfortable alternative.

She avoided coming up by herself. The attic was full of memories she preferred to forget. In the back, in a small, ornate box that had been gathering dust for who knows how long, was a loaded gun. The bullets weren't steel, naturally. Those were a waste of time. There were less complicated ways to kill a human.

But to kill a werewolf with a silver bullet? It was classic.

The gun was heavier than she recalled. Her fingers tightened automatically around it. But she wouldn't be scared. Not this time. She left the manor, walking with a purpose. She hadn't felt so sure of anything before. She reached a house, knocking on the door.

The door opened, a red evening dress catching her eye. The wearer looked up from the gun, and their eyes met. "Are you sure?" Alison asked her again. Surely, the answer was evident in Caswell's face. Alison thrust the bottle in her hand toward Caswell, pressing it against her chest. "He's where I said he'd be."

"Thank you, Alison." Caswell pocketed the little bottle of concentrated wolfsbane, in case she couldn't finish it in one shot. Caswell hadn't had a chance to obtain any on her own with how closely Montana had stuck to her recently. "If I had tried to track him..." she started, trying again to justify putting Montana's human friend in danger. But Alison didn't care. She had volunteered for this. These plans were a few weeks in the making, carefully deliberated. They both knew the risks.

"You're repeating yourself, vampire." Alison flipped her hair out of her face. "Just do this right." With that, she closed the door.

Werewolves were not only the weakest right after the full moon, but they tended to briefly scatter. This was the best time, the only time, this would work. Caswell walked past the playground, into the woods.

She was a hunter. She didn't know how to be anything else. But this time she wasn't after food, nor was she acting in self-defense. Her goal was love, and she was better for it. Sharper, more confident. Prepared to die for her cause, but more prepared to kill for it.

Brick was in a clearing only a few yards from the tree line, hunched over a deer carcass. Though he looked like a man, he was a beast, through and through.

"I can smell you, vampire." Brick growled, not moving from his dinner. "Are you really so desperate to die you're going to lay yourself before me?" He stood, turning slowly to face her. His face was smeared with blood, and his mouth was open in a snarl. "You're the one who kept me from saving Montana."

"Saving her?" Caswell's focus was slipping, but she couldn't stop. The anger inside her was boiling, and her own lips were twitching as her teeth begged her to let them tear his head off. "You're what's killing her."

"I'm not in a good mood today." Brick cracked his neck. "Seeing your face made it even worse."

Caswell couldn't back down now, even if she wanted to. She didn't want to. "If you die, does she get to be human again?"

She had said too much. She shouldn't have been talking at all. Brick finally put all the clues together. His expression changed from disgust to a mocking cruelty, smile wide and ravenous. "Well that's strange. Did the hare fall in love with the fox while I wasn't looking?"

Caswell pulled out the gun. Brick ran toward her. She shot, but Brick was on top of her in a moment, lunging for her throat. They fell to the ground, wrestling for the weapon. He was stronger than Montana. Faster too. Without inhibition. There was deadly intent behind all of his movements.

The same was true for Caswell. Inside each of them was an untamable hatred for the other. And there was a kind of exhilaration in that, in hating so desperately. It felt as though you might never feel passion this strong again, as if all you knew, all you were capable of was hate.

Caswell tossed him off once, but Brick did not let go and dragged her a few feet in the other direction before they fell heavily back into the dirt. Caswell got on top of him and one of them managed to fire the gun, shooting sideways into the trunk of a tree and frightening some birds. The sound distracted Caswell for a millisecond, just long enough for Brick to get the gun in his hands. He grazed Caswell's arm, but she barely felt it with the rage coursing through her. She grabbed Brick's arm, breaking it with only the strength of her grip. Brick bit back a shout but could not keep a perfect grip on the gun.

Caswell quickly stole back the gun, aiming for the heart. As her finger squeezed the trigger, a scream jolted her. Her shot missed by a mere inch getting him in the shoulder instead his heart.

She leapt from Brick and onto the source of the sound. It was a werewolf, she could smell it. Caswell tackled it down, her hands around its neck before they even touched the ground.

There were those golden eyes.

Behind a pair of big, clunky sunglasses.

For the first time, Montana looked afraid of her.

All the rage inside of Caswell wilted instantly. She released her grip and got off Montana in a single movement. Montana coughed, sitting up and scrambling a few feet backward to give herself room to breathe. Caswell had backed off immediately, but she'd still managed to seriously crush her windpipe. She had been aiming to kill, after all. "I didn't know."

"What the *fuck* are you doing?" Montana's voice was hoarse after being strangled, but the sound was still recognizable. The voice of fear was mixed with hurt and anger and betrayal, but Caswell could only hear the fear. She had shown Montana the ugliest side of herself. She could no longer hide behind her own human face. It had always seeped through, like blood through cracked glass. Her eyes weren't human, and her teeth weren't human, and her ears weren't human. And she?

She was a monster.

Remembering what she was doing there in the first place, she twisted around to look at Brick. He was gone. He left a trail of blood from his wounded shoulder, and it was clear he had scampered away when he had his chance. Caswell looked back to Montana. "I was trying to help you! What are you doing here? I told you to stay home!"

"Help me? I was at home, but I heard gunshots!"

Caswell reached out for her, but she flinched and Caswell drew her hands back in. Her veins felt like ice, her body flooding with cold dread. She tried to explain herself. "I would never hurt you, Vic. I'm so sorry. I didn't know it was you. I didn't see you. I didn't pay attention. I was fighting, and I didn't have time to think. But if I knew, I wouldn't have touched you, I swear to god. I was trying to kill Brick."

That did not help Caswell's case. "Why would you do something like that? I thought you said you never wanted to kill." Montana fell into a coughing fit, losing a bit of her forceful tone. "Why didn't you tell me?" She was holding her neck gingerly now. It must hurt to talk, but she was too upset to be quiet and let herself heal.

"I knew you wouldn't understand. I knew you wouldn't be able to do it or ask another person to do something like that."

"I don't need you to make decisions for me! I'm not a child!" The raging sea of emotions from Montana fell still for a moment. She slumped, staring at something Caswell couldn't see. "But I've been acting like one. Brick was right."

"Vic," Caswell spoke softly, unable to say anything else. "Oh, Vic, Vic."

"You've just been pretending for me." Montana breathed out. "And I woulda played along forever because I'm a big, stupid puppy." She looked up at Caswell, and the misery in her expression was so strong it felt like a kick to the chest. "You're not a person." It was an accusation. No, it was an admittance.

Caswell was quiet for a moment. She looked down at her hands. Her long pale fingers and nails like razors. Those weren't a person's hands. In her mind, she saw them around Montana's neck. "I'm not."

Montana started to cry. She sat there trembling, hands clutching her neck, choking out sob after sob. She looked like a broken porcelain doll, a crushed flower, everything gentle and innocent in a state of destruction. Caswell had hurt her, and she could never undo that hurt. "I woulda played with you forever, Bea..."

Caswell stood up. She could feel her heart splintering in her chest. Each step a path over burning coal. She picked up the gun that had been tossed aside so carelessly. When it was in her hands, she hadn't cared what she would hit. What if Montana had shown up a few seconds earlier?

She walked back over. She untied her cape and let it fall soundlessly onto the grass. The early autumn air chilled her neck. All these years, and the bite still felt fresh. She knelt down, setting the gun a few feet away. She picked up the cape and moved slowly, so Montana wouldn't jump. She placed it over Montana's shoulders. Her hands rested there for a moment before she pulled away. "I love you."

She knew this wasn't the time for a confession of love, and it certainly wasn't how she had planned it. She had thought up all sorts of ways to say those words, writing them out and practicing to herself. But she had to say them now, in case she didn't get another chance. In case it was worth anything.

"You don't." Montana squeezed her eyes shut. "You don't know what that means."

Caswell swallowed. She laughed without any humor. "I guess I'm not entirely sure." She took the gun and stood back up. She began to walk away but stopped for a moment. Her voice was soft. "You should go home, Vic."

And there was no possibility that home could be with her.

Chapter Twenty-Three

MONTANA STARED UP AT her ceiling. She had been awake for several hours, but she hadn't moved. She thought she could, at first. She thought she'd be able to stand up and pretend the night had been a horrible nightmare. But then she saw the missed texts from Alison. *Did it work? Did our plan save you?* Her best friend had also gone behind her back. Montana threw her phone across the room, then she didn't move.

Her throat felt fine. She could breathe as easily as she ever could. She didn't know why she needed to breathe as a werewolf. Caswell could speak without breathing. When in Caswell's body, Montana felt love without a beating heart. Maybe that was true because, even in the body of Caswell, she was still Montana, not a real vampire. She wondered what it would be like to switch bodies with a human because she wasn't one of those anymore. She was hardly a werewolf either.

She sat up slowly. She needed to do something. Wallowing wasn't going to help. She tried to think of something she liked, back when she was herself and no other label mattered. Where could she go to escape the complications for a while? Just a little while. She had been so thoroughly smashed by reality last night, she had earned the right to run away from it for a day.

So she went to the zoo.

After a few hours of wandering around a little aimlessly, she settled on a bench, eating Dippin' Dots and throwing bits of a soft pretzel to the birds. She was beginning to space out comfortably when she heard somebody shouting her name.

"Oh my gosh, what a coincidence!" Dot cheered as she approached, as if there were such a thing as coincidence in her life. Some of the birds scattered, but a few favored the pretzel over the threat of humans. A couple hopped closer to Montana. "What are you doing here?"

"Chilling at the zoo, little dude," Montana gave her a high five once she was in range. Behind Dot were Cameron and June, and a taller girl Montana didn't know. "How 'bout you guys?"

"We're on a field trip," Cameron told her.

"Sounds fun." Montana nodded. "You gonna introduce me to your friend?"

"Oh, this is Macy." June pushed her to the front of the group. Macy waved shyly.

"Nice to meet ya, Macy. You can call me Vic."

"She's a werewolf!" Dot interrupted. "Sorry, I got too excited."

"It's cool." Montana assured her.

"You guys know a werewolf?" Macy had no trouble believing this, apparently. "Woah. Does Brian know? His reaction is gonna be priceless. He's been telling people Mr. Drake's a vampire since like, the first week of school."

"Not yet, he doesn't." June told her with a smirk. The two of them were still for a moment before they took off running, presumably both trying to tell Brian first. Watching them have fun lifted Montana's spirits a little. She was glad she went to the zoo at the right time to see them.

"Wait, we're supposed to stick together!" Cameron called after them halfheartedly. He gave up and sat next to Montana on the bench. "Whatever."

"So, you like the zoo, Ms. Vic?" Dot asked sweetly.

"Oh yeah. I love seeing all the animals. Though I'm not sure how I'm supposed to feel about the wolves now. Like, they're basically my people. Should I stage a jailbreak?" Her ears twitched.

"Seems like a horrible, dangerous idea," Cameron told her honestly. "Plus, the zoo would notice if all their wolves went missing."

Montana conceded. "You're right, We gotta start smaller. How about the tree frogs?"

"That's a worse idea. They're not indigenous to these parts." Cameron was cut off by a flamingo running free past them, chased by stressed zookeepers. He dropped the rest of his reasons to end with a simple, "You really don't have to do any jailbreaks when you're with Dot."

"Guess so." Montana grinned. She reached into her pocket, fishing out some cash. "Cameron, could you buy us some Dippin' Dots? I'd go, but after my twelfth cup this hour, the vendor has banned me from getting any more."

"You're going to die." Cameron took the money anyway.

"That's what the vendor said too," Montana said, obviously unbothered by the thought of gorging herself to death on ice cream. Cameron got up and went searching for a stand. Dot stole his seat, and Montana gave her some of the pretzel to throw to the birds. "You've got a good group of friends."

"Yeah," Dot said with a smile, "they're the best."

"Mhm. You ever keep secrets from 'em?"

Dot shrugged, focusing on tugging apart her pretzel. "I guess so. Everyone's got secrets."

"Yeah, I meant more like, secrets that would affect them. Not telling them stuff because you think they'd be better off not knowing." Montana leaned back. "Because you think you know better than they do."

"I don't think you should hide stuff from people, even if they'd be happier not knowing. Like, when you're going to go over a waterfall and they haven't noticed yet. They have a right to know. Plus, then we can work together to get back to shore." Dot accidentally hit a bird in the face with a bit of pretzel, but the bird didn't seem to mind, quickly gobbling up the piece.

"You're a smart kid, Dot."

"Thanks, but it comes from experience. I'm lucky to have gotten so much experience." Lucky felt like a strong word for Dot's life, but Montana didn't push that.

Montana realized she was out of pretzel, so she rested her hands in her lap. "And what do you do about the person who was gonna let you go over that waterfall blind?"

Dot laughed. "Well, I'll be happy we both survived. They'll probably feel bad, so I'd make sure they know I'm not mad at them. Everyone makes mistakes. Then I'd hope they learned for next time."

"How do you forgive them if they were trying to drown you on purpose?" A bird hopped up onto Montana's leg, chirping at her. Dot was delighted by that and distracted from the question. Montana smiled and carefully scooped up the bird, motioning for Dot to hold out her hand. Dot did, biting back her excitement, as Montana gently set the bird down on her palm.

"That's amazing. You're so good with animals." Dot breathed quietly, not moving even a centimeter. Dot glanced up at her. "What were you asking me?"

"Ah, it's okay. I forgot." Montana lied. She watched as Dot giggled, hand outstretched, and the bird flew away. Montana's gaze traced the scars etched into Dot's pale face, all different sizes. Her neck was bare. Montana would like to keep it that way. "Hey, you guys better not visit Beatrice for a while."

"Why not?"

"She's been...real busy lately. It's hard to describe, but all you need to know is she hasn't been able to hang out for weeks, and she can usually make time for me." Montana kept her tone casual, and she masked the painful chasm in her chest with a dismissive wave of her hand.

"Aw, okay. Tell us when she's free again. We can throw her a party." Dot smiled wide. She was the paragon of a good kid, which made it hard to lie to her.

Still, Montana did not flinch. "Sounds great. I'm sure she'll love it."

Right when they needed a distraction, June and Cameron barreled toward them. "June stole your money!" Cameron tattled without hesitation.

"I did not and more importantly, Macy and I found Brian, but he was with Mr. Drake, so now they're all on their way back here. I ran back so I could warn you in case you wanted to bolt." June said it all in a single, quick breath.

"Ms. Caswell did say that Mr. Drake might not be the nicest to you," Dot agreed slowly. Clearly, she didn't like thinking about that.

"I'll be fine." Montana waved off their concerns. Macy showed up with a smaller, stockier kid, presumably Brian, and a grown man who did look very much like a vampire, especially with his black sun umbrella. Upon seeing Montana, Brian fainted and all the kids rushed over to him. Drake approached Montana, his movements sweeping and elegant.

"It's nice to finally meet you." Drake held out a hand.

"Likewise." Montana stood and shook his hand. "The kids told me about you, but I think Beatrice was able to paint a more accurate picture. Ooh, you guys really should invest in painters. They could show you what you look like, y'know, with the reflection thing."

Drake laughed heartily. "Yes, that's a very cute idea." That felt patronizing. Montana was suddenly unsure if the handshake was a normal friendly thing, or the sort of trick you'd try with your pet. Drake lowered his voice, still speaking cheerfully, "I've never actually met one of your kind before, not properly."

"Yeah, well, I'm not exactly the poster child," Montana said. "And I've never met a d—"

"Sit down," Drake commanded, and Montana obeyed without thinking. "Sorry, but you can't say that in a public place like this."

Montana had had a rough night. Her two closest friends had rewarded her undying trust and loyalty with betrayal and a crushed windpipe. She found herself feeling defensive and feeling very sick of that. "Listen, buddy," she growled, "I'm sure you feel very high and mighty with that vampire blood running through your veins, but I'm not gonna be treated like a god damn dog by a guy in a cape."

"Oh no. I'm very sorry. I didn't mean it like that, but please keep your voice down."

Montana stood again. Drake was taller than her, but she had no problem getting up close to him. "Tell me what to do one more time. Make my day."

Montana was ready to take out all her aggression on this schmuck. Over his shoulder, she saw Dot helping Brian up into a sitting position. The kids were all laughing together and taking care of each other. Montana took a deep breath and let it go. She just let it all go. "I think your first concern should be your students." Montana walked right past him. Dot still had her arms supportively around Brian, and the others were crouched around. "Is Brian all right?"

"The werewolf knows my name," Brian said, wide-eyed, before passing out again.

"He'll be fine. This happens a lot." June gave Montana a thumbs up. "He's got bad blood pressure, and he's easily overwhelmed by the supernatural. He just needs some air."

"All right. I'm heading back to my place now. You guys have fun. Set some more animals free and that sort of thing." Montana waved to them. She got a little chorus of goodbyes in response.

As Montana walked away, she ran a hand through her hair, trying to shake off the lingering little voice telling her there's not a vampire in the world who'd respect her. Those thoughts weren't like her. Somebody like Brick would have thoughts like that, not her. She caught her reflection in the gift shop window. Behind it was a shirt featuring a wolf much fiercer than she was.

"Funny," she said to herself, but she wasn't laughing.

Chapter Twenty-Four

MONTANA GOT HOME FROM work completely fatigued. Her body was still adjusting to her new sleep schedule, and her boss had been extra hard on her for the last couple of weeks for reasons unknown to Montana. Maybe his dog had run away or something. Montana would follow suit, but she needed the cash. She just hoped she could relax now that she was home.

But life has a funny way of kicking you in the nuts while you were down. She realized, halfway through a bowl of cereal, that she had poured water in a bowl of skittles. She couldn't bring herself to care and continued to eat. She was hungrier than ever these days, and anything that wasn't meat wasn't making the cut. She was too stubborn to go full carnivore. Not yet. She wanted to last a little bit longer. She didn't know why, or what satisfaction that could give her, but she kept pushing it anyway.

Her suddenly tense body told her someone was going to knock at the door. She wasn't expecting anyone. Her head flashed through every possible option of whom it could be, and she decided she didn't want it to be any of them.

"Little pig, little pig, let me in, or I'll huff, and I'll puff, and I'll kill your damn neighbors."

That was the worst option. *Thanks, life.*

Montana put down her bowl and moved with resignation in her steps. She unlocked the door and opened it, looking up wearily at Brick. She hated that she was so lonely that Brick's smell was almost welcoming. There was another smell. Blood. His shoulder wasn't healed. Would it never heal or did it just take a long time? Montana wondered where Brick had been bitten. Maybe he hadn't been bitten at all. Montana really didn't understand anything about werewolves. "What do you want?"

"You didn't make a fuss this time. Are you warming up to me?" Brick walked past her into her home. "Or have you finally realized what that bloodsucker actually is?" He walked over to Montana's questionable meal, wrinkling his nose at the scent of it. He picked it up and spilled its contents onto the carpet. "Were you eating this? You need some real protein."

Montana closed her door. Brick obviously had no plans of leaving anytime soon. She turned to face her unwelcome guest. "I know how to take care of myself, thanks." Her traitorous stomach growled.

"I really do feel sorry for you, poor thing. Nobody's showing you how to handle your new body. It's not your fault you're stumbling around like a puppy. The closest thing you have to a friend is a vampire! Bet you tried to eat chocolate or something."

Montana did not respond to that one, but her flickering gaze said everything she didn't. Brick laughed. "I thought I'd be mad at you, Montana, and I was. In fact, I was so furious, if I hadn't been injured, I would've grabbed that gun and shot the both of you." Brick made a finger gun to demonstrate. "Because wow, I thought I've seen some disgusting things in my life, but that demented mutilation of love she felt? It still makes me sick to my stomach just thinking about it. But then I realized something. You know what I realized?"

Montana thought the question was rhetorical, but Brick did not continue. Montana sighed. "I don't know what you realized."

Brick stepped closer. Montana instinctively stepped back, her back pressed against the wall before she even registered it. "It wasn't your fault. You had to do what you had to in order to survive. And I take partial responsibility for that. I should've saved you." Brick lifted her chin so she'd look at him.

Montana pushed his hand away, slipping underneath his arm so she had more options than cowering. "I don't need saving." As she walked away, Brick grabbed her tail. He didn't pull, but Montana still found herself frozen in place.

"No, you're right. You've made it this long fine. You could probably live your whole life on your own, no matter what gets thrown at you. I mean, some vampire tries to turn you into a sex slave, and you end up wrapping her around your little finger. That glint in her eyes was repulsive, but I still admire you for being able to put it there. I could never stomach something like that. You don't need saving, Montana, but I think you'd like it. We're social beings, after all. Pack animals."

"I'm not like a vampire." Montana clutched the front of her shirt, turning the fabric above her chest into a tight ball of wrinkles. "And I'm not like a human, but I don't think I'm like a werewolf either." That was the bravest way of saying *I don't know what I might like anymore. I don't even know what I am.*

"I know! They can't squeeze you into any box." Brick let go of her tail, moving so he was in front of her again. "You're just you. It's intoxicating."

Montana wasn't sure she knew what love meant. She thought she knew it before, and she thought she gave it away generously enough. She loved Dot and June and Cameron. She loved the boys and girls who'd talk to her on the train and all the people at the park. She loved the drunk girl who cried on her shoulder and the guy at the sandwich shop who messed up her order and made it up to her by throwing in a free cookie. She loved the birds and the squirrels and even the bugs that had no concept of personal space. She loved Alison. And she loved Caswell. She loved and she loved and she loved. She thought it was easy. She thought it was simple, like making mud out of water and dirt. It was starting to feel more like a hurricane. "Do you think you could ever love me, Brick?"

"I already do." Brick tried to kiss her, but Montana pulled away. A little part of her wanted to let Brick do it. Kissing him almost felt like payback, like she would be getting revenge on Caswell. If she was going to give out her love to anyone who'd hurt her, why not this guy too?

"Why'd you come here?" Montana asked him.

"I told you. I'm going to save you. We're not humans, and that's a good thing. You should learn to be proud of that. Let's escape this boring little town and do whatever we like." He grabbed Montana's glasses, lifting them off her face. "I wish you didn't hide your eyes. They're so beautiful."

Brick was not looking into Montana's eyes at all, even if he thought he was. He didn't know what love was, either. He had nothing he could teach Montana. "Thanks, but I'm good where I am." Montana reached for her glasses, but Brick jerked them away, holding them above his head.

"I don't think you understand." Brick was still smiling. The consequences of their game were becoming very real for Montana, but Brick still had nothing to lose. "Aren't you ready to ditch this sad little life? I think I've given you an impossibly long time to say goodbye. What's holding you back? Is it that little girl with the hair that sticks up in the front?"

Montana lunged for her glasses, but Brick used her shift in weight against her and pushed her down onto the couch. Her shirt rode up her stomach, and the scar that Brick had left her with was visible to both of them. Montana did not look at it. Brick pinned her down. His breath was hot on her face. "Who's holding you back, Montana? Who do you want me to kill?"

Brick had played the game perfectly. Montana's hand was empty. She should've been more careful, she should've been wiser, she should've been anything other than what she was. Whoever she was, whatever she was, it was wrong. "No one." She was exhausted and terrified and out of options, so her body betrayed her once more, and she started to cry. "I'm alone. I'm terribly alone."

"Not anymore."

Caswell was not a human being. She knew that. And yet, she hurt like one.

Montana's words occupied Caswell's every waking moment. Which were a lot more moments than before, seeing as she could no longer eat or sleep. Not even her piano could bring her peace. No matter what she did, it felt like Montana was with her. But she no longer felt any warmth in that thought. There was no warmth in her life at all. Is this how she felt when she could no longer step out into the sun's light? She couldn't remember the sun. She could remember Montana.

"I warned you!" She pointed an accusatory finger at her lack of reflection in the bathroom mirror. She tried to sound angry. She felt too tired to be angry. "If you let them treat you like a human, you'll start believing you are one. Then you have to die all over again. You broke her heart, and you broke your own heart, because you're a selfish coward who'd rather make friends just so they can mourn you than do what you're supposed to do!"

She touched the glass. Mirrors had never bothered her before. But she wanted to see herself, she wanted to see her fingers on the other side of it. Montana had taught her how to want things again. No, she'd never forgotten how to do that. Montana had given her permission to want things again. "You're a lousy vampire, and a lousier friend."

She said, "I bet you want to go say you're sorry. You want to lie to her, don't you? Tell her you know love and that you're some misunderstood creature. You want to lure her back in only for her to suffer all over again because you can't accept the fact that you'll never be human!" She punched the mirror. She didn't mean to do that. She didn't mean to say that either. It sort of slipped out on its own.

Maybe she wasn't capable of love after all. Maybe she was only jealous of Montana. She was a window to the world Caswell had all but forgotten. The world she belittled but missed so intensely that, deep down, she was glad she didn't have to see her own face, or else be reminded that she was not welcome there anymore. Caswell had clung to Montana, leeching off her happiness and humanity. She didn't need to drink her blood to drain her and offer her nothing in return. Caswell was a parasite.

She brushed the glass from her knuckles. It didn't hurt, not like it was supposed to. She wished it did. She'd have to clean it up later. If she was lucky, it would provide a distraction.

But luck was never on her side, and she could not shake the thoughts of Montana.

Chapter Twenty-Five

"I'M SAYING THAT IF you don't know where the frogs—step left, broken pipe—came from, it's entirely possible they're from Kentucky," Dot reasoned as she and her friends walked out of the school. The initial rush of kids desperate to leave the moment the bell rang were already gone, so the walk was a little more relaxing. As relaxing as a walk with Dot could be.

"And I'm saying I feel like that's a stretch." Cameron hopped over a hole in the tiles. "They could be from anywhere, so why Kentucky?"

June pulled out her headphones for a moment. "Do you think, if they were big enough, they'd eat people? They are carnivorous." As they stepped outside, she spotted something and ran off. Dot and Cameron followed, quickly seeing what she did. "Hey, Vic!"

Montana was standing with a man they had never seen before. He must've been a werewolf, due to the physical traits they had in common. They didn't know she knew any other werewolves. The two of them had been discussing something quietly, glancing up at the kids when they heard June shouting. The man's lips twitched into what had to be a smile. "Vic? Is that you?"

Montana did not smile back. "Yeah, it's me." She nodded in greeting as the kids approached. "Yo."

"Ms. Vic, do you think a werefrog would be big enough to eat a person?" Dot asked, as if that were a normal conversation starter.

"Wow, werefrog. Guess a werewolf was not the worst option," Montana joked, but her voice sounded a little hollow. If the mental image of a man-eating frog couldn't make her so much as chuckle, then something was definitely wrong.

"Who's your friend?" Cameron asked. He had casually put an arm in front of Dot to dissuade her from getting closer.

"I'm Brick," the werewolf cut in. "And your names?"

Before they could respond, Montana said, "You know what, we were in the middle of something here, so you guys should scurry home."

"Yeah, we've got homework." Cameron grabbed June's arm, trying to usher both of them away inconspicuously.

"But we need to make sure you're not holding this guy against his will!" June teased. "There's no way you could actually make a friend your own age."

"Hey, wait a minute. I've seen this guy before!" Dot stepped closer and out of Cameron's grasp. "We met at the store, right? All those cans fell on you."

"How did you hurt yourself, little lamb?" Brick stared at a Band-Aid on Dot's cheek. He reached a hand out, but Montana grabbed his wrist.

"Don't touch her."

Brick looked surprised at first, then he laughed, retracting his hand. "You forgetting who's in charge, Vic?"

"You promised." Montana stood her ground but stared at the grass, refusing to make eye contact with him. Cameron slowly reached into Dot's backpack as the exchange took place, careful not to make a sound. He sent a glance June's way, who nodded slightly.

"I haven't broken my half of the deal! I'm not the one who cut her sweet little face. Are you gonna need a shorter leash?" Brick pinched Montana's cheek.

"I don't, uh, I don't think you should be putting your hands on her," Cameron spoke slowly at first, still nonchalantly feeling through the contents of Dot's pack. In one swift movement, he pulled out a can and stepped forward, spraying it directly into Brick's eyes. The burning pepper oil made Brick curse in surprise and let go of Montana. June grabbed Montana's hand and took off running. Cameron and Dot hurried after them, leaving Brick hissing.

"Woah, woah, what's going on?" Montana did not make them stop running.

"Getting you away from that creep, duh." June tightened her grip on her hand.

"Okay, calm down." Montana slowed to a stop. The others paused, too, confused but thankful for the break. "He's not...it's not like that. You kiddos are real good-hearted to worry, but you can't jump to conclusions and pepper spray people. I'll apologize to Brick. You get home. And...stay home. Just for tonight. Don't go outside."

"Do you think we're stupid or something?" June frowned at her. "I thought you were cool, man. Don't treat us like brats."

"I'm not. I just..." Montana sighed in defeat. "Okay, I'm sorry. You guys are clever, talented kids, and a lot better than most adults I know. I shouldn't condescend. I'm in a bit of trouble right now, but I swear on my life I've got things under control. I'm putting a lot of trust in all three of you right now by asking you not to interfere."

"What kind of trouble?" Cameron crossed his arms over his chest uncomfortably.

Montana held her thumb and forefinger close together. "A little, tiny bit. I can't explain it. I don't have time. I need you guys to trust me."

"Is it the same trouble Ms. Caswell is in?" Dot piped up. "If you're telling us the truth, tell us the whole truth."

"She's not in any danger. But if you visit her, you might be." Montana glanced over her shoulder, her ears twitching, listening to something the kids could not hear. "Shit. All right, I gotta go. You have to go too. Please, please stay safe." She pulled them all into one big, rib-crushing hug.

"If you get yourself hurt, I'm gonna kick your butt," June whispered, not sounding as brave as she hoped.

"I know." Montana smiled, giving them one last squeeze before taking off in the direction they had been running away from. Dot began walking with determination in an unexpected direction.

"Uh, Dot? We're under orders to go home," Cameron reminded her.

Dot did not stop. "I'm going to go see Ms. Caswell. Ms. Vic asked us to stay out of it because she doesn't want us to get hurt. But she can't handle this on her own. She was scared. We need to tell Ms. Caswell."

"Why wouldn't they already be working together?" June was already walking with Dot. Those two were ride or die and had been that way since the first grade. If Dot jumped off a cliff, June had probably jumped first. Cameron rolled his eyes and joined them, knowing they'd need a voice of reason to prevent them from doing anything too stupid.

"I think they're having a fight. But when she knows that Ms. Vic's in danger, I know she'll realize this is more important," Dot told them confidently.

They arrived at Caswell's house hours before the sun would go down, and the door was locked. They hoped they'd be able to wake her. Dot knocked on the door, shouting, "Ms. Caswell, please open up!"

Cameron joined in on the yelling, "Let us in!" They shouted and banged on the door for a full minute, until June motioned for them to stop.

"I got this." She gave them a thumbs up, then cupped a hand over her mouth. "CASWELL, OPEN THE GODDAMN DOOR!"

"I thought you didn't swear without permission?" An uncertain voice came from behind the door.

"She was listening the whole time?" Cameron was shocked, and a little offended that she let them scream for a while.

"Normally, yeah, but this is an emergency," June called back, ignoring Cameron. There was no response.

Then they heard the click of the lock, and they breathed a collective sigh of relief.

"Open it carefully, as I doubt I can help your emergency as a pile of ash," Caswell said.

June opened the door a crack so they could squeeze in, quickly shutting it behind them. Caswell stood on the other side of the door, using it as a barrier from the sun's rays. "Dot, is your face all right?"

"Oh, it's only a little cut," Dot assured her. Cameron eyed Caswell suspiciously, moving in front of Dot as a human shield.

"I wouldn't drink a child's blood," Caswell muttered indignantly, but there were more important things to discuss. "Never mind that. What's the emergency?"

"Vic is in danger. There's this other werewolf, his name is...uh..." June glanced at the others for help. She had always been terrible with names. "Clay?"

"Brick." Cameron corrected her. "Close, I guess."

"What did he do to her?"

"Do you know him?" Cameron asked. "Vic's fine for now. But something's going on. They've made some kind of weird deal, and when we tried to rescue her, she went right back to him."

Caswell's sense of urgency faded, her shoulders slumping. "It's none of our business then. She's allowed to make her own decisions. She can keep whatever company she likes."

June was having none of this. She walked closer, stomping on Caswell's foot so she'd double over and be eye level with her. "Do you care about her?"

Caswell blinked in bewilderment. "O-of course."

"Then pull yourself together and get her out of this mess." June folded her arms over her chest. "I don't know what happened between you two, but right now, she needs you. That's more important than anything else, right?"

Caswell straightened back up, smoothing out the wrinkles in her shirt. She chewed on her lip for a moment. "All right. At sundown, I'll go check on her. That's all."

"Good start." June fist-bumped her. "What are we doing until then?"

Caswell began pacing. "Call your parents. I'll do an old protection spell over the foyer, and you three can stay the night. As long as you're in that room, no lycanthrope will be able to smell you. It's not perfect, but it'll keep you safe while I'm out. I've still got the sleeping bags from last time, so don't worry about that." She stopped pacing, remembering the most important thing she had to say. "But no further interference out of any of you. Understood?"

"Crystal clear!" Dot chirped.

"That only works if she says, 'Am I clear?'" Cameron gave Dot a look. As Caswell walked away, they huddled together. Cameron whispered, "Okay, we're totally interfering more, right?"

"I assumed that was a given," June agreed.

Dot nodded along. "Let's get these poor lovebirds back into the safety of each other's arms."

"Birds don't have arms."

Hours later, Caswell was not sure of anything, but she was most unsure of which direction she was going. She had no idea where the werewolves would be. Even if she found their pack, there was no guarantee Montana was with them. She sighed. This was a ridiculous plan. She didn't know why she'd agreed to it. She would turn back, but there was that sludge of dread weighing her heart down that wouldn't disappear until she knew Montana was safe. She hoped Montana wouldn't see her. Or at least, if she did, she wouldn't be too angry about it.

Caswell walked to the playground where they had first met Brick. It stunk of wolves, but she couldn't tell how fresh it was. When she was tackled to the ground by three men, she decided it was very fresh.

The hands holding her wrists against her back were wet and seared her skin. She couldn't hide a wince.

"Not a fan of holy water, huh?" The guy on top of her sneered. This wasn't good. She was underprepared. With the holy water still melting through her skin, she wouldn't even be able to transform. "Don't worry, we've got worse in store for you."

"I bet this is turning the little crossbreeder on. You're a real sicko, even for a bloodsucker." The one on her left taunted. "No wonder Brick's little slut is so messed up."

"Don't talk about her like that," Caswell demanded, and they pressed her harder into the pavement.

"Brick wasn't kidding!" The third one finally cackled. "It really is wet for her! That's sickening!"

"If only it killed you when your mama dropped you on your head!"

A deep, unearthly growl came from behind her and to the right. The sound only lasted a second, but suddenly, none of the three werewolves were on top of her. She heard their screams, but all she saw was a gigantic, dark blur. She tried to focus through her pain and figure out what exactly her savior was.

There, attacking her aggressors, was a huge, black wolf.

Chapter Twenty-Six

IT WAS NOT A full moon.

Even if Caswell were to assume she had made the fatal error of losing track of the moon cycles, the werewolves who had been pinning her down were still in human form. So this wolf had to be a normal wolf. That was the only logical conclusion.

Except this was very clearly not a normal wolf. For one thing, it was much larger than a person, around the size of a grizzly bear. And it was fast and strong enough to hold its own against three werewolves. More than holding its own, it was wiping the floor with them. Caswell sat up slowly, staring in confused awe, as it shook the man who had overpowered her like a chew toy until he was sent flying a few yards into a tree.

Caswell struggled her way up to a sitting position. Her wrists still stung, but it was a major improvement compared to where she was a moment ago. So occupied with her own pain, she didn't realize the wolf was done fighting. Despite its impressive size, it moved with grace, coming to stand in front of her. Caswell flinched, expecting to be pounced, but it moved no closer. It stared at her with golden eyes. She stared back.

"Uh, hi," Caswell said, breathless. "Thank you, uh, for that." She motioned to the unconscious werewolves scattered around. "I'm guessing you didn't do it for me, but it was still nice?"

The wolf leaned its head down, and Caswell thought for a split second it was going to talk to her. Or bite her head off. It did neither of those things. Instead, it licked her whole face with its giant, slobbering tongue.

"Ew." Caswell didn't mean to say it, but she did. She tried to wipe the spit off her face. The wolf's tail was swishing. "Please don't do that again."

Before the wolf could do anything else, someone behind Caswell shouted, "Get off her!" She twisted around to see Alison fast approaching.

The wolf growled, but Caswell tried to calm it. “No, no, it's okay. She's not going to hurt you.” She yelled to Alison, “This one’s not our enemy!”

Alison slowed to a stop, still glaring at the wolf. Behind her was Drake, who was muttering in confusion, “Why are they transformed? It's not a full moon.”

“What are you two doing here?” Caswell tried to stand, but the wolf was looming protectively over her. Caswell wasn't able to move without kicking the wolf, which was on the bottom of her to do list.

“I went to Vic’s apartment since she hasn’t been answering her phone. The door was unlocked, and her place was trashed. I figured the regular police couldn't help, so I went to your house. You weren't there, but this sop was.” She jerked a thumb at Drake.

“Well, Dot, June, and Cameron called me. They were hoping I could use my ‘vampire powers’ to help.” He’d used air quotes. “And they sounded so urgent. I told them I’d do what I could. Your mate doesn't seem to like me very much, but I couldn't let you go into a wolf den by yourself. It's suicide.”

“We’re not mates,” Caswell halfheartedly corrected him. She didn’t know Drake and Montana had met. She didn’t think it was possible for Montana to not like someone. Maybe she really didn’t know anything about her.

“Could’ve fooled me. Well whatever, we came prepared.” Alison lifted her fists, showing off the silver rings and necklaces she had wrapped around her knuckles. They would pack a painful punch, that was for sure. “So now you talk. What's up with the big dog?”

“I...” Caswell glanced at the wolf, trying to figure it out. It continued to watch her. Its very existence was unexplainable. “I have no idea. But it saved my life.”

“And where's Vic?” Alison walked closer, keeping her eye on the wolf. She pulled Caswell out from under it by the shoulders, helping her up to her feet. The wolf did not stop them.

“I don't know that either.” Caswell sighed. “I wasn’t planning on fighting anyone. The kids thought she was in danger, so I came to make sure she was all right. I’m so stupid.” She pinched the bridge of her nose. “What if Vic is in danger? It didn’t sound like she was, but when am I ever correct? I didn't bring anything to defend either of us with."

Drake stepped closer. From his jacket pocket, he pulled out a small object covered with a thin cloth. "I'm not a fighter, nor is this my fight. I can't risk being caught by a pack of werewolves. But I can give you this silver knife, a souvenir of when my parents met." He paused, his heart maybe somewhere else for a moment. "I hope you can find your happy ending like they did." He handed the blade to Caswell, who accepted it gratefully. "I've doused it in wolfsbane," Drake said. "If you all survive this, tell Montana I'm sorry for any misunderstandings between us. I'd be honored if she would give me a second chance."

They watched Drake walk away. Alison pounded her fists together. "I'm not going anywhere. I'm sick of getting sidelined. She might be your girlfriend, but she's my best friend. If you try to send me away, I'll punch you with these."

"Noted." Caswell nodded, hoping Montana wouldn't mind her being in possible danger. The wolf abruptly turned around and ran into the wooded area behind the playground. Caswell sprinted after it, and Alison tried to keep up.

"You're just going to follow it?!"

"Yes, yes I am! I don't know why, but I feel like I can trust it!" Caswell hurried back to her. "Do you mind if I...?"

"Just do it!" Alison grunted, aggravated by many things, including but not limited to, following a giant wolf for no reason. They were losing the giant wolf, and she was the slowest one. Caswell lifted her up bridal style a little awkwardly, and went back to running. The extra weight did nothing to slow her down. They both avoided letting Caswell touch the silver wrapped around Alison's hands.

Caswell skidded to a stop before following the wolf into a clearing. She was thankful she did, since the rest of the pack, including Brick, were present. There were seven of them. But no Montana. Where was Montana? Caswell pushed thoughts of the worst from her mind. She didn't have time to stress.

Brick approached the wolf, grinning wildly. He placed his hands on either side of its face. "Incredible! I've heard stories of well-trained werewolves being able to transform at will, but you figured out how to do it in a year! You never fail to amaze, Vic."

"No way," Alison whispered. Caswell was struck speechless. That monstrous thing couldn't be Montana. It was impossible. But then, Montana herself was impossible.

"What triggered it?" Brick paused, but Montana didn't respond, which seemed natural, but seemed to disappoint Brick. "I guess expecting you to have perfected it is a little much, even for you. Janet, do you think she'll turn back at sunrise or in twelve hours?"

"Sunrise," A female werewolf responded confidently, examining her nails. "I don't get what's so special about her. It was probably an accident."

A few snickers erupted from the group until Brick spoke slowly. "If it's that simple, what's your excuse for not figuring it out yet? I like you, Janet, so I'll give you a second chance. Bad talk our new friend one more time, and I'll rip your intestines out between your teeth." Brick ran his hand from the wolf's—from Montana's—jaw to her right eye. "Never got around to punishing her for insubordination earlier. Who thinks she should lose an eye?"

He received savage cheers in response. "Kill the bastard," Alison said to Caswell, jumping out of her arms. "I'll distract the others." Before Caswell could stop her, Alison had jumped over the brush and punched the closest werewolf in the face. Another one grabbed Alison under her arms, trying to drag her off the first. The rage Caswell felt didn't give her the chance to tell Alison to stop. Caswell barely felt like a conscious being. She was anger, seething and red. She ran at Brick, fighting off that girl who had spoken up, Janet, who leapt at her instinctively.

"Paws off, I want first bite of the bloodsucker." Brick growled, eyes glowing in the low light of the stars. "It's almost nice to see your revolting face, vampire. I'm gonna tear you to pieces for the bullet wound."

Caswell did not speak. She had forgotten how. There was her most hated foe, almost begging Caswell to stab him. And she would be more than satisfied to comply. Alison headbutted the chin of the werewolf holding her back, throwing punches at anyone near her.

"Get the human under control," Brick ordered, then lunged at Caswell. He was intercepted by Montana. Brick shouted, "And grab this idiot before I do something I regret!" All the werewolves fought off Montana, and Alison chased after to defend her. They ended up pouring out of the clearing and into the trees. Caswell tackled Brick to the ground.

But Brick would not stay down. He rolled them so he was on top, not hesitating before punching her in the face repeatedly. He was vicious. "You're gonna regret ever crawling out of the grave when I'm through with you!"

Caswell had her hands around Brick's neck in a moment. Brick made a sound resembling a whimper, and the tension on Caswell's face almost vanished completely. What was she doing? Why was she letting her fangs tell her what to do?

She thought about Montana, who practically lived on her couch, who didn't fear her or hate her because of what she was. Montana who cried at happy endings and didn't think someone like Brick deserved a death sentence. She thought about little puppy-Montana. Too friendly and forgiving for her own good. She had thought that form was ridiculous and that Montana was simply too afraid to be anything stronger. But Montana wasn't the one who was scared. Caswell was.

Caswell's blood stopped simmering. She let go of Brick, taking another hit to the face. "Stop," she said. "This isn't right."

Brick grinned wickedly. In his eyes, Caswell saw herself. Hateful and prideful and so very afraid. "Rolling over already? You deserve to die like a worm!"

Caswell pushed him off, joining him on his feet. "I'm not going to fight you. I have spent enough of this miserable existence letting hatred control me." It was about time she learned something new. Love, she thought, love sounded nice right about now. Maybe Montana could teach her what that really meant.

Brick ran at her again, and Caswell deflected his blows. It was almost funny. Brick wasn't a good fighter, and she could see that now. He was strong, yes, and relentless, but there was no skill or thought behind his movements. Just anger.

"I know you, Brick."

"I don't want my name on your tongue." Brick snarled. "You're scum among scum! Not even another vampire would listen to you!"

Caswell did not stop. She had to try. "We're the same. Losing ourselves to rage because we're weak and we're scared. Scared of you, scared of me, but most of all, scared of losing her."

"She was never yours to lose!" Brick rushed her, grinding his teeth, as Caswell caught his arms again.

"I know." Caswell couldn't help but laugh a little. She pulled the knife from her pocket, ready to toss it to the ground in surrender. "But she isn't yours, either."

Brick snapped. Something subtle in his expression changed. He yanked his shirt down over his bicep, revealing the still recovering wound in his shoulder. Without warning he thrust two fingers in, reopening the wound. His breathing was ragged and his face was twisted, but he was still smiling, gritting through the pain as he dug around. Caswell was too shocked to move.

He dragged his fingers back out, now dripping with blood. He gasped, then lunged, stuffing his fingers into Caswell's mouth. Caswell's whole body seized up, her hand doing the opposite of what she wanted and tightening around the knife. She fell back onto the ground with a thud, unable to move. It had only been a taste of blood, and she would not be down for more than a few minutes. But that would be enough.

Brick laughed. It started quiet but grew into something wild. It was almost a howl. "I'm going to enjoy this! How dead do you have to be to turn to ash? I want to make this last." He pounced, hands up and ready to claw her chest into ribbons. Before he had the chance, he let out a pained cry.

The knife was buried in his side. Brick's eyes went wide, visibly searching for a solution as the wolfsbane entered his bloodstream. He spat blood onto Caswell's shirt, but that was his final offense. His eyes faded from gold to brown, and his inhuman features disappeared.

The curse was rectified when he died.

Just like that, it was over. Caswell could not look away from his corpse, quite literally. They lay in silence, the night continuing indiscriminately without them.

Janet stumbled back into the clearing. She looked the same, no physical changes. The death of the alpha reverting the others must've been another myth. Her expression changed from confusion to glee.

"HE'S DEAD!" She shrieked. "BRICK IS DEAD!" The other werewolves ran to her to confirm this, some looking more bruised and bloodier than others. Instead of crying, she heard howls, wild sounds of *laughter*. Janet motioned the way they came. "The reign of terror is over. Forget the freak. Let's get the others and choose our new alpha."

They left in the direction of the park, howling and whooping, and ignoring Caswell altogether. She wondered if they thought she was dead. She looked rather dead.

Alison came back shortly after, leaning against Montana, who was still on all fours. Alison was roughed up but still kicking. Most of her silver was gone. "Oh my god," she blanched when she saw Caswell and Brick. She pushed off Montana and ran to Caswell's side, heaving Brick off her. His body fell limply onto the grass. "No, no, you can't be dead. Not after all of this."

Montana licked her face again. She prowled around them and got on top of Caswell, as if she were still a lap dog. She crushed Caswell's stomach, whining at her. "You weigh a ton," Caswell finally complained hoarsely, and Alison sighed audibly with relief.

They worked together to push Montana, who was furiously wagging her tail, off Caswell. With a cautious gentleness, Caswell rolled Brick over so he was face up and closed his eyes. She didn't know what she was feeling exactly. Maybe pity. Maybe sorrow. "No more bad blood," she spoke softly. "Find your peace."

"Vic." She stood up, looking at Montana with a fondness she didn't want to hide. Caswell stroked her head with slow and soothing movements. "I don't deserve you. I know that. But I love you. And I didn't even know I could do that anymore. I thought I had forgotten how. But I love you, and I can't make myself stop. If you will have me, I will spend every minute trying to be someone worthy of that."

"That's sweet," Alison interrupted their moment, "but you're talking to a dog. Save it for the Vic we know and love." Her joking tone faded as she took in Caswell's face. "Are you crying?"

"Yes." Caswell laughed through her tears. Her heart was light. She wrapped her arms around Montana's neck, hugging her tightly and never wanting to let her go. She buried herself in her fur. There was that smell. That warmth. She was home. "Yes, I believe I am."

Epilogue

IT WAS NEARING TWO years since Brick died.

Caswell remembered the exact date, and she didn't think she was ever going to forget it. The aftermath was surprisingly uneventful. The werewolves had vanished back to wherever they came from, leaving only one werewolf in town.

Once Montana had arms again, she wrapped them around Caswell and forgave her with such intensity Caswell felt as though she was being cleansed of every one of her misdoings, baptized in a water that would not burn her. They had promised each other right then, without saying a word, that they would discover what love meant. Together.

So things went back to normal. Well, not completely normal. They discovered that Montana could not change forms at will, not exactly. She couldn't make a conscious choice and change. But when Caswell or the children were in any sort of danger, more likely than not, they'd find a wolf at their side. Through her stubborn spirit, Montana had molded her curse into something she could use to protect what she loved.

Things were changing for the children. Dot, Cameron, and June were graduating middle school, which was apparently an ordeal. Caswell didn't entirely understand why, but she was being as supportive as she could, since naturally, it was happening during the day. Montana was trying to stream it to her.

"Okay, Bea, can you see okay?" Montana asked, jostling her phone camera in her excitement.

"I can see your thumb," Caswell responded dryly. She still couldn't believe Montana had gotten her a phone. Her birthday gifts were getting increasingly ridiculous. While it was nice to be able to reach the others during the day, she hardly understood the point of video-calling when her face did not show up on camera. Montana wanted her there, one way or another, and the kids had begged her too. She swore, sometimes their puppy-dog eyes were worse than Montana's.

"Yo, Gregory, my man!" Montana was distracted at the sight of Drake, who was standing with a gaggle of adults by the stage. The ceremony hadn't started yet (Or had it? Caswell didn't know what would signify the beginning of the ritual.) but the teacher was clearly busy. Montana bounced over, completely oblivious. "How's it hanging?"

"Ah, Vic!" Drake gave her a toothy smile. He was dressed like he was mourning, but he always dressed like that. "Dot told me she invited you! I'm glad you could make it."

"Are you kidding? I wouldn't miss it for the world!" She lifted the phone so Caswell could see Drake. Showing up on screens was one of the many perks of his mixed nature, which must be a boon for school picture days. "Beatrice's here too. I told Alison she should come, but she hates kids."

Drake's eyebrows creased into a semi-concerned look. Though he and Montana had gotten past their rocky start and into a full friendship, he and Alison did not interact on a regular basis, and for good reason. Montana was the glue that held all sorts of people together. "All right, well, I'm going to have to ask you to take your seat now. We'll chat later."

"You can bet on it!"

Montana walked down the aisle. She received some odd stares, but nothing too overt. This was the school that Dot went to, after all. The parents and students were used to weirdness. She sat next to Mrs. and Mr. Liang, showing off the phone screen to them. "Oh, hello, Caswell." Mrs. Liang smiled warmly, assuming that was what she was supposed to be looking at. Her eyes wandered up to meet Montana's, her expression gentle but wry. "Are you two still going to be joining us for bowling? We're friends with the manager, so they've already got shin guards and gas masks prepared for us."

From the way the screen jerked, Caswell assumed Montana was nodding. "I bet ya five bucks Bea is gonna break something with her vampire strength before your husband breaks something with his luck."

Mrs. Liang laughed breezily, resting her fingertips on her chest. "Vic, you know I'm not a betting woman!" She said quietly, "Make it fifteen." She squeezed Mr. Liang's hand as the crowd suddenly hushed, and Caswell figured out that meant things were getting started.

A woman up on stage was talking into a microphone about class achievements, only sighing when the sprinklers randomly went off. Of all the strange occurrences around both Dot and her father, that wasn't the worst that could've occurred. The kids started to come up one by one.

This was the big part, Caswell guessed, since everyone clapped. No one clapped as hard as Montana did, who set the phone in her lap, leaving Caswell with a view that made her cover her eyes, too polite and flustered to peek through her fingers. Montana was cheering with all her might for every single child, as if they were her own children.

June was the first of the kids Caswell knew to be called up. She clapped, too, knowing she wouldn't be heard or seen. It was all right. She did the same for Cameron and Dot. When the last child received their paper, Montana stood up to yell about how proud she was of all of them, forgetting a phone was in her lap and letting it tumble to the ground. An affectionate chuckle escaped Caswell's lips.

Caswell found herself picturing how wonderful Montana would be as a parent.

Caswell's view shifted again as Montana picked up the phone, giving her a sympathetic, "I'm so sorry. I totally forgot."

Caswell tried to hide the smile in her voice. "It's not like there was much to see anyway. You made graduations out to be such a grand affair."

Before Montana could tease her, she stumbled to the side, phone tilting in her hand and revealing her attacker. June wrapped her arms around Montana's midsection in either a hug or a tackle, maybe both. Dot and Cameron were behind her, all grinning wide and wearing the same ill-fitting robes as the other kids in the gym. Dot still had her backpack on. Probably a safety precaution on the school's end. Montana dragged them all into the hug, and Caswell could hear their minor complaints and grunts as she crushed their bones thoroughly.

"Oh my god, you guys look so grown up," Montana gushed. "I'm gonna cry."

They didn't look any older to Caswell. Two years was nothing. *Thirteen* years was nothing. They were all so young. Even Montana was. And yet they had experienced so much more life than Caswell had in such a shorter amount of time. She was ready to experience that with them now, the good, the bad, all the pain, and all the love. She was more than ready to live again.

"Shoo, you big dork, we wanna talk to Cas." June tried to wrestle the phone out of Montana's hand as the other two let go of her.

"You're using me for my vampire connections?" Montana gasped scandalously, trying to keep the phone out of her grasp, only for Cameron to yank it away. Montana chuckled. "Wait, wait, let me say goodbye first."

Cameron raised an eyebrow. "You're going to get your phone back in a minute, and you'll see her face-to-face in a few hours."

"This is animal abuse," Montana whined.

"Aw, let her say goodbye!" Dot begged Cameron.

Caswell took notice of the blush that crept onto Cameron's face. After everything the kids had done to help the two of them figure things out, she was ready to pass the favor along. "All right," he mumbled, holding out the phone to Montana.

"See ya," Montana said casually, and they all simultaneously wondered why she was so desperate to say goodbye when that's all she wanted to say. She ran off to make some friends, shouting, "Love ya!"

Caswell sighed dreamily, regaining her composure when she noticed all the kids staring. Not that they could actually see her, but it was the principle of the matter. She straightened her collar. "Right. How's the plan coming along?"

"Fantastic!" Dot grinned. She was missing another tooth, and Caswell was sure there was another impossible story behind it. "We came up with a name!'

"A name?" Caswell wrinkled her nose. "That's not a lot of progress."

June shook her head. "It's the first step to any good scheme! Plus, it's an amazing name. We call it," she paused for effect and motioned for the other two to speak in tandem with her, "Operation Ringtail Lemur

"We're getting a ring on that tail!"

"Oh, that is clever," Caswell admitted. Montana had told her she didn't need a label for their relationship if Caswell didn't want one. But going on three years with Montana led Caswell to decide she'd like to call her something. Caswell wanted Montana to be her wife.

"First, you need a ring. As usual, Dot is going to distract Vic." Cameron turned the phone to Dot, who waved. "And June will help you pick out a ring. She is going to ask you to do many illegal things, breaking laws you might not even know about, so don't do anything she says."

"Boo!" June stuck out her tongue at him. "Stop ruining all the fun."

Cameron continued, unremorseful. "I'll be researching proposal ideas, since I know what's romantic. Dot will also be asking Vic questions on the down-low, to find out her tastes."

There was no way this wasn't going to end in disaster. But if that bothered Caswell, she wouldn't be asking these kids in the first place. Besides, a proposal that ended in flames would be better than an awkward one. Maybe it would make Montana laugh.

"I think it should involve fireworks," June said. "Fireworks are always a good idea."

"Yes, if we temporarily blind her, then she won't see me make a fool of myself," Caswell agreed.

"Aw, come on guys, nobody will be blinded," Dot interjected. Even in hypothetical situations, she wanted things to go right for them.

"Around you?" Caswell gave her a look, pointlessly, but Dot got the idea. "Right, we can work out the rest of the details next time we're together," she said, knowing full well they'd be visiting soon. Her manor was so rarely quiet these days. And that was a wonderful thing. Her sullen tomb had turned into a bustling center of life and laughter. When Montana was there, it really felt like a home, but so did Montana's apartment, and that little cliffside clearing, and the convenience store she'd take her to, and anywhere at all where Montana was. Yes, home was not a place for Caswell. Home was a person.

"Yeah, and we'll give you a hug too," Dot promised, as though she was worried Caswell was jealous that Montana was getting all the hugs at the graduation ceremony.

"Yo, not to interrupt whatever sinister things you nutjobs are working on, but your dad's looking for you, June." Montana came back over, munching on something. Of course she had found food. "He's gonna take you guys for pizza, so like, get on that."

"Wait, are you eating a dog biscuit?" Cameron asked incredulously, lowering the phone without thinking about it. "That's more important than pizza right now."

"Woah, nothing's more important than pizza," Montana said, and Caswell briefly wondered if she should put the ring in her food. It had happened in this unbearably cheesy movie Montana forced her to watch, and it seemed like a decent idea. Montana loved food. But knowing her, she'd probably eat the ring. Were her teeth strong enough to chew through metal? It was possible.

"But yeah, some old lady saw the tail and got real confused. Told me my dog was cute and gave me one of these. It's not terrible."

"That's disgusting," Cameron and Caswell said to her at the same time.

"Do you want another one?" Dot was already reaching into her backpack. June hooked her arm through Dot's to both prevent her from getting out any dog treats and to start her walking in the direction of her dad.

"We can talk about this later. I'm starving," June said with a groan. Cameron gave the phone back to Montana and hurried off with his friends.

They both watched them run off, the energetic murmur of the crowd filling the space. Montana started walking toward the doorway of the gym. She spoke to Caswell. "Need anything while I'm out?"

Caswell hummed thoughtfully. "I could use a kiss."

Montana laughed, stepping outside. She positively glowed in the sunlight. Caswell needed to figure out how to take pictures so she could see this whenever she liked, though there was no great urgency since Montana would never turn down a request to video chat with her. "I better hurry up then. That sounds urgent."

"Very." Caswell nodded solemnly. Montana tapped at the screen, distracting Caswell from their playing. "What are you doing?"

"Ah, it's almost out of battery."

"If that's the case, you don't have to keep talking to me, Vic. Conserve your battery. I'll see you in a few minutes." Caswell couldn't believe they had gotten so lovey-dovey that saying goodbye for even just a little bit filled her with so much reluctance.

"Okay." Montana smiled dazzlingly at her, and Caswell lost any semblance of thought.

"I love you." She said it clearly this time, but just as easily as when she first said it secretly. It was so easy. Loving and being loved. As simple as coming home. If only she had figured it out sooner.

"I love you too."

The End.

Acknowledgments

Thank you to all my friends, family, and teachers over the years who have encouraged my daydreaming habits. You really have no idea what your support has meant to me. My delusions of grandeur are entirely your fault. Thank you to my editor who I drove half mad, thank you to the whole Desert Palms Press team, and thank you my dear reader, for giving my girls a chance!

About the Author

Kayla Gornick is a lifelong Midwesterner with a great love for the Great Lakes. She is also a southpaw, an aspiring librarian, and an all-around oddball. She enjoys a variety of creative outputs, especially ones she is not particularly good at. A self-identified storyteller through and through, she is also delighted to be a part of Weird Little Beasties, a small, independent, and entirely woman-owned visual novel game studio, and she is honored to be a new member of the Desert Palm Press family.

Note to Readers

Thank you for reading a book from Desert Palm Press. We appreciate you as a reader and want to ensure you enjoy the reading process. We would like you to consider posting a review on your preferred media sites and/or your blog or website.

For more information on upcoming releases, author interviews, contests, giveaways and more, please sign up for our newsletter and visit us at Desert Palm Press: www.desertpalmpress.com and "Like" us on Facebook: Desert Palm Press.

Bright Blessings

Desert Palm Press

www.ingramcontent.com/pod-product-compliance
Lightning Source LLC
Chambersburg PA
CBHW030727210726
48505CB00028B/307
9781633040878